Finessed a Dope Boy's Heart

Finessed a Dope Boy's Heart

Racquel Williams

www.urbanbooks.net

Urban Books, LLC
300 Farmingdale Road, N.Y.-Route 109
Farmingdale, NY 11735

Finessed a Dope Boy's Heart

ISBN 13: 978-1-64556-075-3
ISBN 10: 1-64556-075-9

First Trade Paperback Printing September 2020
Printed in the United States of America

10 9 8 7 6 5 4 3 2 1

Distributed by Kensington Publishing Corp.
Submit Orders to:
Customer Service
400 Hahn Road
Westminster, MD 21157-4627
Phone: 1-800-733-3000
Fax: 1-800-659-2436

Finessed a Dope Boy's Heart

by

Racquel Williams

Prologue

Mika

Niggas nowadays ain't worth shit! Now, that might come off harsh. But as I lay here in this bed thinking, I can't seem to shake the feeling of how I ignored the signs of a no-good-ass nigga, all in the name of love. Check this . . . You can be a pretty bitch, phat ass, good pussy . . . You can have money, have a career . . . You could spend your entire life cooking for the nigga, cleaning for him, and sucking his old, dirty-ass dick, and that nigga will *still* find a reason to go out there and find a bitch who has nothing going on for her-damn-self. Not even a pot to piss in!

I wiped the single tear that dropped from my eye. Turning my head, I looked over at Rasheem, snoring as he lay on his back, mouth wide opened. That shit made me sick. You would think after fifteen years of marriage, I would get used to him sounding like a damn freight train. No matter how much I pled with him to lie on his stomach, he would start there, but then end up on his back. I shook my head in disgust.

I remember when I was head over heels over this man. I met him years ago, at a company party. Back then, he was well built, burnt chocolate. As he walked into the room, he caught the attention of many of us—including me. I was just getting over a breakup with my college sweetheart and was looking to get back into the dating world.

Our eyes locked, and he shot me a smile. I was tingling all over, but I remained cool. My bestie, Joy, nudged me in my side and then whispered in my ear.

"I don't know who that lad is, but he is checking you out," she said in her raw British accent.

"Girl, he sure is fine. But there are plenty of fine ladies here, including you."

"Cut the foolishness. I saw how he smiled at you. I can tell when a man is digging a woman."

I didn't respond to her. Joy was in law school and could win any argument. I conceded with my silence and took a sip of the wine that I was drinking. As the evening went on, we danced and partied. My feet started hurting, so I decided to sit down. I didn't realize how much I had drunk until I almost stumbled over the chair that I sat in.

"Here, let me get that for you."

Someone grabbed the chair and pulled it closer to me. I looked up and noticed that it was the tall, sexy brother from earlier. I felt embarrassed. Here, I was drunk, and he had to rescue me. I tried my best to maintain my balance, hoping not to fall in front of him.

"Thank you. I got it," I said politely.

I started to sit . . . and stumbled into him. He grabbed me and hugged me tightly. His strong cologne hit my nose and instantly gave me a high. I felt his warmth, and at that moment, I didn't want him to let go.

"I'm sorry. I didn't mean to hold you this long. Here, sit down," he apologized.

After I took a seat, I busted out laughing. I'm not sure if it was because I was drunk or because he made me nervous. Either way, it was funny as hell to me.

"I hope you're not laughing at me," he said in a sexy, rough voice.

"No, no, I'm laughing at myself. Here I am, stumbling all over the place. I hope no one else notices it. I sure don't want to be the topic of the office jokes on Monday."

"You're good. Trust me. Everyone else is occupied or too drunk to pay you any mind. By the way, where're my manners? I'm Rasheem."

"Hey, Rasheem. I'm Tamika, but my colleagues call me Mika."

"I love the sound of that 'Mika.' Are you from here? Georgia?"

"Oh no, I'm from Mount Vernon, New York."

"Wow! An up north girl. I see where the feistiness comes from."

"What about you?"

"I was born and raised in Atlanta. I'm a Grady baby."

The rest of the night, we continued talking about everything from jobs to personal life. I found out he was a detective at the Stone Mountain Police Station. He was recently divorced and the father of two. That should've been my cue to get to stepping, but my ass was feeling him. His conversation was very interesting, and he was a charmer. The rest of the night, we laughed and talked like we'd been knowing each other for years. When the party was over, we exchanged numbers.

It was hard to ignore that we were definitely feeling each other. One date turned into two dates, and on the third date, he invited me to his house. He was an officer, so I let my guard down and decided to go inside.

After about an hour of drinking and flirting, next thing you know, I was lying in his king-size bed, legs spread wide apart, and his head buried deep into my pussy. I screamed and moaned as he devoured me. He wasn't shy and made sure pussy juice was all over his face. He pinned me down to the bed and punished my pussy, exploring every inch of my petite body.

"Oh my God, I can't take it! Stop, please," I begged as my legs trembled, and I exploded back-to-back.

As if he were just getting started, he lifted my legs in the air and sank his big, black, shiny rod all the way up in me. I wanted to run, but there was nowhere to go. My head was touching the back of the bed, and he had my legs on his shoulders. He thrust in and out of me while he grinded. He looked me in my eyes as he made love to my pussy. This man knew *exactly* what he was doing. Not only was he fucking my pussy, but he was also fucking my soul too.

Growing up, I'd always dreamed of having a big house, the sexy-ass husband, and live a good life. I knew for me to get that, I had to work hard, and I did just that up to my mid-thirties. By the time I met Rasheem, my husband, I had a few dollars in the bank and was at the height of my career. Meeting him was like putting the icing on the cake. He was a well-established detective in the homicide division and a prominent member of his community.

After dating for about a year, he popped the question to me, and I quickly accepted. A few days later, I found out I was pregnant with our daughter Ky'Imani. It was a blessing because, for years, I had problems conceiving. I always call her my miracle child.

After giving birth to Ky'Imani, we had a huge wedding. To be honest, I wanted a small one with only our families and close friends. But not Rasheem Blake. He wanted a big wedding so he could show off. So, that's what we had. The chief of police, lawyers, and other officers were all present. I kind of felt like he did it to earn bragging rights. But I didn't have to pay a dollar, so why was I complaining?

I wish I could've seen the fucking future, 'cause I wouldn't be here in this bed right now. Everything started off good.

We both rented out our houses and bought a six-bedroom house in Snellville. I was excited to be a mom, now I had the husband, and everything was going to be good.

Wrong! I realized this nigga was a fraud, and this was how I got here. . . .

Chapter One

Jakeel

Three Days Earlier
Friday Morning

"Inmate Greene, to R&D. Inmate Greene to R&D," the bitch hollered over the intercom.

I grabbed my things and ran out of the unit. I was well on my way through the compound when a few of my niggas stopped me to wish me well and tell me to make sure I didn't forget about them.

"A'ight, homie. Make sure you fuck plenty'a bitches and send me them videos, bra," my nigga Rell said as we exchanged dap.

"Last call for Inmate Greene. Jakeel Greene, report to R&D."

I grabbed my two manila envelopes, along with the shower bag that contained the few pieces of clothes that I owned. Then I started jogging until I got to the building.

"What were you doing? You must not want to go home," the old CO, Miss Betty, said as she shot me a dirty look.

I wanted to tell that bitch to suck my dick, but instead, I just looked at her and shook my head. FCI Beckley had been my home for the last seven years. The Feds knocked me off with a burner and a few ounces of crack. The bullshit lawyer I had told me it was better for me to cop out instead of going to trial against the Feds. My dumb ass thought I was getting about three to five years. Instead, the judge gave me seven fucking years. I could've walked a year and a half ago, but I caught a few shots that pushed my time back.

I tried to get into the drug program, but because of my previous gun charge, I wasn't eligible. So I manned up and played the hand that I was dealt.

"Here go your bus ticket and a stipend of $200. You're to check in with your probation officer in the Atlanta office at 9:00, Monday morning. Good luck out there."

"A'ight," I said, keeping it short and sweet. I wasn't tryin'a stay in this bitch no longer than I had already. And I damned sure wasn't tryin'a give they asses no reason to put me back in that damn cage. I ain't even chuck her ass the deuces. The way these muthafuckas was, they would accuse a nigga of throwing up some kinda gang sign.

I followed the dude outside to the car. He was taking three other niggas and me to the bus station. The air was crisp, clear, and the sky was blue. I stopped for a moment just to get a whiff of the fresh air. This seemed unreal. It felt good but strange at the same time. I turned around and took one last look at the high barbed wired building. *Fuck these crackers. I ain't coming back.*

This was what freedom felt like after years of being locked up. I paid attention to everything that we drove past. I was like a kid in a candy store. I was eager to reach the station so that I could be away from any and everything that was related to that damn place.

Minutes later, my wish was granted as we pulled into the bus station. I looked to see if I spotted Shontelle. She told me she would be driving a black Dodge Charger.

I got out of the car and looked around. I felt out of place like everyone was staring at me. I tried not to stare back. It was brick outside, so I decide to walk into the Greyhound Bus Station.

"Keel, Keel," I heard someone yell.

I stopped and looked behind me to see who it was in case somebody I ain't wanna see had caught wind that I was getting out today. I was relieved to know that it was Shontelle running toward me full speed. She ran straight into my arms.

"What's good, shorty?"

She grabbed my head and started kissing me passionately. I hugged her tightly and cupped her ass, bringing her closer to me. It felt good to be able to be this close to a female. My dick started to get hard as she pressed up against it. Shit, we needed to get out of here.

"Come on, shorty. Let's get the fuck up outta here."

"Sorry. I'm just happy to see you, baby," she said, smiling from ear to ear. If I didn't know any better, I would think that she missed a nigga.

"Same here, love." I smiled down at her in return, happy that somebody out here gave a damn about me. We held hands while we walked over to the parking lot where she was parked.

I couldn't keep my eyes off Shontelle's hips and the way they swung from side to side. See, Shontelle was my main bitch before I caught my case. She wasn't the only bitch I was fucking but definitely the only bitch that I could say I loved. She'd gained some weight while I was gone, but it made her sexier. I couldn't wait to get to the crib so that I could suck and beat the pussy up. Shit, more like *punish* the pussy.

"Oh shit, this pussy is so good, bae," I panted as I tried to catch my breath while I fucked Shontelle doggie style.

"Daddy, this your pussy," she said in between moans.

I grabbed her hips tighter as I thrust deeper into her guts. I was famished. It'd been years since I had a piece of ass. All I'd known was my palm and some lotion. This was different. It was wet and tight, gripping my dick. I was in straight beast mode. I closed my eyes, trying to savor the moment. I tried my best not to focus on what I was doing, hoping I wouldn't bust too quickly, but I couldn't hold it any longer. My veins started getting bigger, and I felt like my head was about to explode.

"Damn, you tearing out my pussy," she cried out. Shit, just a minute ago, she was bouncing around on the dick. Now, she was crying for help. I paid her no mind. I knew how Shontelle was. Even when the dick was good, she still cried out.

"Fuck! Fuck! Damn! Maaan." I exploded inside her pussy.

I pulled my limp dick out and fell on the bed. I was exhausted and tired, so I just lay there.

"Damn, Keel, you didn't have to fuck me this hard."

"I'm sorry, bae. I thought you were loving it."

"Boy, fuck you. You know I ain't been fucking nothing since you been gone, so my shit hurts like hell." She pouted and got off the bed. Looking at her fine, sexy body made me want to go a second round, but I wasn't a fool. I needed to get my energy back up first.

I sat up and lit a cigarette. This was like heaven. Just got my first piece of ass and now smoking a Newport. I wished I could hit the weed, but I had to see my probation officer Monday morning. I wasn't trying to give her no dirty piss, so this Newport would have to do. It was better than what I had in lockup, so I wasn't gonna complain. And since I sure as hell wasn't tryin'a go back to that hellhole, I wasn't tryin'a test shit 'round here. At least, not until I felt this probation officer out.

I was up bright and early the next morning. In the pen, we had to be up at 5:00 a.m., booted and suited. You didn't want to get caught slipping if a fight popped off. After I took a shower, I got dressed. First things first, I needed to get me a cell and then hit up the mall. When I got torn off, I had a few dollars at my mama's crib. I needed to go over there and grab that.

"Aye, babes, what's your plan for today?" I asked Shontelle, looking over my shoulder at her in the bed. She was laid up with her face resting in her hand, watching me get dressed.

"I thought we were just going to chill." She shot me a dirty look.

"I mean, we can chill later. But I ain't got shit but this bullshit-ass prison gear. I need to go see my mama and them first, then hit up the mall."

"So you want me to take you? I got to be at the shop by ten."

"Nah, I was hoping you'll let me drop you off."

"Drop me off? So you can have your bitches all up in my shit?" She hopped up like the suggestion had really offended her. Standing there, butt-ass naked, she put her hands on her waist.

"Man, come on with that bullshit, babes. That was seven years ago. I told you I've changed. I'm no longer on no bullshit with you. Babes, it's just us."

"Uh-huh, niggas say anything when they locked up. I pray to God you changed your ways 'cause I'm not dealing with you and these hoes any longer. I was the only one that was making those long-ass trips and faithfully making sure money was on your books. I'm warning you, Keel. You better stay away from these bitches."

"Babes, you worrying over nothing. I ain't trippin' off none of these hoes out here."

She shot me a look and walked off. I knew I was a dog back in the day. Yeah, I done fucked multiple bitches. I can't say I'ma be faithful, 'cause I ain't never been the type of nigga to fuck only one bitch. I was a nigga that made money, and with that, the bitches were known to come around, making it hard just to fuck one bitch. But like I told shorty, I'm a changed man. I chuckled to myself, 'cause who I was fooling? I was still that nigga deep down inside, but out of respect for Shontelle and the way she held me down, I was at least gon' try not to let the shit get back to her about what I was gon' be doin' out here in these streets . . . eventually.

It felt weird driving after all these years, but like the old heads used to say, "Once you learn to drive, you can't ever forget." I dropped Shontelle off at work and headed to my mama's house, where I pulled up into the driveway and walked to the door. I rang the doorbell and waited.

"Who is it?" I heard my mama yell.

"It's your baby boy," I yelled back.

The door flew open, and Mama rushed out to greet me. "Boy, I thought I was going to do a pop up on yo' ass. You been home since yesterday, and I'm just now seeing you." She hugged me with everything in her little frame.

"You know I was coming, but I had to spend some quality time with my girl."

"Come on, let's go inside. Your sister is at work. You know she's going to be upset that she wasn't here."

"I'll get up with her later. So what's good, Mama? How you doing?"

"I'm doing okay. Happy that you're home. I can finally rest well at night. You still messing with that same bitch?"

"Ma, chill out. You know I love Shontelle."

"That bitch is bad news. I told you that from the first day you brought her around. I can't tell you who to mess with, but don't trust that bitch. I heard she was messing around out here. I hope you using protection before you run up in her."

"Ma, chill out. Shorty ain't messing wit' no other nigga. People just be spreading lies, trying to put that girl down."

"Hmmm. I hear you, and I see she got your nose wide open. You're my son, and best believe, if that bitch ever do anything to you, I'ma be there with my old ass."

I had to laugh 'cause she was dead-ass serious too. Ma ain't never like Shontelle from the beginning. She said she was around 'cause I had money. That might've been true. But shorty had been there these seven years, more than most of my family, and for that alone, I'm loyal to her.

"What's that smell, Ma?" I walked off to the kitchen.

I was trying to cut the conversation short about Shontelle. I concluded that my girl and my mother would never be cool, and honestly, as long as they didn't disrespect each other, we were good.

"I got some beef stew in the crockpot. It's almost finished."

"Oh yeah, I need some of that." This was one of the things I missed most—my mama's cooking.

After we ate, we sat there, talking for a little while. Mama still had the safe, so I popped it open. When I got locked up, there was a little over twenty-five grand in there. Now, it was only ten grand. I was kind of salty 'cause Mama didn't tell me she used any of my money. I started to say something, but I decided not to. I just grabbed the ten stacks, kissed Mama on the cheek, and left.

I was tight as fuck, though. I was hoping to get back on with some of the money. With only ten grand, there wasn't much that I could really do. Shit, I needed clothes, among other shit, and this was just barely about to cover them.

I spent about three grand at the mall. Got me a brand-new phone, which I had no idea how to work, copped me two pairs of Jays, and the rest was spent on clothes, drawers, and socks.

I pulled in at my homie Jay's auto body shop. See, Jay and I used to run back in the day. Only thing was, he was smart. He made money and got out, using the drug money to start his business. Now, he was running a legit business that the cops couldn't touch. I'd heard that he had even gotten a contract detailing some of the cops' cars. Now, *that* was some boss shit. We spoke quite a few times over the phone while I was locked up. I was definitely proud of the big homie.

When I parked, I took a minute to look around at how my nigga was really out here, getting down. I couldn't believe that he had employees and shit. Finally, I got out of the car and entered the shop. I spotted Jay sitting down by the counter.

"Oh, hell nah. This can't be my nigga." He jumped up and rushed toward me.

"What's good, fam?" We exchanged dap and embraced. "Nigga, I knew yo' days was winding down, but I didn't know you was out."

"I just got out yesterday, fam. I like this." I took a quick glance around his shop.

"Shit, you know a nigga got to make it one way or the other. But, nigga, fuck all that. How it feel to be free?"

"Shit, it feel good as fuck. Still trying to adjust to being a free man."

He sat down, and I took a seat across from him.

"Shit, nigga. It'll take a minute, but you good. First, you need to get you some pussy, then get back to the money."

"Shit, you late. I wasted no time in tearing up Shontelle's fine ass."

"Oh, man, I thought you and shorty was done. Nigga, you need to find you some new hoes." He busted out laughing.

"Well, you know that's a must, but for now, she's the only one that rocked wit' a nigga, so I made sure that she was the one that got this work first. But even when I get some new bitches on the squad, shorty still goin' be my main bitch."

"I hear you, homie. I hear you. Well, fuck all that. It's the weekend. You tryin'a get up in the club? Let's celebrate, nigga."

"Hell yeah, dawg. Shit, I just copped some new gear, so you know I'm ready to jump out there."

"Shit, let's make it happen then, nigga," he said. I handed his ass my phone so that he could lock his number in that shit. I ain't wanna hear him talkin' shit about me, because I wasn't able to work that new technology shit that they had out.

A customer walked in right when he handed me my shit back, so we exchanged dap, and I bounced. It was good seeing my nigga. He was one of the few solid niggas still left out in these streets. The rest of these niggas were either straight pussies or bitches. Shit had definitely changed since I left the streets. Most of the solid niggas were either dead or locked up.

I glanced at the time. It was 6:00 p.m., so I made my way to Shontelle's shop. I swear I just got home and wasn't in no mood to hear her mouth already. After talking to Mama and then to Jay, I couldn't help but wonder. I knew Shontelle said she was faithful to me the entire time, but each time her name got mentioned, it wasn't in a good way. Was she telling the truth? Or was she another bitch out here, fucking and sucking on the next nigga?

Chapter Two

Shontelle

Niggas could be the biggest hoes out here in these streets, but always screaming they wanted a real bitch. When I was younger, I was that real bitch. I was rolling with this nigga Jakeel, helping him make runs up top every two weeks. I helped him count his money and held his gun whenever the police were around. See, I thought I was playing my position as his wifey. That was . . . until bitches started showing up left and right, claiming they were fucking around. One bitch went as far as claiming she was pregnant by him. Of course, he denied the bitch and the baby. I almost had a mental breakdown 'cause he was my first love, the first nigga I fucked. But being the only nigga to get this pussy didn't stop him from slanging dick all over Decatur.

I should've left him, but I was only 18 and was young, dumb, and full of come. So I took his word for it and stayed with him. I was the apple of his eye and the envy of the bitches who wished they were fucking him. I felt proud, especially when he referred to me as "bae." I knew I had to be special for him to bring around all his homies and his family. He also spent stacks on me. When we would hit Lenox Mall, he bought me a diamond ring and bracelets. My account was looking good, and he bought me a brand-new car. At 18, I was in heaven, living my best damn life.

Things took a drastic turn when he got torn off. One of the fiends that he was serving got torn off and decided to rat on Jakeel. My world was turned upside down 'cause all I knew was the life he gave to me. In my mind, I thought he was going to beat the case and come home to me. Wrong! On the day of his sentencing, the judge gave him seven years after he pleaded guilty to drug and gun charges. I remember them leading him away, and I fell to my knees. What was I supposed to do without my man? I couldn't live without him.

Reality soon settled in. Jakeel was gone, and I was in this crazy world all by myself. After days of lying around crying, I got up one day and decided I had to do something. I had to figure out a way 'cause he wasn't coming home any time soon. Jakeel had left some work in a safe. I didn't know shit about selling no powder. But I knew my big cousin Jay was in the streets. I hit him up, and he came over. He decided to get it from me, and he gave me the money. I knew he probably beat me in the head, but he was family, and it ain't like I could just go out there and start selling drugs.

With the money he gave me, I decided to go to beauty school. So I enrolled in Beaver Beauty Academy here Decatur. Within eighteen months, I graduated. I worked in a shop on Candler for about three years, built my clientele up, and saved a few coins. I decided to step out on faith and got my own shop. I hired two other girls and a chick that did makeup. Together, we now had one of the most elite salons on the East Side.

It was hard living without my man. But as time went by and more gossip start circulating, I realized that he wasn't the solid nigga that he said he was. I was out here bragging about how I was holding my man down, and what I didn't know was that I was the laughingstock 'cause everyone in the streets knew how dirty this nigga was doing me.

***

"Girl, I know you happy your boo is home," Liza, one of my closest friends and stylists at the salon, whispered to me.

"Girl, I ain't gon' lie. I am happy he's home, but at the same time, I'm kind of nervous. Seven years have passed, and I'm afraid he's no longer the nigga that I fell in love with. Shit, I'm no longer the young, naïve girl that he left out here. I'm a grown-ass woman, and I'm not up for no games with this nigga."

"Girl, I feel you, but he would be a fool if he comes back out here with the same old bullshit. You held his ass down all them damn years, so he better act right. If he don't, then he will have to deal with me too."

I know her ass was dead-ass serious. Liz and I had been rocking with each other since our freshman year in high school. She was the only bitch that I really trusted 100 percent. Best believe, if she's rocking, then I'm rolling.

Before we could finish our conversation, I heard the door to the shop open. I looked up and saw that it was Keel's ass who'd just walked in. It's crazy how, after all these years, seeing him still gives me butterflies in my stomach.

"Hmm, there goes your boo," Liz teased as she walked off to tend to her client that was under the dryer.

Jakeel made his way over to my booth. "Hey, love, what's good? You're about ready to go?" he kissed me on the lips.

"Yeah, let me clean up my station real quick, and I'll be ready."

"A'ight. I be out in the car, waiting."

As he walked out, I spotted one of the clients who was sitting there waiting, eyeballing him all the way out the door. I couldn't help but wonder if she recognized him from somewhere. I grabbed the broom and started sweeping up the hair from the floor. Then I straightened up my booth and grabbed my purse.

"Hey, Liz, can you lock up and set the alarm for me when you leave?"

"I got you, hon. Go enjoy." She winked at me.

I laughed to myself as I walked out. I looked at the girl that was staring down my man in the face as I strutted by. I didn't recognize her, but I wondered what her story was.

Shit, I quickly put on my coat as soon as the wind hit my face. I swear I hated the fucking cold. I walked hurriedly to the car and got in. I couldn't help but notice he was on the phone, but soon as I sat down, he hung up.

"Who was that on the phone?"

"Oh, just my homeboy. Trying to catch up on old times."

"Oh, okay," I said but wanted to say so much more.

All the niggas he used to roll with were nowhere around when he caught his case. His nigga Mel was the only nigga that gave me money on numerous occasions to send to him. Speaking of Mel, I needed to hit him up later. It's funny I hadn't heard from him since yesterday.

"Do you need to stop anywhere?"

"Huh?" I was so caught up in my thoughts that I wasn't paying attention to what he said.

"You a'ight?"

"Yeah, I'm good. Just a little tired."

"Oh, OK. Do you need to stop anywhere?"

"Yeah, we need something to eat. What you feel for?"

"Anything is cool with me. Shit, I've been gone so long, everything tastes better than prison food."

"Okay, we can do Applebee's. There's one on Memorial Drive, near the highway."

"A'ight, bet."

On the way to Applebee's, his phone started ringing. He ignored it like he didn't hear it. Matter of fact, he cut the music up louder, but I wasn't going to let him do this. I cut the music down some as the phone continued ringing. I guess whoever it was wanted to talk to him badly. I tapped him on the shoulder.

"What's up?"

"Your phone is ringing. Why you ain't picking it up?"

"Man, I can hear it. I'll call back whoever it is later."

That's when it hit me. He just got the phone today. I don't even have the number. So whoever was calling him just got the number. I looked over at him suspiciously.

"Who you gave your number to already?"

"Damn, Shontelle, what are you? The fucking police?"

"Nah, I'm your fucking woman, and I asked you a fucking question."

"It's no-fucking-body, okay? Shit, it might be my mama or my sister. You ain't the only trying to see me or talk to me. Can you stop with all the damn questions? Do I ask you who calls your phone?"

"You know what? Fuck you, Jakeel."

I was not in the mood to fight with this nigga, but I hoped he didn't think I wouldn't make a note of his attitude. He pulled up at Applebee's, and we got out and walked in.

It took no time for us to order our food. I was still in my feelings, so I just kept quiet and ate my food. The atmosphere was tense, but I didn't give a fuck. His ass was going to watch how the fuck he talked to me.

After dinner, we headed home. I was exhausted from working, so I got in the tub as soon as we got in the house. Then I made me a glass of hot chocolate and got in bed. I knew he could tell I was avoiding him 'cause he stayed in the living room, pretending like he was watching television. Either way, I didn't give a fuck.

Chapter Three

Mika

Three Days Later . . .
Monday Morning

I glanced at the clock on my nightstand. It was 3:42 a.m., and here I was, wide awake like I didn't have work in the morning. This wasn't nothing new, though. Lately, my sleeping pattern was off. I was concerned to the point where I spoke to my doctor about it. He went ahead and prescribed Ambien. The first time I took it, I was out of it at work. The entire day I was sluggish and could barely function. That was the first *and* the last time I took those pills. Soon as I got home, I threw them in the trash. This wasn't good at all. Being a probation officer was a tiring job, and most days, I was in the field for close to twelve hours. Don't get me wrong. I love what I do. But not being able to sleep at night was putting a strain on me, physically and mentally.

I looked over to the side of the bed and noticed this husband of mine still hadn't made it home. Shit had gotten really bad in the last year. First, it would be little lies that he was "working," and then he was "hanging out with the boys." I tried to give him the benefit of the doubt . . . until one night when he came home, and I saw lipsticks stains all over his crispy white shirt. When I pointed out the shit to him, he tried to say it wasn't lipstick. I looked at him and shook my head. This nigga must've thought I was a fool. That night, I grabbed my pillow and headed to the guest room. I buried my head in my pillow and started crying. I loved this man. We were a family. Why would he step out on his family?

Just thinking about that night made me upset all over again. I grabbed my phone and dialed his number. It went straight to voicemail. I shook my head and threw the phone down on the bed. I just lay there in the dark, looking up at the ceiling.

The alarm kept going off, and, as usual, that's the time I started feeling tired. I silenced it and decided to give myself an extra twenty minutes. I must've dozed off, 'cause a banging on my door awakened me.

"Ma, are you up?" Ky called out to me.

"Yes, baby, I'm up." I quickly sat up.

She walked into the room, looked at me, and shook her head.

"What is it?" I asked, the look on her face frustrating me.

"Hmmm, so Daddy didn't come home again?"

"Baby, listen, your daddy is a grown man and free to do what he pleases. Now, you need to get ready. Don't you have an early class this morning?"

"Yes, I do, and I'm ready. Ma, I love my daddy, but I have no idea why you put up with him."

"Girl, get the hell out of my room. When you get you a husband, *then* you can talk to me about marriage stuff."

"Hmmm, no disrespect, but if this is how married life's supposed to be, I'll be single forever."

I looked at that girl and walked off. I rushed to my closet and pulled out a pin-striped pants suit. This was one of my favorite outfits, and I'd probably worn it more than I should have. Ky must've sensed that I don't want to talk about her daddy 'cause she walked out of my room without saying another word.

I love my child, but she needed to stay out of grown people's business. I married this man for better or worse, and just because we were going through a little rough patch didn't mean we didn't love each other. I tried to convince myself there was no other woman that could replace me. My husband and I had put too many years of hard work into our marriage. I was sure neither one of us wanted to let it go.

I heard a knock at the door and lifted my head to see who was there. Joy peeped her head in the doorway.

"Hey, you, I didn't see you come in." She came in and closed the door behind her. She placed a cup of hot chocolate in front of me and took a seat across from me.

"Girl, I wish I didn't have to be here today. But until I hit the lotto, I have to be here. Today, I got three new intakes. I just hope this day goes by fast."

"What's going on, girl? You look like you've been run over by a tractor-trailer. Are you still having problems sleeping?" she quizzed.

I took a sip of the hot chocolate and looked over at my friend. "I can't remember the last time I got a good night's sleep, and to top it off, this so-called husband of mine didn't come home last night."

"Say *what?* What you mean he ain't come home? Was he working?" she shot me a surprised look.

"No, he was not working. He barely works the night shift, and when I called his phone, it went straight to voicemail."

"Tamika, I don't mean to pry, but do you think Rasheem is screwing around?" She gave me a suspicious look.

"Hmmm . . . What else can a married man be out doing all night? I know what—fucking and sucking on one of these little trifling-ass young bitches. Girl, he's been careful so far, but I'll catch on to him soon enough."

"Tamika, I'm so sorry you're going through this. I mean, these men nowadays are straight-up dogs. Here, this man has a beautiful family and is still trying to fuck it up. Girl, that's why my ass been using my dildo. I tell you, sometimes it gets lonely. But I refuse to lie up with one of these old, two-timing-ass niggas. But if I were you, I would confront his ass. You know men are good at cheating but bad at hiding it. We women can go out and fuck a whole basketball team. We get home, prepare dinner, wash clothes, clean the house, wash our asses, and fuck your man like your ass wasn't just sliding down on another man's dick. These men, soon as a bitch give them a little attention, they start fucking up. They stop coming home on time, and stop doing the shit they're supposed to do. They think they're the smartest. But in reality, they are dumb as fuck."

She went on a whole tangent, and I had to say that I was grateful for her. Joy, just like her name says, was always a good time. And whether or not she knew it, she brightened up my day, just that quick. The hot cocoa and the conversation warmed my quickly freezing heart. The best part about it was that she was dead serious. And I wished I had the balls to cheat on my husband the way that he was doing me. Give his ass a taste of his own medicine. Maybe then, he would get his act together. But knowing Rasheem, he would just kill my ass and move the bitch that he was fuckin' into my bed before my body was found. Who was gonna check him? He was that powerful.

I couldn't do that to Ky. She wouldn't go for some random bitch coming in and playing house with her daddy. So she would probably end up out on the streets, and he'd stop paying her tuition. She didn't deserve that. To be motherless, homeless, and her future cut short because I wanted to get even with her daddy . . . I was better than that. But thinking of Ky made me smile. I knew what she would be with, and I planned to talk to her about it tonight.

Coming back to my current environment, I saw a smirk cross Joy's face. I hated when she did that . . . well, when I didn't want her to. That was something that came with being best friends for decades. She could read me like a book, and I knew that she was gonna be on my ass like white on rice if I didn't tell her that I was thinking what she thought I was thinking. Regardless of whether I did, though, she was already planning the stealth mission that would catch my husband in his bullshit. With no prenup and fifteen years married, all I needed was proof, and I would be in there like swimwear.

I knew that I couldn't hire anyone to do it because all the private investigators were either former cops or had some kinda cop connection, and they *all* knew Rasheem. He made sure that they did. Hell, even the ex-cons that I worked with knew who my husband was. They never gave me any problems because they didn't wanna have to face his ass. That was the kinda life I lived. I was pretty much a prisoner in a miserable-ass marriage, and couldn't do shit about anything because of *who* my husband was.

"So, when we getting this shit started?" Joy asked, making me laugh. I loved the way her British accent sounded when she cussed.

"I don't know if it's a good idea—" My phone started ringing, and I couldn't say that I wasn't glad. Usually, I hated when our sessions were interrupted by work. But this time, looking at the expression on her face, I was happy for the excuse to put this conversation on pause.

I excused myself and picked it up. It was the receptionist telling me that my 9:00 a.m. parolee was there.

"Work calls," I said, hanging up the phone.

"We might be finished . . . for now, but we ain't done," Joy threatened, motioning her finger back and forth between her and me. Blowing me a kiss, she left, and I grabbed the file in front of me.

I took a few minutes to read over it carefully. I liked to find out who I was about to come in contact with and what their story was before talking to them.

"Joanne, please tell Mr. Greene to come in," I paged the receptionist.

"OK, Mrs. Blake, gotcha."

I left his folder open and sat there waiting. Sipping my hot cocoa, I started to wonder if he'd gotten lost on the way to my office or had made a stop at the bathroom or something. Either way, I was becoming impatient, and this was a bad way to start things off with me. There were two kinds of parolees: the ones who wanted to get their probation over with and didn't give me any trouble at all, and the ones who wanted to let me know that they weren't gonna answer to no bitch. I didn't want to pass judgment before he got in here because I always gave them the benefit of the doubt. But I would've been foolish not to pay attention to these kinds of things. They were usually precursors to later, more blatant acts of defiance.

I heard a knock and tried to give him a clean slate in my mind. Sitting upright, my hands folded over his file on my desk, I made sure that I had on my poker face.

"Come in, Mr. Greene," I yelled enough for him to hear.

A dark-skinned brother walked in. I surveyed him from head to toe. His pants sagged, and his hair wasn't combed. He just wasn't making this benefit of the doubt thing easy for me.

"Good morning, Mr. Greene. I'm Officer Blake. Please, take a seat."

"What's good?" he asked. "My bad about the delay. I had to take a piss." He added an explanation for the delay in his arrival, but the way he was speaking was too informal for the environment we were in.

This was his first mistake—well, his *third* at this point. I wanted to tell his ass we're not in the hood. That shit might work among his boys, but I wasn't one of the boys, and it wasn't working with me. Instead, I took my personal feelings out of the situation and got right down to business.

"So, you were released on Friday from FCI Beckley. I'll be your probation officer. First, I need a urine sample from you. Then I'll make sure you understand the rules and regulations of being on probation. If you violate any of these rules, I will come to get you personally and send you back to prison. Do I make myself clear?" I took a cup out of my drawer and placed it in front of him.

He stared at me and didn't respond right away. His lack of response made me meet his eyes to make sure that my meaning was clear. But as I looked him in the eyes, I quickly looked away. Something unexplainable was happening. It was like this convict was burning a hole inside of me. My panties started becoming uncomfortable. Like . . . They were all of a sudden too tight for my ass. I wanted to stick my hand under my skirt so that I could fix them, but I couldn't. So I crossed my legs, trying to manipulate them into a better position.

"Officer Blake, can I ask you a question?" he grabbed my attention.

"Yes, you may." I continued to avoid eye contact by looking at the computer screen, pretending like I was reading.

"What is a beautiful woman like you doing in this position? I mean, do you *like* your job? Locking up people and all that?"

I smiled and clasped my hands together. Uncrossing my legs, I forgot the reason that I'd crossed them in the first place . . . and crossed them again, expeditiously. "Well, yes, I love what I do. I get to keep criminals off the streets and help those that want to come home and get rehabilitated. So, now that you brought that up, which category do you fall in?"

He looked at me and smiled. "I mean, I'ma get me a job and stay outta y'all way. You know what I mean?"

"Well, I do hope so, 'cause you will find out, I'm not the officer to play around with. Let's go so you can take this test."

I got up, snatched the cup, and walked out the door. He followed me to the bathroom. I stood with the door ajar while he pissed in the cup. My mind kept wandering off, but I managed to get it under control.

He handed me the cup, which barely had enough urine in it to test. I guess he wasn't lying about using the bathroom before coming into my office. But that didn't make sense. He had to know I was gonna test him, so why wouldn't he hold it? Looking at it, and then at him, he smiled and gave me a shrug as if to say, "I told ya so," to which I smirked before I could catch myself. Turning on my heels so that he didn't see all the way through my soul, we walked back into my office.

Putting the test strip into the cup through the hole in the top, I went over everything with him.

"Your curfew is at 9:00 p.m., nightly. If there's going to be any delay, you need to send me a text to this number here." I pulled one of my business cards from the holder and highlighted it. "You're expected to find employment and only go to work and home. Seeing that your crime was drug possession with the intent to sell, you are not to be around any drugs of any kind. Are you following me?" I asked to make sure that he understood. When he didn't respond, again, I looked up into his face, and he hit me with a quick head nod to let me know that he got what I was saying. His eyes were so intense that this time, I sighed involuntarily before looking back down at the paperwork that I was going over with him.

"Now, you are being paroled to your mother's house, a Miss Mary Greene, is that correct?"

Again, no answer. Again, our eyes met. Again, he nodded.
"OK, good. I can come to check on you at any time, without notice, and if I find anything that conflicts with the terms of your parole, you will be thrown back into jail to serve out the remainder of your sentence."

Not waiting for him to respond, I handed him some papers to sign. After he finished, he gave them back to me. I handed him my card with my work cell number highlighted, and when he grabbed it, he held on to it long enough to make me look up at him again before taking the card and putting it into his pocket. I slid him what I called my "Welcome Packet" across the desk to avoid any more physical contact with him. I didn't think that my panties could take another glance.

"Okay, Mr. Greene, you're free to go," I offered, practically rushing him out of my office. "Keep me posted on the job hunting. In one of those pamphlets are some places that hire felons, and they work with us with new releases. Oh, don't you forget to call color code each day after 5:00 p.m., to see if your number is called. If it is, you need to report the next day and provide your urine." I finished up before I stood, ready to send him on his way. He stood up too and stared at me all over. It kind of made me uncomfortable.

"What does a man like myself have to do to get with a woman like you?" he finally spoke, and the question that he presented made my heart skip a beat and my stomach flutter.

"First off, I'm a happily married woman," I deflected. "And second, you're out of line. I'm an officer, and you're a criminal. There is no way in hell that we can have anything. Now, go on out of here before I violate you for crossing the line."

"Oh shit, and you feisty also. Oh, you should check those panties. They probably in bunches by now." He smiled and winked at me before walking off.

I quickly closed the door. The nerve of this punk! What did he know about the Victoria Secret thong that I was wearing? I hurried to my seat and calmed down my nerves. His picture was looking at me in the still-open file. I sat there and stared for a few seconds before I closed it and put it where the rest of the files were.

The rest of the day went by fast, and I was eager to get out of there. Once I got off the elevator on the first floor, I checked my phone and realized that my husband hadn't called me all day. So, this nigga didn't come home and hadn't called either. I thought about calling him but decided to do it once I reached home. I stopped by the local Publix and grabbed a rotisserie chicken with some greens and mashed potatoes. I had a slight headache and didn't feel like cooking. The kid and I could eat this for dinner. As for Rasheem, he could eat wherever the fuck he was at or eat shit. I was so angry with him that I could care less about him right now. Next, I stopped by the liquor store and grabbed myself a bottle of D'ussé. I needed something to calm my fucking nerves before I did something I regretted.

As I pulled up to the house, I spotted Rasheem's truck in the driveway. That was very strange. He barely made it home for dinner, so why the hell would he be here now? I pulled into the garage and parked.

I walked up the stairs and into the kitchen. The house was quiet. I put the stuff on the counter, then walked over to the living room and kicked off my shoes. I sat down for a few seconds, but something kept tugging at me. I needed to confront this nigga. I got up and rushed up the stairs.

I heard the shower running, so I walked over to the bathroom door. His clothes were on the floor. I picked up his shirt and smelled it. It was sweaty but also smelled like perfume. Nothing that I recognized, but I knew it was some cheap-ass shit. It smelled like musk and stale pussy. I then picked up his polo drawers and could see visible come stains on the front. I heard the water cut off, so I hurriedly threw his nasty drawers down and cut the lights off in the room. Then I grabbed the bat that I kept behind the bedroom door and sat on the bed.

A few minutes later, he walked out of the bathroom, dick hanging and all. Any other time, that shit would've turned me on, but knowing that his dick had just been inside some random, trashy-ass bitch, it disgusted me. He was on the phone laughing and talking like he didn't have a care in the world. I didn't know if he didn't expect me to be home, or he just didn't give a fuck. But I was about to find out. His mouth dropped open as he saw me sitting on the bed.

"Ummm . . . Let me call you right back," he whispered in the phone.

"Hello, husband, don't hang the phone up. Is that her, the whore that you been with all night?"

"I'll call you back." He hung the phone up and started drying off.

I stood and hit him across his knees with that damn bat with all my force.

"Oh, fuck! What the fuck?"

I turned the light on so that he could look me in the face. "Damn, Mika, what the fuck you do that for?" He lunged toward me.

"Back the fuck up, nigga!" I hit his ass on the arm.

"You fucking crazy bitch! I swear, I'ma beat yo' mother-fucking ass!" he yelled as he tried to walk off.

"I don't know where the fuck you going, but I told yo' ass before, I'm not going to be with you if you around here fucking everything. You can pack your shit and get out, for real," I said as I raised the bat again.

"Bitch, I done told yo' crazy ass that I'm not cheating on you. I was working a case all night, that's all. But, nah, you want to act all crazy and shit. I fucking love you."

"Nigga, shut the fuck up. You fucking something, and when I find out, I'm going to demolish yo' ass!" I yelled as

I walked out of the room, leaving his ass there to tend to the bumps and bruises I left on his ass by his damn self.

I was too fucking heated. I needed someone to talk to, but it was too late to call my girlfriend, Lexi. She was the only one that I could trust with my business. As much as I loved Joy, if I told her, the whole office would know what the hell was happening in my household. She would mean well and want people to see how fucked up a person Rasheem was. But I knew that shit would backfire, and they would see me as weak and dumb as hell for staying with him for as long as I had. I'm sure that some of their asses already knew about the shit that Rasheem was doing, anyway. Hell, some of them might be fuckin' his ass behind my back.

I sat in the living room awhile to cool off, then went back to my bedroom. Shaking my head, I stomped over, locked my bedroom door, and threw the bat down since Rasheem wasn't in there. I was mentally tired and drained. Fuck, I had to work in the morning, and there I was acting a fool.

Half an hour later, Rasheem knocked on the door. Reluctantly, I let him in. "You know that was a business associate, and you acting like a jealous schoolgirl. What is wrong with you, Tamika?" this old, psychotic-ass nigga said.

I walked over to where his clothes were and grabbed them. "Nigga, you see these? They have a bitch written all over them. Your shirt smells like cheap-ass perfume that I would never wear, and these fucking drawers that I bought have come stains all over them. So, unless it's a nigga you were with . . . Who's the bitch?"

"You're crazier than I thought," he chuckled. "You going around checking my dirty drawers. Is this the kind of woman I married? You're worse than these project bitches—"

"Rasheem, I don't give a fuck about what you're talking about. You're a fucking married man, and you're running around here like you single. If you don't love me, why the fuck don't you just leave? Get your shit and get out," I yelled at the top of my lungs.

He looked at me like he was shocked and took a few steps toward me. "Get out? Hold up. Wait. Did you forget *I* bought this house? Yeah, you losing your damn mind."

"*Your* house? In case you forgot, we are *married*. I'm going to call a lawyer tomorrow, and I want you out of my life. I'm not living like this anymore."

"You know what? I tried for years to deal with your over-bearing ass. The truth is, I love you, but you're boring, and all you do is nag. You know why I stuck around? 'Cause of Ky'Imani. I wanted my child to have her parents in the same home! But she is damn near grown, and I don't need to deal with your shit anymore."

"Boring? 'Cause I don't swallow your come or let you have your threesomes? What the fuck I look like eating pussy to please you? Are you willing to suck one of those big, black, ten-inch dicks to please me? Don't ask me to do some shit that you ain't willing to do for me." He lunged toward me and grabbed me by the throat. "You better get your fucking hands off me before I report your ass. Your name will be plastered across the television tonight as a detective that beats his wife."

"Bitch, you wouldn't," he said through clenched teeth with his fist raised.

"Try me, nigga."

He must've known I wasn't bluffing 'cause he let me go and walked off. He started grabbing things and throwing them in bags.

"I'm divorcing yo' ass, and I'm asking for half of every-thing *and* alimony."

"Bitch, I'll kill you before you get a dime from me. Now, call and tell whoever the fuck you want to."

I sat on the bed looking at him and wondering how we got here. This can't be my loving husband treating me like this. The tears wanted to flow out, but I tried my best not to shed one of them in front of this nigga. I pulled my nightstand drawer open and took out my Glock that was inside. I held it in my hand while I sat there.

"Hmmm, what the fuck you take that out for? Don't forget who the better shooter is, sweetheart."

I knew he was looking for a reaction out of me, but I held my composure and ignored his ass. Finally, he grabbed his keys and left. I walked over to my window and watched as he pulled out of the yard and down the street.

That's when I broke down. This was the actual moment that I realized that our marriage was over, and I needed to figure out my next move.

Chapter Four

Jakeel

It was my first weekend as a free man, and I was out with the niggas up in the club Blue Flames, one of Atlanta's elite strip clubs. This was one of the clubs that TI frequented. Mel and his cousin were showing me a lot of love tonight. We were in the VIP area, chopping it up. Big bottles of Patrón and Grey Goose were on our table.

"Yo, shorty, come here," Mel hollered at one of the stripper bitches. She was a bad little bitch with hair down to her ass.

She must've known there was some money over here 'cause she smiled and strutted toward us. She took a seat next to Mel. He whispered something in her ear, and she giggled. I pretended like I wasn't eyeing shorty, so I started playing around on my phone.

"Hey, sexy, my name's Mia. What's yours?" she reached over and touched my hand.

"Hey, beautiful. I'm Keel. Nice to meet you."

"Your boy told me you fresh out of the pen and could use some company."

I looked at Mel, and he busted out laughing. I couldn't do anything but shake my head. My nigga ain't changed at all.

"Come on, let's go have some privacy," she said, taking my hand and helping me up.

I followed her, watching her ass jiggle, and her hair swung from side to side with the sway of her hips, giving me peeks of that phat ass in that thong. Feeling my eyes on her, she winked at me, leading me behind the curtain. This was where it went down for a lap dance. She slightly pushed me back on the couch and started grinding on me. "Shake That Monkey" by Too $hort was blasting through the speakers.

I grabbed her hips as she gyrated on my lap. My dick started getting hard as I sat there, trying to stay focused. She grabbed my hand and led it between her legs. I moved her thong out of the way and slid my finger in her wet, slippery pussy. *Oh,shit!* She started grinding on my fingers. My dick was rock hard and needed to be released.

Seconds later, the song ended. That was some fucked-up shit. She looked at me and smiled.

"Don't worry, love. It doesn't have end here. I have somewhere quiet where we can chill and get to know each other better."

"How much I owe you?"

"Your boy took care of me already. Take my number. I'm going to text you."

"Oh, yeah! *That's* what's up!" I slapped her on the ass as we walked out of the room.

I made my way back to the table, and all along, I was hoping my dick would go down some. Shorty was definitely a bad bitch, and I wanted to fuck her. Mel's and his cousin's faces lit up as I sat at the table again.

"Nigga, you good? Shorty took care of you?"

"Yeah, I'm straight. Good looking out, bro."

"Ain't no thing. Did you fuck?" Mel busted out laughing.

"Hell nah, that shit was too fast. She gave me her number, though. We about to link up."

"That's my nigga."

We all busted out laughing. I could tell Mel was the man up in here tonight. Dancers kept walking up to the table, greeting him, and kissing on him and shit. I remember those days when we were grinding together, that's how I had the bitches all over me. I missed the attention and was eager to get back in the streets. I was out of the game long enough and was ready to get back to the bag. I was just gonna make sure that I didn't get caught up this time.

"Oh, yes! This dick is soooo good. Give that dick, daddy," Mia, the stripper, yelled as I fucked her from the back.

Shorty was dead serious that we could meet up. After the club closed, I parted ways with my niggas, and we rolled to a motel.

"Take this dick, bitch! This how you want it, huh?" I said as I thrust in and out of her slippery pussy.

She threw her ass back on me, matching my thrusts. This was some good pussy, and she wasn't backing down. She definitely knew how to bounce on the dick.

"Awwwww, fuck me harder, daddy. Awwww, fuck me," she yelled and eased her ass all the way back on the dick. I slid into her guts while gripping her hips. The pressure started building up in my dick. My veins began getting harder and started throbbing. Oh, *shit! Oh, shit!*

I exploded.

I took the condom off and walked to the bathroom, flushing it. Then I leaned on the wall, taking a few seconds to regain my strength. I was still under the influence of all that alcohol, so I walked back into the room. I needed a few minutes to lie down so I could get my energy back.

"You good, babes?" she quizzed as I walked into the room. She was lying there butt-ass naked. I thought about going for a second round, but my body wasn't up to it, and I wasn't going to embarrass myself.

"Yeah, I'm good, shorty. Just need to lie down for a few."

"Well, go ahead. We have the room for the night." She got up and walked off to the bathroom.

One of the rules that I lived by when I was in the streets: Never fall asleep around bitches, especially ones that were strangers. I wished I wasn't feeling like this, but the shots of Patrón crept up on me, along with fucking, so I just needed to chill.

I picked my pants up off the floor and took my phone out. Shit, there were over twenty missed calls from Shontelle. There were even more texts from her. Fuck! I knew some shit would go down if I didn't go home last night. Fuck it, though. I'll deal with that when I wake up.

The ringing of my phone woke me up. I opened my eyes and looked around. Shorty was wrapped up beside me, so I eased off the bed, trying my best not to wake her. I grabbed my drawers and put them on, then snatched up my phone. I had more miss calls from Shontelle. I glanced at the time. Shit, it was after 10:00 a.m. How the fuck did I let myself sleep this late? I was supposed to be home hours ago. I hurriedly put on my clothes and rushed out the door. I knew shorty would probably be mad when she woke up that I left like that, but I needed to get to the crib.

I tried to prepare myself for the imminent argument. I thought of the lie that I was about to tell, making sure there would be no holes in my story. I called Mel's number, but it went straight to voicemail. That nigga was probably still sleeping and shit. Fuck it. I threw the phone down on the seat and headed home in Shontelle's car.

I opened the door and walked in. The house was quiet. I knew it was Sunday, so she wasn't at work. Plus, I had her car, so I knew she hadn't gone anywhere. I walked into the room and heard the shower on, so she was in the bathroom. I took off my jeans and got in the bed. Maybe if I pretended that I was sleeping, she wouldn't bother with the beefing.

I heard when she walked into the room, and a few seconds of silence passed. I was relieved . . . until she broke through that shit with her voice shrill with frustration.

"Where the fuck you been? I've been calling your phone all damn night, and you just bringing yo' ass in here now," she yelled.

I sat up and looked at her. She was angry and ready for a fight.

"Yo, my bad shorty. I was out with the fellas. We were chilling and shit. I should've called."

"Your bad? You took my fucking car and was gone all night, and all you can say is 'Your bad'? I done told your ass I'm not going through this with you this time around. Whatever ho you was laid up with, you need to be with 'cause Shontelle ain't dealing with your shit no more."

"I told you, I was with Mel and his cousin. I wasn't wit' no bitch. I ain't got time for no bitch," I yelled, trying my hardest to convince her that I wasn't fooling around.

"You a fucking liar, boy, and I don't know why you keep screaming Mel's name. That nigga's a whole ho out here. Birds of a feather sure flock together. But I know one thing . . . Them bitches stupid. I'm not staying with no cheating-ass nigga."

"Shontelle, a'ight, man. Believe what the fuck you want. I told yo' ass that I wasn't with no bitch. Goddamn, you acting like my mama, like I can't go out and hang with the homies. A nigga been gone seven long years. Shit, I need to breathe."

"Nigga, I'm not your motherfucking mama and never want to be her ass, either. If you feel like you want to be free, you need to go stay wit' yo' old trifling-ass mama and leave me the—"

I jumped off the fucking bed and yanked her by the throat. "Bitch, don't you ever in yo' fucking life call my mama out of her name. You fucking hear me?"

"Get the fuck off me," she yelled.

I let loose and shoved her away from me. I played many games, but disrespecting my mama was not one. I understood her ass was mad, but that didn't give her a pass to disrespect my mama.

"Boy, I'ma call the fucking police on you. You going back to jail, you hear me? I fucking hate you!" she yelled with straight venom in her voice.

She reached over for her phone that was on the nightstand, but I grabbed it up before she could. I didn't want her to make a dumb-ass decision because she was mad. I mean, yeah, I shouldn't have put my hands on her, but she knew better than to talk shit about a nigga's mama. I was starting to see what everybody was talkin' about. She was gonna get a nigga hemmed up, and I couldn't take that chance, no matter how much I loved her ass. Right now, though, I had to get her to calm down so we could talk this shit out, or at least so she wouldn't call the folks on me when I left up outta here.

"Man, shorty, I'm sorry. I snapped. I swear, I'm sorry."

"Boy, fuck you. You put your hands on me behind your hoes you fucking. Get the fuck out of my house," she yelled.

"Man, you wildin' out, and I say I wasn't with no bitch. I'm sorry I put my hands on you. It ain't like I hit you."

"You sound stupid, you know that? Get out now, or I *will* call the police."

"A'ight, man, do what the fuck you want." I threw the phone on the bed and walked out.

I didn't want to get locked up, but I wasn't going to beg no bitch. Shontelle's ass was acting crazy right now, so I needed to let her breathe. She screaming that police shit right now, but she would be the same bitch coming down to the jail telling me how sorry she was.

I walked out of the apartment and dialed my mama's number. I hated calling her, but shit, I needed a ride. My mama decided to pick me up, so I sat on the stairs, waiting. I was pissed the fuck off. I understood I was out of pocket for coming home late, but that bitch didn't have to go that hard. I pulled out a Black & Mild and lit it.

I'd been home for a week, and I was already feeling stressed out. One, I needed to get me a fucking ride. Two, I needed to get back on. I couldn't live like this without no money. My fucking probation officer expected me to get a job. But where the fuck was I going to work? I hoped that bitch didn't think McDonald's. I chuckled when I thought about her. Even though she was older, there was something about her that grabbed my attention.

Suddenly, a horn honked. It was my mama. I got up and jogged to her car. As soon as I sat down, she pulled off.

"Boy, you know I got to work tonight. What the hell happened? She must've put your ass out."

"Ma, I don't want to talk 'bout it, a'ight?"

"Hmmm, I hear you. I have no idea why you ain't bring yo' ass home in the first place. I told you, that girl ain't no good. Not for you to be over there wifeing her up. If you ask me, she just a gold-digging heifer. Boy, you goin' learn."

"Mama, just chill. I'm grown enough to choose who I want to be with. I get it. You don't like shorty, but it ain't like you have to deal with her."

"I hear you. My mama used to tell me, a hard head make a soft ass."

I didn't want to go back-and-forth with her, so I didn't respond. See, once her mind was made up, it was hard to change it. I didn't care if they liked each other or not. I was only trying to get my shit together.

My mind was racing hard as hell. I hated to be out here like this. I needed to get back on my grind real soon so that I could get my own crib. But first, I needed a ride ASAP. This bitch was stuttin' on me, and there's no way I was going to kiss her ass just for a place a stay. Ain't no way . . .

Staying at my mama's crib was the last thing that I wanted to do, but a nigga got to do what I got to do for the time being. But best believe, I'ma lift up outta here ASAP. Once my mama pulled up, I hopped out of the car and walked into the house. God knows, I knew my mama probably was going to continue preaching. But to be honest, I didn't want to hear that shit.

Walking into my old room was like déjà vu. I felt like I'd taken a thousand steps backward, and in reality, I had. But a real nigga never stayed down long, so I knew it wouldn't be long before I was back on my shit, and then it would be my turn to stunt on Shontelle's ass. As soon as I got my shit together, I knew she would be the main one tryin'a be the main bitch, but there was something that was telling me that I couldn't trust her ass. I pushed that shit to the back of my mind and lay back in my old bed, staring at the ceiling. I couldn't tell you how many nights I did this when I was plotting on my come-up. It seemed like I had to come all the way back to my roots to get back to where I was. There was something that I had to learn, but what was it? I was thinking long and hard, and soon, my eyes started to get heavy. Before I knew it, it was lights out.

Chapter Five

Shontelle

I knew something was up when I kept calling Keel and not getting him. The old me would've not thought anything about it. But the new and improved Shontelle was hip to the little games niggas be playing. I stayed up most of the night calling this nigga, and not once did he pick up the phone. I sent him multiple texts, and he ignored those too. So to see this nigga walk his ass up in here the next day acting like shit sweet was crazy as fuck. And then to lay his nasty ass in my bed when I knew he'd just fell up outta a bitch was even more disrespectful. This nigga must not have gotten the memo that I ain't the little young, naïve bitch that he left out here. I'm a boss bitch now. Shit, I made my own fucking money and didn't need him for shit . . . and I mean nothing!

I knew when I put his ass out that he was going to call his old, bald-ass mama to pick him up. About fifteen minutes later, I heard a car pull up, and lo and behold, it was her old ass in that twenty-year-old Honda. I knew the bitch didn't like me, and I didn't like her ass either. I just tried to get along with her 'cause her fucking son begged me to. That old hag could kiss my fine ass. If you asked me, the ho was just jealous 'cause of how her son treated me. She tried competing, but there was obviously no competition. I watched as he hopped in her car, and they pulled off.

I then walked to the front and locked my door. Putting
the chain on the door, I grabbed a Smirnoff and headed
back to the room. Shit, it was Sunday, and I was supposed
to be chillin'—not arguing with my nigga. So, I planned to
do just that now that his ass was outta the picture. Picking
up the remote from the nightstand, I scrolled through the
channels, hoping to catch a good movie. Nothing grabbed
my attention, so I picked up the phone and dialed this
nigga's number.

"Yo," he answered the phone.

"Damn, nigga, why I ain't hear from your ass?" I quizzed
playfully.

"My bad shorty, but I thought you was goin' be busy. You
know, with yo' man home and everything."

"Boy, whatever! I already told you what's up, but believe
what you want."

"A'ight, shorty, chill out. What you doing?"

"I'm in my bed, horny as fuck and need you to come suck
on this pussy for me."

"At your crib? Where your peoples at?"

"That nigga stayed out all night, and once he got here,
we got into an argument, so I put his ass out. His mama
picked him up."

"Yo, you got to chill, yo. You keep acting like that, and
bro goin' know something going on."

"And you think I care? That nigga don't own this pussy
no more. Anyways, I ain't tryin'a discuss him. Can you
slide through?"

"Yeah, I'ma make this run, then come through. Yo, make
sure that nigga over at his mama house fo' sure."

"You sound like you scared. Not Mr. Street Nigga."

"A'ight, shorty, go ahead on."

He hung up the phone before I could say another word.
I wasn't too worried where Jakeel was. He stayed out,
probably fucking and sucking on one of these nasty-ass

hoes, and I was about to do the same thing. What's the fucking problem? He shouldn't have an issue with that shit for two reasons. First, this was *my* fuckin' crib, so I could do who and what the hell ever I wanted to in this bitch, and he ain't have shit to say about it. Second, these niggas did that shit all the time. They fucked friends and family, and then would come back and lie up with their bitches like that shit was the move. But when a bitch did the same shit, they were called hoes.

I hated that shit, and I wasn't about to live by them dumb-ass rules. I was a boss bitch, and boss bitches made their own rules. And you saw that them niggas was abiding by that shit too. Running to be all up in this good-ass pussy. Whoever said pussy ain't rule the world was a muthafuckin' liar. And I was proof of that shit.

I kept my pussy waxed and made sure I took my daily vitamins. So, it's safe to say I got that sugar pussy. This pussy has gotten me cars, money in the bank, and designer clothes. I ain't no ho, but if I saw an opportunity, my ass was going to jump on it.

I'd already bathed but decided to take a quick wash off. I oiled down real good and threw on a silk pajama top from Victoria's Secret. I didn't bother wasting any time putting on no panties. They were going to come right off anyway. I thought about cutting my phone off but decided against it.

I must've dozed off because when I heard the doorbell ringing, it woke me up. I jumped up, and as I walked to the door, I thought, *What if it's not who I'm expecting?* I dismissed that thought immediately. I looked through the peephole and wasted no time in opening up the door. I yanked my company in and shut the door before anyone could see him.

"Damn, shorty, you good?"

I didn't respond. Instead, I started kissing him while I pulled him to the room. Yes, I fucked Jakeel a day ago, but it wasn't the same. *This* was the nigga that had been sucking and fucking me for the past couple of years, and I couldn't seem to get enough. I didn't know if it was the dick itself, or it was the fact that he's supposed to be forbidden. Either way, this dick had this chick gooooone.

He wasted no time throwing my legs over his shoulders and burying his head deep inside of me. I grabbed his dreads and pulled his head deeper in, almost suffocating him. My pussy was throbbing, almost like my skin was in heat. He twirled his tongue around in a circular motion all around my pussy walls. My toes curled around as my body tensed up on me. I couldn't hold it anymore.

"Oh shit, yes, Zaddy. Yes, Zaddy." I held on tight to his dreads while cream poured out of my pussy. He didn't raise his head. He just started licking slowly, cleaning it up. My body started convulsing, and I wrapped his ass up in a leg lock. I was coming so hard that I thought I was about to pass out. And his ass didn't let up. He sucked harder, more aggressively, like he wanted to make sure he got every last drop that my body shot out.

After he was sure that I'd finished nutting, he flipped me over on my stomach. He slid his dick into my ass, and I groaned out in pain and pleasure as I tried to stomach the pain of getting fucked in the ass without any lubricant. I loved it when he fucked me, but lately, it seemed like that's the only hole he was interested in. I mean, I loved getting fucked in my ass but slowly, not the way he just pushed in me without lubricant. Shit, he could've spit on my hole or his dick or something. I closed my fist and braced down on the bed to ease some of the pain.

"I know you love when Zaddy fuck you in the ass, don't you, baby?"

"Yes, I love it, boo," I lied.

"Oh shit, I'm 'bout to come. oh,shit," he panted and yelled out before he exploded in my ass.

I fell flat on my stomach. My ass was on fire, and I needed something to cool it down ASAP. He must've read my mind 'cause I felt when he slid his tongue between my ass crack. He licked from front to back, and his tongue definitely brought some comfort to me. I was ready to head to the shower and wash myself off, but he wasn't done. He licked my ass better than he'd licked my pussy, and when he stuck his tongue inside and moved his head back and forth, making it go in and out of my asshole, I came harder than I had when he ate my pussy.

After he was finished, I got up and limped to the shower. After a few seconds of being in the water, I heard the bathroom door open, and he stepped into the shower with me. He took the washcloth and started washing me. I loved it when he did that shit. Usually, it was the woman who was washing the nigga off, but he wasn't like that. He was the kind that thought about me just like I would about my nigga. I had to say that this may be part of the reason that I was feeling him so much. I returned the favor, making sure to pay special attention to his dick. I mean, it had been in my ass, after all.

After we washed each other, we ended up fucking some more, right there in the shower. I wrapped my legs around his waist and rode that dick while he grabbed my hips. He slow fucked me, and I squeezed my pussy muscles and popped the pussy on him. I swear I ain't never been fucked this good, and I wished it didn't end.

After we got out of the shower, we got dressed and lay together on the bed. I was worn the fuck out, and he looked like he'd been around the block a couple of times himself.

"Aye, babes, you know we goin' have to chill with all this," he said as he looked over at me with a serious expression on his face. I sat up and shot him a half-dirty look.

"What you mean?"

"Come on, shorty, you know I'm digging you and e'erything. But you know my nigga out, and the last thing we need is for him to find out we been fucking behind his back."

"Oh, really? Now you give a fuck about him? I thought we've been talking about leaving and starting a life together. Now the nigga home, you on some different shit?"

"Shorty, you know the nigga was like a brother to me. I mean, it sounded good when we were talking about it, but that shit ain't possible. This nigga still love you, and plus, I got a situation with my baby mother. I can't just up and leave my daughter like that. I'm sorry, bae."

"Sorry, nigga. You really talked a good game. Three years you been fucking me. *Three fucking years,* and now, 'cause you scared of this pussy nigga, it's fuck me."

I jumped off the bed and was ready to bust this nigga in his head with the lamp. I grabbed the lamp, but the nigga grabbed my hand.

"Shorty, chill the fuck out. I fucks with you hard. I have feelings for you. I just don't think now is a good time to keep on fucking around."

"Boy, fuck you! You talk that good game, how you would treat me better than how he treats me. Hmm, now, look at you—just a piece of shit like him. Get the fuck on, man," I collapsed on the bed and started to cry. I thought that he would comfort me like he had on the many nights when I'd cried over Jakeel.

Instead of feeling his hand on my back, trying to soothe me, I heard his footsteps leave the room. Next, I heard the door shut, and just like that, he was gone. I felt the ultimate betrayal . . . He was Jakeel's right hand, and after Keel got locked up, at first, he would call and check up on me. Then he would drop off money for his boy.

One Saturday evening, he stopped by the shop, and we started talking. He came clean to me about a lot of the shit Keel was doing to me. Said that he couldn't lie for his nigga but didn't want me to leave Keel hangin', doin' that time by himself. The nigga said that he loved his nigga, but he was feeling bad because niggas out here in these streets wished that they had a down-ass bitch on their team like me. Flattery got his ass everywhere, and he started taking me to dinner and shit so that I wouldn't be sitting in the house bored out of my damn mind because I really didn't have a life outside of Jakeel at the time. So, automatically, I thought this nigga was for me.

That's how all this shit had started in the first place. He took me to see Keel, and when we got back into the car, I broke down. I didn't know how I was gonna make it without Jakeel. He had been my everything. That was right after all the bitches came out of the woodwork, claiming to have fucked my nigga. I made Mel take me there so that I could confront him about some bitch named Lauren, who was claiming to be pregnant with his child. That had been the last straw for me. If that nigga ain't come clean about all the shit that he'd done, I was gon' leave his ass up in there to fuckin' rot.

Of course, Keel lied, and like the good homie Mel was, he vouched for the nigga. Said that she had been fuckin' with some cop, and that's who he thought the baby's real daddy was. It didn't make that shit hurt any less. Maybe that kid wasn't his, but the other bitches had screenshots and all other kinda proof of the shit that he was doing behind my fuckin' back. I wept in Mel's arms when we got back to his crib . . . and one thing led to another.

We started fucking around, and it went on. We talked about moving away and starting a life. Now, all of a sudden, this nigga talking about his bitch and daughter. Boy, fuck you, that bitch, and that monkey. I swear I hated fucking niggas. How was I so stupid to let this nigga play me like that? I was so sure he was different . . . I couldn't stop the tears from flowing; my heart was hurting so badly. This was the ultimate betrayal. Four years later, this nigga was leaving me hanging because his nigga was out, and he was scared of Keel's ass. That was the real reason, 'cause I knew he ain't give a damn about that bitch or that bastard that he ain't even really know was his for real. I guess the saying, "bros before hoes," was true.

Chapter Six

Mika

After that big fight between Rasheem and me the other day, I thought that was the end of us. But he came back home that night with flowers. He got on his knees and cried and pleaded. How could I not forgive him when I took the vows for better or for worse? That was two weeks ago, and he had now returned to his bad behavior. This shit was getting old. He started not coming home every night, and when he did, it was three or four in the morning.

I hadn't seen him in two days. He didn't call. Instead, I received a text telling me he was doing some undercover work. OK, even though I was suspicious, I didn't have any proof. Earlier in the day, he called, and we talked. I still didn't believe him, but I kept my feelings to myself.

He promised he would be home as soon as he finished his paperwork. So, me being the supporting wife, I decided to throw a roast in the oven. I took a shower and waited. . . .

That was five hours ago, and I was *still* sitting here waiting. I was so fucking pissed off that I was shaking uncontrollably. I took a sip of the cranberry vodka that I was nursing as I paced back and forth in the living room. I called his phone, and it kept going to voicemail.

About six hours later, I heard the garage door going up. It was either his ass or our daughter. Ky was here, so I knew it wasn't her. I emptied the glass of liquor, preparing myself to confront this nigga. I'd been letting too much shit slide over the years, but not coming home was the ultimate disrespect—especially when I knew his ass *wasn't* at work.

He stepped into the house and hung up his key. I walked toward him with my arms folded.

"So, this is what we're doing now?" I asked in a fierce tone.

"Mika, what are you talking about?" he asked like he didn't have any idea what I could be so upset about. He proceeded to walk off, but I ran up behind him and grabbed his shirt.

"Don't you fucking walk off while I'm talking to you!"

"I'm just getting home, tired from working all goddamn day, and instead of greeting me like a good wife's supposed to do, here you go coming at me crazy. All you live for is drama. I'm getting sick of this shit."

"You're getting sick of this shit? No, *I* should be the one saying that. You're a married man, and your wife has not seen you in two days. And before you open your mouth to lie that you've been 'working,' I checked that shit already," I lied.

"So, now you a detective, checking up on me and shit. I'm not one of your little convicts that you need to check up on. I'm a grown-ass man, and I'm free to do what the fuck I want to do."

Slap! Slap! I couldn't take him talking crazy in my face anymore. I slapped his face twice.

"Don't you talk to me like I'm one of these filthy pussy bitches out here that you're screwing. I'm your fucking *wife,* and I deserve to be treated as such. I will *not* tolerate this shit."

He grabbed my hands and shoved me away, causing me to stumble backward. I regained my footing and leered at him while I debated whether I wanted to smack his ass upside the head again or not. He was really pushing it, and even though I knew I was wrong for putting my hands on him, I was over him and his bullshit. Honestly, I felt like he'd lost his damned mind, and I was trying to knock him back to his sense . . . back to the man that I'd fallen in love with.

"Don't put your fucking hands on me. I ain't no Ike, but don't think I won't beat your ass. You should know I ain't one of these weak-ass niggas out here. Now, get the fuck out of my way. Let me know when you start behaving like a wife and not a jealous-ass schoolgirl."

"Fuck you, Rasheem. Fuck you! I'm the best fucking thing to ever happen to you. You should be worshipping the ground I walk on. Fuck youuuu," I yelled as he walked up the stairs.

I crumbled at the foot of the stairs. His words were as cold as ice. Rasheem was known to have some fucked-up ways, but this was his second time talking to me in this manner. I didn't have an ounce of empathy for him, nor he for me. This was far from the man to whom I had given my heart. Who the fuck was this, and who was he fucking with?

After a few minutes of crying my eyes out, I got my emotions under control. I made my way up to my room and noticed he wasn't in the room or the bathroom. I walked to the mirror, and when I saw one or two wrinkles visible, I knew it was stress. I'd always taken care of my body, so my well-toned body was appealing. I wasn't the kind to just go around sleeping with different men, so I knew my pussy wasn't worn. It didn't get wet like it used to, but with the help of a little Vaseline, I was good. I knew I sucked dick well, and despite my age, I still knew how to ride the dick. I was saying all this to say that I didn't understand why my husband would be out there fucking around on me. Tears filled my eyes again as I searched my brain for reasons. If this man had everything at home, who was he risking our marriage for?

I walked to my bed and got into it. I was hurting badly, but I was determined not to let him see me like this. Men loved when they felt like they had the woman at a weak point. He walked into the room and went into his closet. I closed my eyes, trying my best not to look at this cold-ass bastard.

I heard when he walked to the bathroom. I opened my eyes then. He undressed at the front of the bathroom door like he always did before he walked in, I was assuming, to take a shower, and slammed the door.

A few seconds later, his phone started ringing. It stopped but then started ringing again. I jumped off the bed and tiptoed to the bathroom. I was scared and nervous, but nonetheless curious. I grabbed his pants and removed the ringing phone. I didn't recognize the number. I waited for it to finish ringing, and then I checked the texts.

Can't wait to see you later, babes.

It didn't stop there. The texts continued. As I read them, tears rolled down my face. Just when I felt my heart break, I also heard the water cut off. I quickly put his phone back into the pocket and threw his pants where I found them. Softly, I tiptoed back to bed. *That was close. Almost got caught.*

I closed my eyes and pretended to be asleep. I pulled the covers halfway up my face so that I could hide the silent tears that were rolling. I listened as he moved around the room. I assumed he was getting dressed for his date. He even put some cologne on, 'cause the strong stench of Old Spice hit my nose. That was a sign that his ass was too old to be out here gallivanting with all these young bitches. Nobody wore Old Spice anymore. But he swore by that shit. Could smell his ass coming a mile away.

A few minutes later, he walked out in his shoes. I knew then he was on his way. When I heard him walk down the stairs, I jumped out of bed and ran to my closet. I pulled out a pair of black sweatpants, a black T-shirt, and quickly got dressed. I ran down the stairs, put my slippers on, waited until I heard his car pull out of the driveway. Then I rushed out the door. I jumped into my car and pulled out of the garage. I knew I had to speed up a little if I wanted to catch up with him before he got out of the subdivision. I caught him right at the light, spotting his dark blue Chrysler Jeep two cars ahead of me.

He made a right on Walker Road. One of the other cars made a left, which only left one car between us. I tried to keep my distance so he wouldn't spot me. He was a detective and was trained to notice if someone was tailing him.

All along, as I followed him, my heart was beating rapidly. I didn't know where this man was heading. All I knew was that I was following him. What if I were wrong? What if he were on his way to do some undercover work, and here I was interfering with his job? I thought about turning around and going home. Shit, it was too late now. He'd turned off on Church Street. Wasn't that shit ironic? His ass needed to be headed somewhere to get right with Christ, but I knew that was the furthest thing from where he was going. Now, it was only our cars on the road. I slowed down because I couldn't afford for him to see me. A few minutes later, he made a turn into Hampton Inn & Suites Atlanta Decatur/Emory.

He parked, and I pulled in and parked a few cars down. I scooted down in my seat as he got out. I looked up a little and watched as he got out of his car, looked around, and hurried into the hotel. Quickly, I cut the car off, jumped out, and ran to the hotel door. The lobby was busy, which was good for me. I could blend in with the rest of the people. He walked around the corner, so I hurriedly ran after him. He walked down to the last door and knocked. I hid beside the ice machine but peeped around to see

what he was doing. The door opened, and a blonde came
to the door. They hugged and started kissing passionately.
I blinked twice because I knew I had to be seeing shit.
This *couldn't* be my husband, who claimed he hated white
bitches. My heart didn't want to accept it, but the proof
was right there in front of me. They walked into the room
and closed the door. I had to lean on the wall for support.
My legs felt weak, and tears filled my eyes.

"Are you okay, ma'am?" someone tapped me on my
shoulder.

I looked around and saw it was one of the hotel workers.

"Yes, I'm fine. Thank you." I shot him a fake smile.

I quickly straightened myself up, wiped the tears from
my eyes, and got myself the fuck together. I couldn't be falling apart out here with all these people around. There was
no telling who knew whom, and the last thing that I needed
was for the word to get out that I was breaking down and
shit in public. And with the way people were recording shit
with their phones, it would be nothing for that shit to be
recorded and shared all over social media. I could see the
caption now: *"Probation Officer Has Nervous Breakdown
After Catching Husband Cheating At Hotel."* Nope, that
wouldn't be me. I wasn't about to be the next viral sensa-
tion or hashtag 'round here. Especially not looking a mess
in my sweatpants, T-shirt, and slippers. Honestly, I had
no business out here with this shit on anyway. My career
would be over. I would be made a laughingstock. None of
my parolees would take me seriously ever again. And all
them bitches who knew that I didn't have a perfect life
would have something to gossip about around the water
cooler.

Sucking it up, I did what real bitches did when the shit
that their intuition told them was right in their faces. I
needed to figure out my next move. But instead of taking
my ass home and packing my things, my feet seemed to

have a mind of their own and led me in the opposite direction of the exit. Without thinking, I made my way down the hall and stood in front of the hotel room. Mind racing, filled with rage, I knocked on the door. At first, no one answered. I knocked on the door again, this time harder.

"Who is it?" a woman yelled.

"It's room service," I yelled, changing up my voice.

"We didn't order any food," she yelled back.

"The manager asked me to deliver this bottle of Dom Pérignon as an appreciation for you staying with us."

I guess the mention of champagne piqued her interest because the door flew wide open. A white bitch stood there in her robe, blinking slowly. She looked at me, then past me like she was waiting on someone to come down the hallway with a bucket of iced champagne.

"Who are you, and where is the champagne?" She looked confused.

"I'm Mika, and I'm here for my husband." I looked dead into her face.

"Your husband? Lady, I don't know what you're talking about. I'm in here with my fiancé—"

I pushed that bitch out of the way and made my way into the room. There my husband was laid out across the bed with his dick in his hand.

"You trifling-ass nigga," I yelled as I lunged toward him.

He opened his eyes, looked at me, and jumped up off the bed. "What the fuck are you doing here?"

"I should be asking *you* that. I'm your fucking *wife,* and you laid up in a hotel room with this cracker bitch. How could you do this to me?"

"Baby, please explain this to me. Who is this woman, and why is she saying you're her husband?"

"This is my wife—"

"Your *wife?* I thought you were divorced. Why did you propose to me?" she asked before she started crying.

"You a lying piece of shit. You left me at home to come to screw this old crackhead-looking bitch." I looked at him and felt pity.

"Bitch, I ain't never smoked crack a day in my life. Rasheem, you better get this ho before I stomp a hole in her face."

"Bitch, how about I get *you?*" I let all professionalism go at that moment. I ran up on that ho and punched her a few times in her face.

"Stop! You're not thinking clearly. You have your job to worry about," Rasheem yelled. This nigga grabbed me and put me in a bear hug.

"I'm pressing charges on you, bitch! You're going to jail," that ho yelled.

"Shut the fuck up, Gina," he yelled in anger.

"Get the fuck off me. Matter of fact, you need to get your shit out of my house. I want a fucking divorce, you hear me? I'm done, Rasheem." I yelled as I head-butted him with the back of my head, and he dropped me. I caught myself before I fell because the last thing that I needed was this bitch to catch me slipping and try to sneak me on some payback shit. Giving her the look of death, I couldn't even look at his ass as I made my way out of the room.

I hadn't had a physical fight in years, but because of this old cheating-ass nigga, I was in here acting a damn fool. I slowly walked and tried to calm myself before I went into the lobby and controlled my temper just enough to walk out the door. I got in my car, and then it came out. I didn't cry in front of that nigga, but now that I was alone, I let it out.

I gave this nigga all these years of my life. Fucked him good, sucked his dick. Washed, cooked, and cleaned for him, and here he was laid up with this white trash. How could he disrespect me like this? How . . . I slammed my hand on my steering wheel to relieve some of the frustration that I was feeling. I sat in the parking lot a good five minutes before I was able to pull off.

"Fuck you, Rasheem. How could you do this to me?" I screamed aloud as I cried all the way to the house. I kept trying to make sense of all the shit that just went down. I knew we had some issues in our relationship. Yes, I thought he was creeping around, but to see it with my own two eyes just ripped my soul into tiny pieces. "I loved you, never cheated on you, and *this* is how you do me?" I asked the empty seat of my car as if Rasheem were sitting right there beside me.

I pulled into my driveway, got out of the car, and dashed upstairs. I ran into my bedroom and buried my head in my pillow. I was hurting so damn badly. I tried to control the tears, but they just wouldn't stop.

"Mom, are you okay?" I heard Ky's voice. I tried my best to wipe the tears away quickly, but I couldn't. "Mom, you're crying. What happened?" she rushed over to me and wrapped her arms around me while I sobbed. "Mom, talk to me. What's wrong? Did Daddy do this to you? Did he hurt you?" I could tell that she was becoming more and more panicked with every question that she asked that I couldn't compose myself enough to answer. Taking a deep breath, I pulled myself together long enough to answer her questions for her.

"I found your daddy with his mistress," l let out between sobs.

"You did *what?* He had a woman here?"

"No, I followed him to the hotel, and I saw him kissing another woman. I can't believe he did this to me." I started sobbing harder.

"Are you serious? I'm going to call him. How could he do this to you? How?" She hugged me.

I wished I didn't bring my baby girl into our shit, but I was hurting, and it felt good talking to someone else.

"Mom, I swear I kept telling you. You need to leave him. We can move up north. I would love to live in New York. I love my daddy and all, but he's been no good for you. You're beautiful, you're strong, and you have your career. What do you really need him for?"

I heard the words coming out of my daughter's mouth, but it didn't make my heart hurt any less. I married this man because I loved him and wanted to spend the rest of my life with him. I didn't plan on divorcing him. But what other option did he leave me?

Chapter Seven

Rasheem

"Hey, baby, I wasn't expecting you back so—" Lauren said, but I cut her ass off. I wasn't there for a conversation. I was there to get some stress off my chest.

"Suck my dick, bitch," I commanded, and just like the good, obedient bitch she was, she dropped to her knees and snatched my joggers down.

I hadn't even made it all the way in her house, and the door was still wide open. But she ain't give a damn. She was servicing a nigga like suckin' my dick was her full-time job. And it was. I paid all the bills in this bitch, just like I did at home. The difference was, I got all the pleasure with none of the fuckin' naggin'. If she had some class about herself, I would leave Mika's ass for her. But there was a difference between the bitches you fucked and the ones that you wifed up.

Right now, I was pressed. Both of my bitches were mad with me, and I knew that I could get Gina to come back, but Mika, I was pretty sure she was done with my ass. I knew I was being reckless with how I was moving, staying gone for days at a time. But I had to keep both of my bitches happy. I mean, I watched these niggas out here in these streets with multiple bitches, and they all just went with the flow. But not my two mains. They wanted to be the only ones.

For a while, Mika was enough for me. But when I asked for a threesome on my fiftieth birthday a few years ago, and she said no, I told her that I was gon' have one with or without her, and I'd meant that shit. Lauren had been with the shit, and she'd brought her friend to make my fantasy a reality. That friend was Gina. And the way that bitch sucked and fucked me had a nigga hooked like a drug. I didn't do white bitches and never expected to take her ass seriously. But a couple of threesomes later, and we started sneaking and hooking up behind Lauren's back.

She was everything that Mika wasn't, and something outside of my norm. Unlike my black bitches, she never talked back—well, not until tonight when Mika's ass busted up in the hotel room on our asses. She showed me why niggas fucked with white bitches. It was just . . . easy.

I never really intended on marrying her, but after fucking with her as long as I had, she wanted some kinda commitment, so I got her ass a ring and put on the whole romantic scene and shit. It was so easy to sell some of these bitches dreams. But that dream wouldn't ever become a reality because—well, it couldn't. They would never take me seriously at work if I came up in there talking about I had a white bitch on my arm. They may have been status symbols in some places, but I was still in the South, and I mean the *Deep* South. They woulda tanked my whole career behind some shit like that. And a nigga's reputation was all he had.

That's why Mika was so necessary. She fit the whole mold for my success in my career and life. And it wasn't like she wasn't bad in bed, either. She just wasn't down for all the shit that a nigga wanted to do. And being my wife, there wasn't shit she should've denied me. I took damn good care of her. She only worked because she wanted to. She upgraded her car every fuckin' year. She had more name-brand shit in her closet than them Kardashian bitches, and she wasn't even fuckin' me like I knew they were fuckin' their niggas. I mean, hell, they had to be doin' something special, 'cause them niggas lost their minds. And *that's* what I needed from Mika—that mind-mushing fuck. But she wasn't with the shit. And that's why her prudish ass had to spend some nights at home alone.

I never woulda thought she woulda gone all secret agent on a nigga. I thought she was too classy for that. But I should've seen it coming with the way that she had been on a nigga lately. I should've just laid this pipe on her ass, and that would've got some get right in her. But instead, I'd left Gina's crying ass at the hotel and came over here to Lauren's house. I knew I should've gone home, but the way that Mika was, I didn't want to give her grounds to kill my ass. If I went home right now, it could be considered a crime of passion, and I wasn't tryin'a go out like that.

"Ooooh shit! Hum on them balls, baby! Just like that, Mika," I moaned out, grinding harder into her face.

Pop! The sound of my dick aggressively exiting her mouth made me look at her like she'd lost her damn mind.

"I *know* I don't look like no damn Mika to you!" she snapped, rolling her eyes and getting up off her knees. It wasn't until then that it registered on me what I'd said. Now I knew that my wife was the woman for me. Why it took another bitch's throat to be massaging my dick for me to get it, I had no idea. But I got it now, and I knew that I had to make shit right with Mika. "Do I look like some old-ass bitch who can't keep her man satisfied?" Lauren kept saying, and it was pissing me off the more she talked.

Was this what people thought about my wife? I guess I had never considered how this shit would make her look to these bitches out here. All I was tryin'a do was get my dick wet from time to time. But the words that Lauren had just spat at me made me realize what I'd really done—to Mika, to our marriage. I had her out here looking like she wasn't shit when she was really my backbone. She was the reason that I woke up every morning. She was the mother of my child. Well, my first one anyway.

"Did you hear me, Sheem? Or you over here fantasizing about that bitch?" she was in full ratchet mode at this point, rolling her neck, popping her lips, and pointing them long-ass nails in my face.

"You better simmer the hell down, Lauren. You still need to realize who the fuck you talkin' to. I get it. What I just did was disrespectful as fuck, and I'm sorry. My head just ain't where it's supposed to be. But you're talking about the mother of my child," I said, and as soon as the words came outta my mouth, I wished they hadn't.

"Just get out, Sheem," she said, her attitude fully gone, and her eyes starting to brim with tears. What the hell was it with me making all my bitches cry tonight? I was really slippin', and that wasn't like me. I knew that I had to make it right with Mika. Once shit was good with us, then the rest of them would be easy to get back on track.

"I'm sorry, Lauren," I said, pulling my joggers up and finally closing the door. The last thing that I needed was these messy-ass folks out here all in my business.

"Just go home, Rasheem. *To the mother of your child,*" she repeated, the words choking her, and the tears finally pouring from her eyes.

"You knew what I meant—"

"No, actually, I *don't* know what you meant, nigga. *I'm* the mother of your child too. And why are you here, anyway? Ain't this your time with Gina?" she asked, laughing and crying at the same time, looking like a madwoman. I guess the look of shock on my face was funny to her. "What? You didn't think I knew about you and her? About the proposal that she couldn't wait to throw in my face? Nah, nigga, I been knew. But you pay the bills over here, and you keep a bitch real comfortable, so I let you do what the fuck you wanted to do. I knew you wasn't gonna leave Mika's ass, so if Gina wanted to be happy with that delusion, I let her ass. I tried to tell her you had a wife, but she told me that

I was just mad that you chose her. Guess her ass gotta humblin' tonight, huh?"

The more she talked, the harder she laughed. She was giving me the business, and that shit was hitting me in the gut. Every word was a lick to my ego. I realized that how I was seen was worse than they could ever see my wife. I was just a cash cow, an old nigga who was willing to pay for some young pussy, and they passed my ass around like the collection plate on Sunday mornings. I stood there speechless, feeling like *I* was the one who had been played, all the while thinking that *I* was the one doing the playing. Nobody wanted to be my wife for real, but Mika. Nobody would put up with me and my shit the way that she did. Nobody knew me, matched my grind, and shared dreams of a real future but her. And here I was, out here playing the fuck outta her *and* myself. And for what?

"You ain't got shit to say now, huh?" Lauren kept on with the verbal abuse. "That's a'ight. You can go home to your wife and not come back here ever again. My *real* baby daddy is out now, so you ain't gotta buy that lie no more," she said, and that made me close the space between us in a few steps and pick her ass up by her throat. I squeezed tight enough to stop her ass from talking, but it didn't make her stop laughing.

Did this bitch just say that the child I had been taking care of for the past seven years wasn't mine? I knew I *couldn't* have heard her right.

"You . . . might . . . wanna . . . put me down. I *own* you, Sheem," she eeked out, with a smile on her face. I dropped her ass on the floor and turned to leave the house. "And I still expect my checks to come every week in the same amount too, boo. Or it's *over*—for more than your fuckin' marriage," she yelled at my back, laughing again.

I didn't respond—I just opened the door, walked out, and slammed that bitch behind me. I didn't wanna hear her voice or see her face, or I might've done some shit that I would regret. I knew before this was all over, I was gonna have to murder Lauren's ass. And Gina's ass too. Those bitches really could ruin a nigga, and I knew that, now, they had no reason not to.

My shit was falling apart, and the only person who could make it better, I had betrayed in a way that I might not be able to come back from. Mika didn't know this, but a nigga was willing to kill to keep her. And I damned sure planned to kill her ass too before I lost her and let another nigga have the great woman that she was . . . the woman that I'd been taking for granted.

As I got in my car driving as fast as hell to get home before Mika left for work, the words that stood out most of the shit that Lauren was spitting at me replayed in my mind. *My real baby daddy is out now* . . . I didn't know that nigga was free. I was gonna have to take care of his ass too, before Lauren got to him and told him that *I* was the reason he'd lost seven years of his freedom.

Chapter Eight

Mika

I must've fallen asleep last night when Ky'Imani was talking to me. I woke up, still dressed in my clothes, looked over beside me, and noticed Rasheem was not in bed. Everything that happened last night flashed back in my head. I felt the tears forming, but I tried my best not to let them out. I was hurting and disappointed, but I wasn't no weak bitch and wasn't going to sit around here crying over this man. God knows I'm a good woman, and I deserved better than what he was dishing out. The face of the white bitch flashed in my head. The bitch wasn't no model-type bitch. She looked more like white trash—the kind that will suck your dick for twenty bucks. He was a stupid-ass nigga. How you go from classy to trashy?

The alarm started going off. This was my cue to get my ass up and take a shower. I hated going in today, but I had a job to do. There's no way I was going to sit at home, moping around.

After my shower, I dried off and took a glance at myself in the mirror. For me to be this age, I had to admit that I was still a baddie. After having my daughter, I had a breast implant, so my breasts were sitting up lovely. These squats over the years definitely gave me a plump ass. My stomach was flat, even though I had a few stretchy marks. Looking at me, you couldn't tell that I was 45. Numerous times, I got compliments from men telling me I looked like I was in my twenties. I would just look at them, smile, and walk off, all along, smiling inside.

I was so caught up in my thoughts that I didn't notice him sitting on our bed as I walked into the room. As soon as I saw him, my spirit changed.

"What are you doing here? You got some fucking nerve. You spent the night with your bitch, and now you come up in here?" I shook my head at his ass as I clutched my towel tighter.

"Listen to me, Mika. I'm so sorry. I swear that bitch don't mean a damn thing to me. Me and you was fighting, and she was just something to do," he tried to plead. When he saw I wasn't buying his shit, he jumped off the bed and walked up to me, grabbing my arms.

"Let go of me. We've been married for fifteen years, and you decided to throw it away behind a cracker bitch. You the same nigga that sat up here talking 'bout you would never fuck a bitch outside your race. Hmmm . . . You a lying piece of shit!"

I pulled myself away from him and walked to my side of the bed. I started getting dressed. Had I known his ass was in the room, I wouldn't have come out of the bathroom undressed.

"Mika, baby, please hear me out. I love you, but I have needs. You bury yourself in your work. All I hear about is your cases, your new releases. I'm your husband. I need some of your time. When we do have sex, it's like I'm forcing you. I didn't know what to do."

"You know you sound like a typical man. It's *always* the woman's fault that you take your dick out and stick it into a whore. I knew you were fucking around on me. I just didn't have proof until now. Hmm, I'm so disappointed that I allowed you to drag me like this. How many of your friends are looking at me, laughing? I bet *everybody*

knows you're slanging dick around town except me. oh,-
God, I'm such a fool." I placed my hands over my face,
embarrassed. I was having second thoughts about going
to work now. I was going to think that every whisper
around the office was about me.

"Ain't nobody laughing at you. Look, that bitch don't
mean nothing to me. You and my daughter mean the world
to me. We can go to counseling. I'm willing to try anything."

"I'm done. I want a divorce. I want half of everything.
I'm done with you."

"You can't do this, Mika. I love you. We can't split up."

"You heard me. I'll be contacting a divorce lawyer some-
time today."

He jumped in front of me as I tried exiting the bedroom. I
crossed my arms over my chest, pissed. He had some nerve
trying to come to me begging now. He could've talked to
me about this before he stepped out on me. He could've
tried and given me the chance to deny him or some shit
before he went to another bitch. Talking about needs . . .
needs, my ass. This nigga was selfish, plain and simple.
The only reason he was trying so hard now was that his ass
got caught. If he hadn't been, he probably would've been
laid up in that hotel room with the trashy, pasty-ass bitch,
and I would be in my bed, in our home—alone—waiting
for him to come home. Now, *he* was the one who wanted
some of my time.

Hell, he could've even been honest with me that night we
had that big fight when I was sniffing his drawers like some
kinda bloodhound. I shook my head at what I'd become. I
was better than having to sneak and check his damn phone
and look for nut stains in his underwear. When I thought
about it, the perfume that the white bitch was wearing
wasn't even what I smelled on his sweaty-ass shirt that
night. That let me know that there was more than just her.
Damn, I was feeling dumber and dumber by the minute.

"You can't do this. You and my daughter are my life. I take care of you, and *this* is how you act? All I did was get a little pussy from the bitch, and you want to walk away from what we have? Fifteen years, Mika. *Fifteen years!* Don't no other bitch have my heart but you."

"Get the hell out of my way. Don't come screaming about no damn fifteen years. She ain't the first ho that you fucked. I should've left your ass a long time ago, but I was in denial. I was blind as fuck. I didn't want to believe my precious husband was stepping out on me. I wonder how many nights you done fucked and sucked on them hoes and still came to lie up beside me in the bed. You a nasty-ass nigga that runs around here with your detective badge, acting like you all high and mighty. Fooling everybody . . . with your old nasty-ass dick."

I shoved him out of the way with my purse and walked out of the room. It was too damn early in the morning for me to be this upset. He was still saying some shit, but I wasn't listening to another word of his lies. I quickly dashed out the door and headed to my car. The whole way to work, all I could think about was the shit he was spouting out of his mouth. But every time I thought about forgiving his ass, I would see that white bitch standing in that hotel room door with her robe on. And then his ass lying in bed with his disloyal-ass dick in his hand. I had lost everything and had done nothing but be a good woman to his ass. This was the kinda bullshit that made women end up on damn *Snapped*.

I hated starting my day off in an angry mood. My job was pretty stressful on its own, so adding to it was not a good thing. Things definitely needed to change up. I couldn't go on living like this. I had given this nigga fifteen fucking years. Our daughter was 18, and this was how he ended us? She was almost out of the house, and we should've been planning for retirement and traveling the world together.

But here I was, contemplating divorce. This was *not* how I saw my life going.

I'd put on a good front in front of him, but I was hurting badly deep inside. He had no idea how much I loved him and how deeply he had hurt me. I felt my eyes getting watery, but I used my inner strength to stop the tears from flowing.

"God, all I ask of you today is to give me a little strength to get my job done without breaking down," I whispered a prayer to God before getting out of my car and walking toward the building. One thing I knew was that when everything else failed, prayer would help. I wasn't no religious chick by far, but I knew the power of prayer and the peace that it could bring. And I needed every ounce of that power and peace today to keep my shit together.

"So, what's going on? You've been sitting there looking at the food on your plate for the last ten minutes. You've barely said two words to me today, and your eyes look puffy, like you been crying," Joy said as we sat in the break room at work.

I looked at her and looked down at the food on my plate. She was right. I just sat there thinking. As much as I tried to hold the pain in, it was still visible. I was hurting badly. I wanted to break down. I want someone to wake me up and tell me this was all a dream, but I knew that it wasn't. And knowing that—knowing that this was my reality—was tearing me apart on the inside.

"Hmm, just a rough night."

"Rough night, huh? Is Rasheem on his bullshit again?"

"I followed him to a hotel, and he was there with a white bitch," I blurted out. I figured there was no reason to keep that shit in now. Word would get out soon enough that my happily ever after was over and done with. Might as well get the shit over with now.

"A *white* bitch? Did you beat that ho's ass?" She looked at me with her mouth wide open.

"I wish I did, but where would I be this morning?" I lied. I didn't know how Rasheem had gotten the bitch to not press charges, but she hadn't. So, I sure as hell wasn't taking the chance of being overheard admitting that I'd laid hands on her cracker ass. "Everything I worked for would go down the drain. As mad as I am at that bitch, she don't owe me a damn thing. He disrespected me. *He* brought that bitch into our lives."

"You know what? You're right. I'm just so angry. You gave that man your all, and *this* is how he acts? Cheating is wrong on every level, but fucking a *white* bitch makes it worse. What's wrong with these so-called brothers nowadays? So what he had to say?"

"Girl, a bunch of bullshit. You know what hurts the most? After catching him, the average nigga would've run after his wife and tried to make the shit right, right? Not him. That nigga stayed at the hotel. Then he have the nerve to walk into the house this morning, professing his love for his family."

"You know, for a minute, I thought he was one of the good ones out there. The way he looks at you and often brags about you . . . I didn't see this shit coming. I'm still shocked and angry at the same time. I know you love him, but you deserve so much more than this. I'm sorry you going through this."

"Yeah. I thought we were going to be together forever. But over the years, the love wasn't as strong. At first, I blamed myself. Shit, maybe I didn't screw him good enough. Maybe if I just spent more time with him, he would be happy. This nigga wasn't happy because he was too busy out there fucking around on me."

"Baby, listen to me. I know how much you love him, and if you think it's worth fighting for, then fight for it. But if you feel like you need to walk away, then do it. I have a big place, and I'm there by myself. If you need to get away for a few days, you more than welcome to come. You and Ky'Imani."

"Thank you, love. Let's keep this between us. You know I don't want the entire office in my business. Plus, Rasheem is close with a few officers over here."

I knew that I was asking a lot of her, but this wasn't an argument. This wasn't him spending too much money on a new car or gun. This was the end of fifteen years of my life. Looking at her, I could tell that she would respect my wishes. The last thing I needed, on top of everything else, was bullshit at work. She reached out and grabbed my hand, giving it a reassuring squeeze. I gave her a faint smile, and then let my eyes travel back to the uneaten food on my plate.

"Girl, you ain't got to worry about me telling your business. You the only friend I got in this building. Anyway, lunch is up, and you still ain't eat. I know you hurting, but you still have to take care of yourself. If you dead and gone, that nigga will still be out here screwing around. Oh God, I hate that he's doing this."

"I'm going to be okay. I just needed to vent a little. I have two more releases today, and then I'm going to do three home visits. I think getting out of the office will do me some good. And it'll save me having to act up if he decides to bring his dumb ass up in here, trying to put on a show and shit. As a matter of fact, I might take you up on that offer to stay with you. I'll let you know. Thanks, babes, for being a great friend. I swear those are hard to come by."

We exchanged hugs and walked out of the break room. I was ready for this day to be over. I needed something strong to help with this pain. As a matter of fact, talking with my mother always soothed my soul. In the past, I'd tried not to put her in our business. Maybe it was because my mother always thought he was a piece of shit, and I was too good for his ass. . . .

I guess Mama knows best, after all.

Chapter Nine

Jakeel

"Baby boy, you can use my car to get to where you need to be. I talked to your probation officer yesterday when she came to do a home visit. I told her you were out looking for a job. That's what you need to be doing instead of moping around here behind that little fast-tailed girl," Mama said, standing in the doorway to my room.

See, this was the kinda shit I was talkin' about. I felt like I was 'bout to be late for school the way she was standing there with her hands on her hips and her forehead wrinkled. I knew that she meant well, but she was in my business, and that was something that I didn't want my mama to be involved in. She was in the clear, and they didn't search her shit last time because of it. It was better that she didn't know shit because then, she wouldn't be perjuring herself on the stand.

"Mama, leave that boy alone," my sister Toya said, coming up behind Mama. She was three years older than I, but she looked out for a nigga. She knew what I was into, and even rode with me on a couple of nights when Shontelle was mad at me about some shit. She never snitched me out when I was younger and had bitches in my room when Mama was at work. She just made sure a nigga had condoms, so I ain't pop up with no babies 'round here. She even took me to the clinic the couple of times my hardheaded ass ran up in them nasty bitches raw, and they asses gave me something. Then, she promptly dropped me off at the house and proceeded to the bitches' houses to beat their asses. She was the original rider in my life, and I would always love and respect her ass for that shit.

"I won't leave him alone, neither. Me leaving him alone cost me seven years with him in a cage. This time, it might be worse. His ass might end up—"

"Now, you know you always taught us that there's power in the tongue. Don't speak that over Keel, Mama. He got his head on straight now, don't you, Keel?" she asked me, nodding her head so that I would agree.

"Yeah, Mama, I got my shit straight this time. Promise," I said, holding up my hand like I was swearing on a Bible.

Mama rolled her eyes like she didn't believe us, and she was right not to. There was never any telling what was gonna come out of Toya and me when we teamed up. But she couldn't do anything but let us be until she had evidence to the contrary, which she would never get. Unlike me, Toya wasn't the kind to leave any evidence—or witnesses—for that matter. She was savage as hell.

"Well, you can take his ass job hunting, then," Mama said, shaking her head and looking at Toya over the rim of her glasses. "Since you wanna act like a babysitter, you can be one," she stated, before walking off to her room. I knew Mama was getting ready for bed because she had to work. She always had to work. That's why Toya's and my ass were always into some good bullshit.

"I got him, Mama. Promise," Toya said to her back.

"Y'all can keep them damn promises wit' y'all lyin' asses," she snapped before slamming the door to her bedroom. She was at the age where she should be enjoying retirement. Instead, she had an ex-con for a son and a lesbian for a daughter. I bet she fell to her knees many nights, wondering what she did wrong.

The truth was, she hadn't done a thing wrong. Our mama was the best mother a pair of knuckleheads like us could ever have wanted. She was a lady, and an example of what a good woman should be so that I would look for that, and Toya would be that. But being a single parent, her absence when she worked all the time left plenty of space for us to get into mischief. And with kids, there was nothing that would make us turn away from the chance to get into some shit.

"I finally get to see my little brother, huh?" Toya said, her lips pursed, shaking her head at me. "And it took for that little stanky-pussy-havin'-ass bitch to put ya ass out for that to even happen? That's fucked up, bro, real shit."

She came and sat down at the foot of my bed. I had to laugh because I knew that Mama was gon' tell her ass what happened between Shontelle and me. . . well, as much as she knew of what happened. She wouldn't have come and picked my ass up if she knew that I'd put my hands on that bitch. She ain't like Shontelle, but she didn't raise us to be on no fuck shit like that, either.

"Maaaan, gon' with all that. You spend seven years around a bunch of bitches, and you'd be ready to—wait, never fuckin' mind," I stopped myself before I even finished my statement, because her ass would be in heaven if she were locked the hell up. So, my point was no longer a point.

"Glad you stopped that dumb shit before it came outta ya damn mouth. One, a bitch ain't neva been caught slippin' and won't neva get caught slippin', so me being in a cage is a no-go. And two, being locked down and surrounded by desperate bitches would be like heaven to me, you know that shit," she spoke, and I just nodded my head in agreement, laughing.

"Man, you a trip. I missed yo' ass," I said, pulling her over to me to hug her. We wasn't into that mushy shit, but this was a special case.

"Man, gon' on now," she said, pushing me off of her. "I wanted to visit you, but I couldn't stand to see you in a cage," she admitted, and I couldn't be mad at her for that.

"Nah, I get it. Yo' ass would be tryin'a bust a nigga out and shit. Then we'd be on the run. I needed to do that time. I really did get my shit together."

"I hope you did, man, 'cause even though I ain't let Mama speak that shit, you know she speakin' truth. I knew them charges was on some bullshit. That cop had it out for you, but there was nothin' we could do with the evidence that they had stacked up against you," she said, and again, I knew she was speaking the truth. See, what had happened to me wasn't on no regular search-and-seizure shit. The cop that got me locked up—check this—that nigga was a homicide detective. And, nah, I hadn't been caught on no end-a-nigga-life kinda shit. In all my years of dealin', I hadn't had to take a single life. I'd beat some ass within an inch of that shit, but I ain't have no souls on my shit.

His ass was mad with me because we were both fuckin' the same ho, and he'd caught me in her house. I was on my way home, and this nigga had sicced one of his damn patrol officers on my ass after catching me in that bitch's crib. So, a nigga was literally caught in some pussy, and it cost me seven years of my life. And, yeah, I know what you sayin'. While I'm over here talkin' about I learned my lesson and shit, I done got out, and I'm back on the same shit. That's partially true. I was on the same shit, but I wasn't goin' nowhere near *that* bitch.

"Get up and get dressed so I can take you to Jay's shop, and he can hire yo' ass," Toya fussed, and I wanted to kick my own ass because I hadn't thought about that shit. I knew he would put a nigga on, without a doubt. But I also knew that I was tryin'a get back on in this dope shit and didn't want to bring no heat to my homie's legit business behind me doin' some shit I had no business doin'.

I stood up, and my phone started vibrating on my bed. I looked down at it and blew out a sigh. It had only taken a day for Shontelle to start hittin' a nigga up. I wanted to respond and go back to my bitch, but the more I thought about shit, especially with her threatening to call the cops on me, the more I realized that that wasn't the kinda shit a nigga wanted to have hanging over his head. That let me know that I couldn't trust her, and that wasn't something that I could have with the shit that I had on my agenda.

"You walkin' around here lookin' like don't nobody love you, baby bro. That bitch ain't help you get your shit together. Don't want nobody else to have you, huh? I swear to Gawd, I'll never understand bitches like that, rather have you lookin' homeless, hopin' the next bitch won't see what's underneath. Don't she know bitches into upgrading niggas nowadays?"

I looked down at my threads and had no idea what she was talkin' about. I thought I'd done all right with my little shopping spree. I had to ball on a budget, seeing that more than half of my money was gone from the safe.

"I mean, Mama spent some of the money that I had in my safe, so a nigga had to work with what he had," I told her with a shrug.

"Mama did *what* now? She ain't need yo' money, nigga. Where you get that shit from?" she asked me, looking like she was ready to square up with a nigga. I was confused as hell, tryin'a figure out what I had done wrong.

"I just assumed—"

"So, you got some money missing, and your first thought was that *Mama* took it? Did you ever think that your *bitch* took it, just like the bricks that she took outta that safe, saying that you told her ass to take it and sell it and split the money three ways, some on your books, some to Ma, and the rest to her."

"She said *what* now?" I asked, looking at my phone, wanting to call her ass and go the hell off.

"Well, that shows that her ass was lying," she said, shaking her head. "Like I didn't already know that shit when we ain't see a dime of that damn money."

I couldn't explain how pissed I was with Shontelle's ass right now. And it didn't help that Mel had told me that *he* was the one who was putting money in her hands to put on my books. But let *her* ass tell it, *she* was bringing me money that she'd worked long and hard for. *She* was sacrificing for a nigga. I was starting to see the bitch as the snake that she was.

"Don't call that bitch. We 'bout to handle this business. Don't give her ass no attention and move the fuck around. Sometimes, you make a bigger impact by *not* doin' shit and lettin' a bitch see what she missed out on by being a shady-ass ho."

I heard her talkin', but that ain't make me wanna beat this bitch's ass any less. I hated that I'd fallen for her shit, but in reality, I had made her the savage bitch that she was, so I couldn't blame her entirely for her actions. But that didn't mean that I had to put up with the shit, either. We had both done our dirt, and that made us even. But at the same time, that shit was kinda sexy to a nigga. I had taken this naïve young-ass girl and turned her into a real savage. But even a savage had a degree of loyalty. I was conflicted, and I guess it showed all over my face because Toya popped her lips and rolled her eyes. She placed her hands on her hips, and her demeanor let me know that she didn't have the patience for my bullshit. So, not wanting to get popped upside the head or cussed the hell out, I walked past her mean ass and out of the room.

When I walked out the door, I was shocked to see a new car in the driveway. There was Mama's old-ass Honda that she wouldn't upgrade for shit. Then there was Toya's loud

pink-ass Dodge Charger. The last one was a blacked-out
Expedition sitting on chrome rims that were blinding my
ass in the sunlight.

"Welcome home, li'l bro," Toya said, and I looked at her
like I knew she was fuckin' lyin' to a nigga. There was *no*
way that this was my shit.

"Dead assed?" I asked, so excited I felt like a little-ass
nigga at Christmas.

"Dead assed," she said with a smile, holding the keys
out for me.

I snatched them bitches before she could change her
mind and ran to that muthafucka, pushing the key fob
to pop the locks. When I opened the door, that bitch was
decked out on the inside and had that new car smell to
it. I hopped in and looked around. It was all electronic
everything in that bitch, and the sound system beat as
soon as I turned the key in the ignition.

Hopping back out, I ran to Toya and picked her ass up,
spinning her around. She squealed for me to put her down,
and I did, but only long enough to kiss her ass on the cheek.
I didn't know where she'd got the money from to get me
this damn truck, but I planned to pay her back, and then
some.

"So, you gon' drive around to handle this business,
a'ight?" she instructed me. "If I gotta babysit that ass, I
might as well do that shit in style."

I ran around the front of the truck and opened the
door for her. She walked over and got in, a huge smile of
accomplishment on her face. I loved her ass more than she
would ever know. She was the one that taught me the game
with the dope and the bitches. But she got out as soon as
she'd made enough to start her clothing line, just like Jay.
I wanted to do the same, but I had to get back up before
I could do that shit, and I had to find something to invest
my money in to clean all the cash that I made.

"Where to first?" I asked, smiling, ready to put some miles on the dash of this bad bitch. It was fresh off the lot and ready to hit the road for a nigga.

"To Jay's, and then we gon' get your damn hair cut and hit up Lenox."

"I ain't got no money, sis," I admitted, and the words left a sour-ass taste in my mouth on their way out.

"Who said anything about all that?" she asked, looking at me like I'd offended her.

"A'ight, I hear you," I said, throwing up my hands in surrender at the stop sign at the top of our block. "Where you get the money for this shit?" I asked when she laughed at me because I was throwing in the towel. I wasn't one to argue, so I changed the subject to something more pleasant.

"Investments, bro. Stocks and bonds and shit," she said, sounding like a real hood-ass businesswoman.

"Damn, you gon' have to teach me that shit," I said, meaning it. I was a risk-taker and knew that stocks were a risky game. But it was also one that could pay off in real numbers. The kinda money that some niggas wouldn't see in a lifetime of hustlin'.

"Sure will. Anything to keep yo' ass outta these streets," she said, and her tone told me that she meant that shit. She ain't want me to put my life and my freedom out there no more. That's how I knew she loved a nigga. And in times like these, I was grateful to be loved.

Pulling up to Jay's shop, it was like he was expecting us or some shit. That's when I realized that Toya had planned the whole day out for me, in real life. We walked in, and he dapped me up before leading us to the back of the shop. When we walked into his office, I had to say I was impressed. Looking at him in his coveralls, with oil and grease and shit all over them, I didn't expect his shit to be laid out like it was.

I walked over to the display case and couldn't help but smile. He had all the model cars that we'd put together when we were younger in a glass case. I thought that was so damn dope. He'd always had a thing for cars and had turned that shit into a legit hustle. When I turned around, they were sitting and looking at me like they were waiting for me to sit my ass down. I made my way over to the seat that was beside Toya, and Jay leaned forward and placed his hands on his desk.

"So, why ain't you come to me to ask me to put you on, my nigga?" Jay asked, looking at me like I was trippin' not to have thought of that shit.

"Keepin' shit a hunnid, Jay, man. I ain't wanna fuck up what you got goin' on."

"Fuck it up how?" he and Toya asked at the same time.

"Man, I gotta get my money up and fast. I didn't wanna bring no heat to your spot. Especially with you bein' legit now."

"Do you hear this shit? I *know* I can't be hearin' this shit. Jay, you better talk some sense into this nigga before I knock some sense into his ass," Toya said, jumping up out of her seat and standing over me. I could tell she was ready to bust me in my shit, and I could understand why. But what I didn't get was why her ass was actin' like she was all surprised.

"I hear his ass, and I really think that the prison food altered his brain or some shit. Or, aye, maybe his ass like being locked the fuck up with them niggas. You must got you a boyfriend you tryin'a get back to in there," Jay said, and it was now *my* turn to jump up. That was some disrespectful shit to say. And this nigga knew that I was the furthest thing from fuckin' gay. Not that there was shit wrong with the shit, because my sister was gay as hell. But that wasn't my fuckin' move.

"Sit yo' simple ass the fuck down," Jay said, and the tone of his voice was one that I only heard when I knew he was about to take a life.

"Man, nah. Why you say that disrespectful-ass shit, nigga?" I asked, still standing in defiance to his demand. He had me all the way fucked up.

"So, you the only one in the room who can let dumb-ass shit come outta your mouth, huh?" he challenged, rising from his seat slowly. I could tell by the way that his fists were pressed into the top of the desk that he was just as pissed with my ass as Toya was. But I wasn't paying her ass no mind. It was Jay that I had beef with because he'd flat-out called me a fag-ass nigga to my face.

"Man, you ain't have to say no shit like that, though," was all I could think to say, because I was hip to what he was tryin'a do.

"I'm over here tryin'a give yo' ass a damn job, to keep your probation officer off ya ass. Ya sister done bought you a car and takin' you shopping and shit. Ya mama lettin' you stay in her shit 'cause you won't listen to no-damn-body and ran right back to the bitch that put yo' ass out in the streets less than a week after you got the fuck free. And you repay us by goin' back to the same shit that got you hemmed up in the first fuckin' place?" He called me on my shit. It hit me so hard about what he was saying that I had to sit my ass down. Nigga knocked the wind outta me with the truth.

"It's all I know, my nigga. All that I'm good at," I admitted. My ass wasn't good at school or sports or none of that other shit. But I was good with cookin' up them damn drugs and hustlin' my ass off. I'd climbed the ladder quick as hell and was on my way to the next level when I got popped.

"Then learn something the fuck else, nigga. Lemme teach you 'bout these damn cars or how to run a legit business. Get ya fuckin' GED or some certification in some shit. I know you ain't sittin' here tellin' me that Shontelle got more hustle about herself than you do."

The sound of her name made my temples start to throb. That bitch had hustled with my fuckin' money, so there wasn't no comparison. I had never worked a day in my life. I made that work, work for my ass instead. Not that a nigga was lazy, but who the fuck worked hard when they didn't have to?

"That's what the fuck I thought," Jay said, taking my silence as confirmation that what he'd said had hit home. "Now, you gon' fill out this paperwork. You gon' be my apprentice. And you gon' find a legit hustle. Or me and Toya here gon' have to take you the fuck up off this earth," he said, and I knew that he wasn't making an idle threat. Sometimes, being loved was a pain in the ass. I wanted to be grateful, but I had just spent seven years being told what the fuck to do every minute. I'd be damned if I was gon' take that shit now that I was free.

But I would go with this shit for a li'l bit. At least, I would be able to stack my money back up so that I could buy back into the business that I loved—the business that had my heart and soul. And if they didn't like it—well, by then, I wouldn't give a fuck. I would be doin' me.

Chapter Ten

Rasheem

"Detective Blake, there's someone here to see you," I heard one of the rookies say, knocking on the open door of my office. My face lit up, hoping that it was Mika or at least Ky'Imani. None of the women in my life were speaking to me, and that shit would be a nigga's wildest dream come true . . . if it wasn't behind some shit that I'd done wrong.

I had tried calling them all but didn't get a callback. The one that fucked with me the most, though, was Mika. I had been by her office, but she made it her business to spend most of her days in the field, and they weren't able to tell me where she was because of that confidentiality bullshit. I mean, we were on the same side, so I didn't know what the issue was with telling me where my wife was. It was in moments like this that I realized little shit like her sending me her location when she was out in the field just so I would know where she was, was good. It was funny how you missed the shit that at one point got on your damned nerves before. All I could do was hope that she was missing a nigga the same way.

She was about to have me staking out her ass. I didn't know where she was staying, and the bitches in her office weren't telling me shit. Not even my little mole, Joy, who would let me know if one of her parolees got outta hand and tried to holla at my wife. That was when I realized that she had told them what was goin' on between us. That was when the shit became real. But I was tired of this shit now. It was time for my wife to bring her ass the fuck back home, and we work this shit out. She would just have to look stupid to all them bitches that she'd chosen to tell about our personal business. That was *her* fault. She knew better than to do that shit anyway.

"May I come in?" a soft, sweet voice broke me out of my thoughts and brought me back to reality.

I looked at the innocent-looking woman standing in the doorway of my office, holding a manila envelope. She was beautiful, and even though I was already in the doghouse for the bullshit that I'd been into, I still took note and wanted to play the hero to this damsel who was obviously in distress. Her eyes were wide, and she looked like she was ready to cry. I didn't think anything of it because she didn't look any different from any of the other young, beautiful women who walked into my office with evidence of foul play.

"Yes, you may," I said, standing up from my seat, waiting for her to come into my office.

Instead, she broke down in tears, right there, in the middle of my door. I rushed to the rescue, helping her stand up from the crouched over position that she was in. I even tried to help by taking the envelope that she was holding out of her hand. She took a couple of deep breaths, then stood to her feet as she looked deep into my eyes.

"Thank you so much, Detective . . ." she dragged out, waiting for me to introduce myself properly.

"Blake. My name is Detective Rasheem Blake, beautiful," I said with a proud smile. I wanted her to remember that name because if I had my way, she'd be screaming it at the top of her lungs later. With my whole roster not speaking to me, I decided to start drafting a new team.

"Perfect," she said, and I stared at her, finding it strange that she'd regained her composure so quickly. "Detective Rasheem Blake, you've been served."

She pointed at the envelope that I had so willingly taken from her hands. She didn't even have to force the shit on me. I had to say that I'd seen my share of process servers do their jobs in my career, but this bitch was good. Damned good.

She left my office with a giggle and left me standing there on stuck. I was too embarrassed to chase her ass through the station and didn't want anyone to know that I had just been played like that. Instead, I walked back to my desk and dropped the folder on top of it. I didn't want to open it because I had a bad feeling that I already knew what was on the inside of it.

At first, I didn't want to touch it at all, like it had a deadly snake inside of it or some shit. In reality, though, I knew that there was some kinda death in there, even if not a physical one. It was the death of my happily ever after. And even though I knew that the shit was coming, I thought that with a little time and space, maybe Mika would give me another chance.

Finally, I sucked it the hell up and picked up the envelope. I flipped it over and over again on my desk, wondering how I had missed the signs that this may have been from Mika's divorce lawyers, and on the back side, as plain as day, there was a stamp with the attorney's contact information.

If I hadn't been thinking with my dick, I might not have missed the shit. But I was distracted, too easily for my chosen profession, honestly. And now, for the first time, I was embarrassed for the way I had been behaving. Yeah, it should've bothered me that I had failed my wife. But me failing at my job was more of an issue for me. Getting caught slipping in my marriage was ending in divorce.

But being caught slipping on the job could end my entire existence.

Opening the envelope, I pulled out the paperwork and started to read it. I'd expected her to ask for half of everything. That was what I'd hoped for, anyway, so that I could drag the shit out in court contesting the division of assets. That was the plan to buy me some time so that I could get her to change her mind. But as I read the paperwork, I saw that she didn't want shit. Not even alimony like she'd claimed in our last argument. Not child support for Ky'Imani, even though she asked that I continue to pay our daughter's tuition for any degrees that she wished to pursue, at any university that she chose to attend. *Just like Mika, thinking of others before herself. If her ass had thought about* my *needs, we wouldn't be in this damn situation in the first place,* I thought bitterly, getting pissed off.

I think the thing that was making me the angriest was the fact that my wife wasn't asking for any of the things that we'd attained in the last fifteen years. Not even my last name. The only part of me that she seemed to want to keep was our daughter. And if that was what I had to bargain with, then I would fight for K'Imani with every fiber of my being. I knew she wouldn't want to leave her mama to come live with me, but it wasn't about that. It was about buying time for Mika to come to her senses. I mean, who the fuck walks away from fifteen years of being happily married—for the most part—because of a minor—well, a couple of minor, but she only knew about one—indiscretion?

It just didn't make sense to me. She was so loyal to me. I never would'a thought that she would leave me. There was no reason for her to want that. I mean, she had everything that she could ever want. And it wasn't like she was religious, and my affair was against her beliefs or no shit like that. I was sitting there, trying to make sense of it, and I was coming up empty.

I mean, it wasn't like I was flaunting the bitches around or no shit, and I drove to Alabama to get Gina's ring, so I knew that wasn't the issue. No one could've seen me buy that. And the shock that was on her face when Gina was calling me her fiancé let me know that she hadn't been aware of it. I couldn't figure it out. There was nothing but her ego that was keeping us from repairing our marriage. I'd told her I was willing to do whatever I needed to in order to make this shit happen. But she wasn't biting, and I was getting tired of this game. She wasn't about to divorce me. That wasn't gonna happen. This shit was 'til death do us part, and she needed to get over what the hell happened so that we could continue on this journey together. She knew none of them bitches held a candle to her. That's why she was in the house, with the kid, access to all the accounts, the clout, and had the ring—well, the last name, at least, because technically, Gina had a ring too. Regardless, she knew I wasn't about to marry that white bitch. She couldn't be that damn stupid. This was evidence that Mika wasn't a real hood bitch, or she would've been happy with her position and played her fuckin' role. But noooo, her ass wanna go file for divorce.

"Boss, we gotta problem," Detective Moore, my protégé, said, coming into the office without knocking.

I hadn't moved since that bitch had served me these damn papers and left the office. I had been reading the paperwork over and over again, trying to make sense of it. It wasn't that I couldn't understand what it said. It was more that I couldn't believe that I was really reading divorce papers. Mika wanted to end our marriage, and I knew she wasn't playing with my ass. She had moved out, and now she'd hired a lawyer. She wasn't one to waste money just to make a point. I had to get to her ASAP and talk her outta this shit.

"Damn, Sheem. Are those what I think they are?" Moore asked, looking down at the same paperwork that I was reading for the twentieth time in an hour.

"Man, she just tryin'a scare a nigga straight, that's all," I said, putting the papers back in the envelope that they were in and looking at Moore, who had sat his ass down on the opposite side of my desk.

"What's this problem that you're talking about?" I asked, hoping that it was something that could distract me from my misery. Maybe I could take out some of my aggression on some nigga who had the nerve to be out here tryin'a break the law.

Moore got up and closed the door, looking out before he did to make sure that no one was coming our way. I knew it had to be serious, then, because I never closed the door to my office. When he sat back down, the look on his face confirmed it. I gave him my undivided attention, waiting for him to tell me what we were up against.

"You remember that li'l nigga you had me pull over and plant that shit on because he was fuckin' with yo' bitch?" he asked, and I nodded. He knew that I knew who he was talkin' about because that was the case that got him promoted to detective, with my recommendation, of course.

"Jakeel Greene, right?" I asked, and it was his turn to nod.

"Well, he's out."

"Damn, has it been seven years already?" I asked, and he nodded.

"But that's not the big problem."

"OK, what is it?" I asked, tired of him playing this game with me. I needed him to spit the shit out.

"Guess who his probation officer is."

I didn't want to hear the words because that would make it real. What the fuck were the odds of this nigga that I set up behind my side bitch being one of my wife's parolees? I needed to get the two of them away from each other. I knew that Mika was all about being professional, but if Jakeel's ass found out who she was to me, she could be in danger. I couldn't chance her being hurt by more of my bullshit. But how was I supposed to protect her ass when she wouldn't even answer my damn calls?

"We gotta get him reassigned," I said, and Moore looked at me like he knew that shit was impossible. Because, well, it pretty much was. Either there would have to be some kinda line crossed between the two of them, or he would have to pose a danger to Mika for that to happen. And she was too professional for the first to occur. The second one, though, was possible.

"How you gon' tell them that you feel like your wife is in danger without telling them why?" Moore posed the question like he was reading my mind. "You know that shit is gonna bring light to you and shit," he spoke the truth.

"Maybe we can catch his ass on a violation," I said, rubbing my chin with my hand. That seemed like the only thing that would work, given the situation.

"Yeah, that could work. What about Lauren? Would she be willing to help with that shit?" Moore asked, and I looked at him and then back down at the envelope. "Aaaah, man, don't tell me she mad at yo' ass too. What you been out here doin'?"

"Got cocky and started movin' real reckless," I admitted, and he shook his head.

"Well, you need to make up with her, and with Mika, so that we can get Jakeel's ass out of the way—ASAP—before we both end up fucked up. I took that nigga down for you, but I ain't 'bout to do no time behind that shit."

I looked at him across my desk, because I didn't appreciate the threat that he'd just let slip from his lips. It seemed like everybody was tryin'a test me lately. I was gonna let that shit slide . . . for now. But what he didn't know was, if this shit hit the fan, he would be the *only* one under fire. Not me. I had insurance to make that shit happen, as well as the pull to make sure that he was the only one that would be culpable for any of it.

But I didn't plan for it to come to that. I had some schmoozing and begging to do to all three of my bitches because even Gina was gonna come in handy in this little mission. This was about to get expensive as hell. But I was willing to pay any price to save my career, keep my freedom, and even, hopefully, get back in my wife's good graces.

"Get the fuck outta my office so I can make sure you covered all the fuckin' bases," I snapped at him, and he chuckled a little bit before turning to head out. "And, Moore," I yelled at his back right as his hand touched the handle to my office's door.

"Yeah?" he said, looking back at me, his eyes getting big as hell.

"If you ever make another threat to me, you won't get the pleasure of being behind bars. You'll be in a fuckin' box," I said, holding my Glock in my hand, aimed right between his fuckin' eyes. "And one more thing before yo' scary ass go change ya drawers 'cause I know you just shitted on yourself . . . Never turn your back on a nigga you make a threat toward."

Reaching behind himself, he twisted the doorknob and opened the door just wide enough for him to ease out. I laughed at his scary ass when the door slammed behind him. He must've forgot who the fuck he was talkin' to and about. I picked up the envelope. It seemed that all of them had forgotten who the fuck they were dealing with. I felt like it was time to give their asses a reminder. Beginning with Mika's ass. If anybody should've known damn better, her ass should've.

Chapter Eleven

Mika

After catching up on some work, I glanced at the clock on my desk. I had a client that was supposed to be returning in another five minutes. I wasn't looking forward to dealing with no-damn-body after the day I had, but I needed to check on his progress and see if he made any effort in finding a job . . .

I decided to use the restroom and freshened a little bit before I headed back to the office. Then I opened his file up and waited. I hoped his ass didn't show up late 'cause I planned on getting the hell out of here. . . .

The phone started ringing so I picked it up. "Mrs. Blake, your three o'clock is here."

"Send him right in, Joanne."

"Okay."

A minute later, Mr. Greene walked in. I looked up and almost didn't recognize him. It was like he got an entire makeover since the last time I saw him. This brotha that was standing in front of me looked like he was supposed to be in a *GQ* magazine. But not as one of those men in suits; instead, a gray-sweatpants-white-tee kind of brotha.

"Mr. Greene, you look . . . different," I blurted out before I could catch myself. Rasheem had knocked me all the way off my square because that was unprofessional as hell. Trying to regain my composure, I didn't make eye contact with him immediately, because I could tell that he'd caught that slip up too. "Please take a seat. How are you doing?"

"I'm good. How about you, beautiful?" he smiled at me.

God, please make this man stop smiling like this, I whispered and scooted all the way back in my seat.

"So, how's it been going? Have you had a chance to check out the job leads?"

"Yeah, but to be honest, I ain't tryin'a to work no seven dollars an hour and shit. No disrespect, but I'm a grown-ass man. What the hell that's supposed to do for me?" he stared me down.

"You ever hear the phrase, 'You have to crawl before you walk'?" I glanced at my computer, took a quick read, and then continued speaking. "You're a convicted felon that did seven years in prison for selling dope and having a gun. You don't have a high school diploma and no skills or technical training. Now, tell me what kind of jobs do you think you're qualified for?" I took my glasses off and stared at him, waiting for a response.

"Damn, shorty, you think a degree of the white man makes a motherfucker more qualified? Shit, I was making thousands per day in these streets without a damn degree. You can't talk to me about making no money. I can walk my hood ass into any establishment and talk money with the best of the best. See, all y'all look at is a nigga's record. I ain't got to be book smart to be able to make money."

"I see you still have that street mentally. When you walk into an establishment looking for a job, you can't tell them how many keys you done sold or how much crack you've cooked up, or how many guns you've slung. That shit doesn't matter. What you need is a real job. It doesn't matter if you flipping burgers or cleaning toilets. It's a legal job that won't land your ass back in the pen. The choice is yours. You can either do it the right way or go out there and do the same dumb shit that will land you right back into the arms of the white man."

This shit was pissing me off. In front of me was a fine-ass man, but the shit that was coming out of his mouth sounded dumb as fuck. I wished I could reach over and slap the hell out of him for talking dumb like that.

"I hear you," he mumbled.

I'd hit a sore spot with him. I was sure that his mother had been on him about doing things the right way. She was a sweet lady, and I could tell that her son being locked up had aged her and broken her heart. No mother wanted her children locked up in some cell. It made them feel like a failure. But if he knew what was good for him, he would listen to her—and me. He had to change his ways to not end up in the same place that he'd just gotten out of. And, fine or not, I would put his ass right back there.

I could tell he wasn't liking the way I was talking to him, but hell, I didn't give a damn. I was one of the few probation officers that gave a damn, and I was sick and tired of seeing these black men come in and out of these doors. I was tired of seeing the mothers breaking down 'cause their sons are led away in shackles. If me being a hard-ass on them can help one client, then, well, my job is done. . . .

"What are your weaknesses? Why do you think you can't find a job?"

"I mean, like you said, I ain't got no skills." He shrugged his shoulders.

"You know what? Your attitude is standing in the way of you being great."

"Yo, I'm about sick of yo' slick-ass comments. I'm a grown-ass man, and I'ma figure my way out like I been doing since I been 15. I don't need no fake-ass caring from nobody and especially not from the law. Are you done with all yo' preaching so that I can get out of here? I got some places to be."

"Hmm, I see you one of the brothers who are not used to having a woman that cares," I said, and that let me know that he was used to holding shit down on his own. He had trust issues, and that could be because of the life that he'd lived. I couldn't blame him for that, because, at this point, I had my own trust issues.

"I got plenty of bitches that care about a nigga," he said, and that made me look at him with my head cocked to the side. I wondered if he realized how stupid he sounded. It was then that I realized that you could take the nigga out of the hood, but those ways were almost impossible to shake. That was my husband's issue too. No matter how many promotions and accolades he received, he never got outta that street mentality, where shit is measured by credibility and how many hoes you had hangin' off ya dick. That shit was sickening.

"One of them places you gotta be needs to be a job or beating the streets 'til you find one," I said sternly. I started typing up some notes, and he slid a business card onto my desk.

"Nah, shorty, I don't have to beat no streets for shit."

Looking down at the business card, I looked back up at him, confused. I didn't know why he was giving me a card to a detail shop. But his smile let me know that there was a reason behind the action, so I just waited on him to fill me in.

"I gotta job, man. I was just fuckin' wit' you," he said, flashing me a proud smile. I couldn't hide my own smile too. "But it's nice to know you care about a nigga, though. The only other women in my life who seem to give a damn about me are my mama and my sister."

"None of them bitches that you were just braggin' about?" I asked with my eyebrow raised.

"Nah, all they care about is clout, green, and keys. But that shit don't matter when you're behind bars," he said, and I knew the tone in his voice all too well. That was the tone of disappointment. Someone had let him down recently, and that shit was bothering him. But it seemed to be humbling his ass too.

"Well, it seems like something is starting to sink in for you, Mr. Greene, and that makes me happy," I said, looking over my laptop at him.

"Oh yeah? Well, what else makes you happy? A nigga wants to make sure to do more of that," he said, and I had to giggle. "Something is different about you too, Mrs. Blake. You ain't got that stick up yo' ass like you did when I first came up in here."

"Uuuugh, is that how you talk to all women? You do know that only works with ratchets and chickenheads. You'll never pull a *real* grown-ass woman, talkin' to them like that."

I didn't know if I was telling him that because I wanted him to step up his shit for me or for the next real woman that he came across. The fact that I couldn't decide was unsettling.

"Well, then, Mrs. Blake, would you allow me to learn how to address a woman properly of your caliber from you? Saaaay, over some TGI Fridays?"

That made me stop typing and damn near stop breathing. I knew that I had to be hearing things. There was *no way* that he was asking me out.

"Are you asking me on a date, Mr. Greene?" I asked, smirking at him.

"No," he said, holding his hands up in surrender. "That would be unprofessional. But . . ." he paused, giving me that million-dollar smile again, "if the two of us just so happened to be at the TGI Fridays at Lenox Mall, in like an hour, and the hostess just happened to seat us both at the same table, then it would be a wonderful coincidence."

I had to laugh at that. He was handsome and funny, and right now, I needed that. Thinking back to what Ky had said about me going out, I didn't see the harm in us "happening" to be in the same place at the same time. I knew I wouldn't let it go any further than that, because it would be putting my career at stake.

"Make it *two* hours," I said to him, and I could tell that he didn't expect me to agree.

"Dead assed?" he asked like *he* was the one hearing things at this point.

"Dead assed," I repeated, trying to sound hip.

"Damn, that shit sounds sexy as hell with your accent," he complimented, making me blush.

"Don't push it," I threatened. I couldn't deny that it made me smile, though, that he'd picked up on my accent. It'd been forever since someone said something about it. Everyone else that I was around every day was used to it. And it had been more than a decade since Rasheem said anything about it, to the point that I thought maybe it was gone.

"A'ight, then lemme get outta here before you change your mind," he said, rising from his seat. "And it's on me, Mrs. Blake?" he said my name more as a question than a statement because I'd just agreed to meet up with him. "Ya know, since a nigga gotta job and shit."

"Goodbye, Mr. Greene," I said, shaking my head at him and rolling my eyes.

"You mean, see you later, Ms. Blake," he said, removing the "Mrs." from my name.

Before I could say anything else, he was up and out of my office, closing the door behind him. My head felt light like this was all a dream. The only thing that let me know it wasn't was the scent of his sexy-ass cologne that I'd fought not to sniff too hard while breathing, and the smile that stayed plastered on my face. I had an internal struggle about whether this was a good idea, but I decided not to question it. I was about to be single soon, so he could be practice. And it wasn't like I was sleeping with the man. After all, it was *just* dinner.

I'd been cautious all of my life and had no negative marks against me my entire career. So, even though Mr. Greene seemed to be harmless enough, if something did come to light, it would probably only result in a verbal reprimand—if that. And it wasn't like I would be the first in this damn office to sleep with a parolee. Hell, some of them had to transfer the niggas to another officer because they started full-blown relationships.

"It's just dinner, Mika. Chill out," I said to myself, looking down at the card that he'd left on my desk.

I picked up the phone to call the number and make sure that he had really found a job. That would be my last task of the day before rushing home to freshen up before I had to get to Lenox Mall for this little rendezvous.

I had to admit, I couldn't remember the last time that I'd been this excited about anything.

Chapter Twelve

Gina

"Well, look who it is," Lauren said, looking me up and down like she was ready to hit me. I couldn't say that she didn't have a good reason to. I stood in her doorway with a handful of toys for Jasheem and some Applebee's and a bottle of Moscato for her. She had been my best friend since we were little, almost her son's age, and I had committed the ultimate betrayal.

"Can I come in?" I asked her humbly. I knew she was gon' read my ass left to right, and I deserved every damn bit of that shit.

"I'on know. The last time I let ya ass in my shit, you stole my man," she said, loud as hell, popping her lips with her hands on her hips. I knew she was putting on a show for the hood, and I didn't try to stop her. She had every right.

"Girl, bye. His ass for *everybody*," I said, rolling my eyes. I mean, if I was gon' be on the outs with my best friend, it wasn't gonna be behind a muthafucka that had lied to both of us.

Rolling her eyes, she stepped to the side so that I could come in. I walked in and looked around. I could tell that she was in her feelings because she had her "Fuck That Nigga" playlist on blast and was cleaning her house. There was sage burning and all, which let me know that she was trying to get any hint of his ass out of her space. I hated this for her. I hated this for both of us.

And I wanted to give Rasheem's ass a taste of his own medicine. That was why I was there. Well, other than to apologize. I was there to let her know about the plan that I'd come up with to get back at his ass for breaking our hearts.

I went into the kitchen and put the Moscato and food on the counter, then left and headed down the hallway toward Jasheem's room. When I walked in, he was lying on his bed, reading on his tablet. That was one thing that I loved about Lauren. She was a great mother. While most moms bought their kids gaming systems and sat them in front of the TV, she was the kind that took him to museums, and he had a Kindle with a subscription so that he could download as many books as he wanted to. Lauren wasn't a typical project mom. She was just a mom who happened to live in the projects.

"Well, what fantasy world are we visiting today?" I asked, after standing there watching him for a few minutes. He was a really good kid. I wished she knew who his father was so that she could get some real support and not just handouts from Rasheem's ass. But because she didn't know, she'd named him after the two possibilities—Jakeel and Rasheem.

"Auntie Ginaaaa!" he hollered in excitement. He placed his tablet down on the bed before hopping up and running into my arms. I hugged him tightly because it had been months since I'd seen him. When Lauren had found out about Rasheem and me, she'd told me to stay out of both of their lives. That was a pain that hurt worse than what I'd felt when Rasheem's wife had busted into the hotel room. I was losing not only my best friend but also the child whose life I had been in since before he was born. I couldn't have children of my own, so he was all I had.

"I bought you something," I said, holding out the gift bag that had an art kit, canvases, a sketchpad, and some journals in them.

Jasheem loved to draw, sketch, and paint, and he loved to make up his own stories. He was a little artist in the making. But he got it honest because Lauren used to dance and sing. She got sidetracked from leaving here and going to art school when she started messing with Jakeel and then came Rasheem, and she was stuck here, having to put her dreams on pause to raise a child alone, like so many other mothers.

Taking the bag out of my hand, he went back to his bed and dumped the contents onto it and looked back at me with the biggest smile on his face. Rushing back over to me, he gave me another tight hug that made me smile from ear to ear. I loved this little boy and his mama more than life itself, and if there was one thing that I would never do again, it was let anything—or anyone—come between us.

"What do you say, Jay?" Lauren asked, making me jump and turn around.

I hadn't heard her walk up behind me. She gave me a smirk that let me know that she could've fucked me up if she wanted to, and probably would've if her son wasn't in the house. Instead, she handed me a wineglass filled to the brim with the Moscato that I'd brought. She'd put several cubes of ice in the glass since it wasn't chilled enough when I brought it.

"Thank you, Auntie Gina!" he said, looking up into my face with his little arms still wrapped tightly around my waist. "I was about to it, Mama. Promise," he whined.

"You are so welcome, baby boy. And she knows you were. She's raising you right, so she just had to make sure," I told him, trying to ease his busy little mind. "Now, why don't you go draw me a picture, and maybe later, you can read me one of your new stories?"

Pulling away and nodding, he rushed to his bed and started ripping the plastic from the packages. For some reason, I caught myself doing what I'd always done from the moment that he was born. Staring at him, I was trying to see features that told me who his father was. I didn't know who Rasheem was at the time that Jay was born, but now that I knew him—intimately—I found myself searching for his features in my nephew's face.

It was weird, because he looked like Rasheem *and* Jakeel, depending on the angle and the way the light hit his face. But more than anything, he looked like Lauren. Giving up, just like I had on trying to get her ass to get a DNA test, I looked at him for a few moments more before turning to look at his mama. Lauren was smiling at her son too. But that smile vanished from her face when her eyes met mine. I felt like I was her child and hadn't said, "thank you." But I knew that what I'd done was way worse. She motioned with her head toward the front of the house, and I followed her, knowing that this conversation wasn't about to be a pleasant one for me.

When we got back to her living room, Lauren walked over to her door, making sure that it was locked and put the chain on it. I knew that she wasn't expecting anyone to come in, so she was making sure that I wouldn't be able to get out so quickly. *That* made my heart skip a beat. I sat on the couch, hoping that we would at least be able to talk this shit out civilly. But I knew that Lauren had a temper, and all it would take was one wrong word, and she would be upside my damn head.

Sitting down in the chair across from me, she took a couple of sips of her wine. I couldn't tell whether it was because she liked to watch me squirm, or because she was trying to calm her nerves. Knowing Lauren, it could've been either. Or both. Finally, she picked up the remote and turned the volume down on her television that was playing songs from her Spotify playlist called "Fuck That Nigga," just like I'd said. That made me giggle, but when she looked at me, my laughter caught in my throat, and I waited for her to speak.

"You know I ain't gonna be as quick to forgive you as Jasheem was," she started, and I nodded my head.

"I know," I said just above a whisper before gulping my wine. I had a feeling that I was gonna need about three of these just to be able to get through this conversation.

"Slow down on that shit. I want you to remember this fuckin' talk so that we never have to deal with this again," she said, and I nodded and put my glass down. I gave her my undivided attention.

"Listen, I am so sorry, Lauren. I should've never fucked you over for Rasheem. You're my best friend. Nah, fuck that, you're like family. I should've never let a man come between us." I stated my apology before she lit into my ass.

"You're right. We *are* family. How long have we known each other, G?" she asked me, and I let my eyes roll back in my head while I did the math.

"Fifteen years."

"Who took you in when yo' daddy put ya ass out because you were fuckin' niggas?"

"You."

"Who would be in the middle of the bullshit with you when them muthafuckas would do you dirty?"

"You."

"Who put you in rehab when that last one got you hooked on meth?" she asked, and I was feeling worse and worse by the minute.

"You."

"And who beat the bitch ass who was in yo' fuckin' house, actin' like shit was sweet when you got outta rehab?"

"You."

"Whose shoulder did you cry on?"

"Yours."

"And who kept yo' ass from relapsing. Even handcuffing you to the bed to make sure you ain't go cop no shit?"

"You—"

"And how many times have I ever fucked you over?"

"Not one."

"So, why in the hell would you do me like that?" she asked, and I felt so bad because the hurt was evident in her voice. Before I could respond, she burst into tears. I would've never imagined that she cared about Rasheem as much as she did, and it made me wonder if she knew about his wife. She couldn't if she was this fucked up behind him and me.

"L-Boogie," I called her by the nickname that she'd gotten in high school because she could sing like the singer Lauryn Hill. She looked up at me with wet eyes, and my heart broke for her. I hated to be the one to tell her this part because I was sure it was gonna devastate her. "You know he's married, right?"

She burst out laughing, but there were tears still spilling down her face as well. I was so confused at that moment. I didn't know if my friend had just lost her mind because there wasn't shit funny about what I'd just told her. Picking up my glass, I started sipping on it again while I waited for her to stop laughing. A few sips later, she was still laughing hard as hell. It was crazy. She would seem like she was about to stop laughing, and then, right when I thought she'd got herself together, she would bust out laughing once more.

Shaking my head, I got up and went into the kitchen to refill my glass. When I got in there, I picked up the bottle, about to pour some more into the glass, but decided to just bring the whole damn bottle with me.

"Grab those other two bottles out of the fridge, biiiitch. We gon' need them," Lauren yelled from the living room. I didn't know how she thought I could carry three bottles of wine *and* a glass, but I figured that shit out. When I came back into the living room, her glass was empty too, and I knew it was half-full when I'd left the room. "Whew! All that laughing had me parched."

She fake fanned herself and took one of the unopened bottles and popped it open. Pouring her glass damn near full, she put it to her lips and drank that shit down like it was water. Shaking my head, I refilled my glass halfway and sipped it, waiting for her to tell me what was so damn funny.

"Gina . . ." she started, looking at me like I had to be dumb as hell. "Baby . . ." she said, and I knew she was about to talk to me like I was stupid. "Yes, I knew the nigga was married. I also know that he has a daughter that ain't too much younger than us. Why do you think that nigga stay droppin' stacks on me? You think he wanted his perfect life disrupted by a possibly illegitimate child? He was paying to keep me quiet," she said, refilling her glass, her eyes glued on me, giving me the chance to soak up what she'd just told me.

"That shit would ruin his life and his reputation," I said, my face lighting up.

"Exaaaactly. And he's still payin' a bitch to keep that shit a secret. Personally, I think he's dumb as all hell to be paying on a baby that may not even be his. Especially when they have take-home DNA kits at the pharmacy nowadays. I believe he's paying for the delusion of having a son, since his wife only gave him the one child, and it was a daughter."

"His ego is—"

"Bigger than his dick," she said, and we both busted out laughing. "And that's big as fuck because that nigga is hung like a damn horse."

"Say that," I said, and she quickly shot me a look. I didn't do shit but shrug, because she couldn't get mad at me for speaking facts. The only reason I knew was because she'd brought me into their sex life to appease his ass.

"So, imagine my shock when word hit the hood that you were engaged to his ass. One, I was pissed because I was like, nah, my main bitch wouldn't do no shit like that behind my back."

I hung my head because I had hoped that the conversation about what I had done would be over. But I knew that was wishful thinking because what I did was fucked up.

"Then . . . then . . . When I saw that shit on Facebook, I kinda felt a way because I had been dealin' wit' his ass for years, and he gave *you* a ring and *not* me. But theeeen, I had to bust out laughing, because I knew that he knew I would've thrown that shit back up in his damn face because I knew he couldn't marry me when he was already married. I wanted to call you and bust your little bubble. But I knew that, eventually, you'd find out, and that way, you wouldn't be tryin'a make a bitch seem like I was hatin' on yo' ass."

"Well, that shit slapped me right in the damn face . . . literally," I said, shaking my head.

"That bitch popped you, huh?" she asked with a giggle. "I always told his ass he was underestimating her. She may be professional and shit, but no woman takes disrespect at the level that he was doin' that shit. Honestly, I been watching the news, expecting her to shoot his ass if she ain't left him already."

"Oh, she left his ass, 'cause he been callin' and textin' me, beggin' me to forgive him. Talkin' about he finna get divorced, so we can really get married now," I said, shaking my head. "I'm surprised he ain't been hittin' you up too."

"Oh, I wouldn't know if he has or not. That nigga been blacklisted," she said with a shrug, and I could tell that she was through with his ass. Honestly, I was too. I wasn't about to lose the only real family that I'd had behind his fucked-up ass. And all he was gonna do, if I did take him back, was do me like he'd done his first wife. And then *my* ass would be on an episode of *The First 48*.

"I'm surprised you ain't fall for the okey doke, though," she said, looking at me over the rim of her glass.

"Nah, I'm done too. I ain't about to lose you and Jay behind his ass. I mean, he was fuckin' you behind her back, and went behind your back and was fuckin' me. It ain't worth it."

"I hear you, boo," she said, and I could tell that she didn't believe me. I could show her ass better than I could tell her. "You wanna know what's worse, though?" she said, and I was there for all of it. I'd missed my best friend and couldn't wait to tell her about my plans.

"What, bitch?" I asked, chomping at the bit for the tea.

"He was behind getting Jakeel locked up because he caught him in here with me. Set him the fuck up," she said, her speech starting to slur. "And what got me was, that nigga had a whole wife. How the fuck he gon' be mad that I had somebody else when he had a whole fuckin' family at home?"

That was it. I was waiting for the missing piece of the puzzle. I wanted to ruin Rasheem, and she'd just given me the ammo I needed to make that shit happen.

"So, you wanna get some payback on that ass?" I asked, and she smiled brightly, letting me know that she was down for the bullshit.

"What do you have in mind?" she said, taking slower sips from her glass so that she didn't miss any of my plans. Karma was a bitter bitch, and, in this case, it was *two* bitches.

Chapter Thirteen

Shontelle

I felt like I had been going through the motions for the past week. Jakeel wasn't responding to me, and Mel had me on the blocked list. I had been tryin'a suck that shit up, but it was starting to weigh on me. I'd tried to pop up at his mama's crib, but she was rude as fuck and told me that he was at work. When I asked where he was working, she wouldn't tell me, and that shit pissed me off. I was about to cuss her old ass out for all the years that she'd been a pain in my ass, but here came his dyke-ass sister walking up on me and shit. It wasn't like I was scared of her ass or nothing, but I wasn't about to fight for no damn reason.

"Girl, you a'ight?" Liza leaned over and asked me. I had been combing the same spot on my client's hair for the last couple of minutes, caught up in my thoughts.

"Nah, I'm not," I admitted, but before I could go into detail, the door opened, and two women came in with the cutest little boy I had ever laid eyes on. One of the girls was white, and the other was black. I had never had a white woman in here, and that shit had me both nervous *and* excited at the same time. This could be the next level for my salon.

They sat down, the little boy climbing up into the black girl's lap, but playing in the white one's hair. The way that the black girl looked at me was really familiar. I wondered if I knew her, but I saw so many people come through this shop a day that she could've been someone who had been coming in to get her brows done or buy bundles, and that's why she looked so familiar.

"We'll be with you ladies in just a second," I greeted them. I made it my business to welcome all of my customers. Yeah, I was the shop owner, but that personal interaction with each client, regardless of whether they were sitting in my chair, was the added touch that I felt made a huge difference and brought back the customers. Well, that and the free wine with their service.

I finally got my head together and back in my business, where it should've been all along. I had built this shit without Keel, and if he didn't want to be in my life anymore, that just made room for a nigga who *really* deserved me. At least, that was the lie that I was telling myself. I had never thought about my life without him, and even though that seemed like it may be what was happening, I just wasn't ready to accept it.

"Liza, can you put her under the dryer for me, please?" I asked after I'd whisked through putting the curlers in my client's hair.

The woman who was holding the little boy had been staring me down, and it made me curious about how she knew me. But, then again, a bitch was fine as hell. So, she might've just been admiring all this fineness. Who knew? But I was about to find out.

As soon as my client was out of my chair, both women were on their feet and walking in my direction. The black girl was holding the little boy's hand, practically dragging him across the shop before someone else got into my chair.

"Hello, ladies," I greeted them, but I was getting a bad vibe from them by now. "My name is—"

"Shontelle," the white girl finished for me. "I'm Gina, and this is my sister, Lauren."

"Sister?" I asked, confused as hell. Their mama must've been an old-school ho to have two kids of two different races.

"Yeah, my sister," she said like it was a dumb question. My spidey senses were tingling, and I could feel the bullshit brewing. "And this is my nephew. He needs a haircut," she finished, pointing to the little boy.

I turned my attention to him in order to not cuss this cracker-ass bitch out. If she knew who I was, then she knew she was in my shop, and I could beat her ass or refuse service as I saw fit. That was one of the perks of having your own shit. You didn't have to take shit off nobody. And I wasn't going to, either. I'd had it up to here with folks damn trying me.

"Well, I'll be more than happy to give you a haircut, handsome little guy. I'll make sure that you're fly as hell for the girls at school," I said with a smile, and he blushed. "What's your name?"

"Jasheem, but my friends call me Jay. So you can call me Jay," he said in the cutest little voice ever.

"Jasheem?" I asked, making sure I had heard him right.

"Yes, ma'am," he confirmed, making me smile again because it was so rare that kids his age had manners nowadays. He must've gotten that shit from his daddy because his mama and damn auntie were rude as fuck.

"Cool. You know how you want your hair cut?" I asked, putting the stool down so that he could step up into my chair. I put the cloak around his neck when he was settled in, and he moved his tablet from up under it. Looking down at it, I was shocked to see that he was reading a book instead of playing a game like so many of the little badass kids did that came through here.

"Yeah, I want my hair cut like my daddy's," he said like I knew who his daddy was. The way that the "sisters" giggled, I knew that they'd coached him to say that shit.

"Well, I don't know your daddy, honey. So you're gonna have to be more specific. Look at that wall right there," I said, pointing to the pictures of the posters that had different haircuts displayed.

While he studied them, I looked at the two women who had brought him here. As if sensing that I was in trouble, Liza came back to her station beside me. She picked up her broom and started sweeping up the hair from the pixie cut that she'd just finished on her client, but her eyes were glued on the women that were staring at me.

I wheeled the chair around so that Jasheem was facing me and leaned down a little bit so that we were face-to-face. I didn't want to look at them bitches anymore because they were about to get cussed out. Apparently, they asses were never taught that staring was rude as fuck, but I was about ready to let their asses know.

"Didn't see anything that you liked?" I asked him, studying his face to see if I could choose for him.

"That one," he said, pointing. "And that's my daddyyyy! You know my daddy?" I wasn't sure if that was a question or a statement, and I didn't want to be the one to tell the little boy that his mama was a ho who fucked other bitches' men, so I chose to say nothing.

I froze for a second before turning around and looking at where he was pointing. It was a picture collage of Jakeel and me from when we first started dating 'til right before I'd put his ass out. I had *just* added that picture, and that was the one that he was pointing at. It all hit me at once, and I had to suck in a deep breath. When I looked back at Jasheem, I saw it. He looked just the fuck like him. Then my eyes drifted back to his mother, who had a huge smile on her face. I didn't feed into her shit, but I did recognize her, though. She'd gained a couple of pounds in all the right places and apparently upgraded her life a little bit because she was dressing better and had her hair laid and her lashes looking like Sunday morning church fans. But she was the bitch who had claimed to be pregnant by Jakeel when he first got locked up.

Wheeling Jasheem back around, I grabbed my clippers and cleaned them. I had to keep my shit together before I lost all professionalism and showed the hell out in my shop. And I knew that was what she wanted. Why the hell else would she bring this little boy in here? She must've heard about Keel and me and wanted to start some shit. See, this was the kinda shit that made me wanna leave Keel alone for good. His past and the shit that he'd done were still impacting us in the present.

"Now, this is gonna be kinda loud, honey. I don't want it to scare you," I said before I flipped the clippers on.

"It's OK. I'm a big boy. It won't scare me," he said before his eyes went back to his tablet.

"I hear you, big boy," I said with a smile, and that kinda hurt my heart. I wasn't the one to give Jakeel his first child, and I'd always wanted children with him. But if we did get back together, I was happy that this well-spoken, intelligent little boy was his child. The mother, though, she was gonna be a problem for me, and I could tell that shit.

About fifteen minutes later, I'd learned so much about Jay, as he'd asked me to call him. He was 7, loved to read, write, and draw, and wanted to be an artist when he grew up. He was sweet as pie. I'd given him a Mohawk and used the sponge on his pretty curly hair that I knew he'd gotten from Jakeel. I hadn't given his mama the pleasure of seeing me sweat. Instead, she was seeing that she would never be on my level, because she came here to start drama, and

I handled my business and was even kind to my man's bastard child.

"So, you ready to see the finished product, Jay?" I asked him, and he smiled and nodded his head.

I turned around and grabbed the mirror and the recent picture of Jakeel and me. Holding the mirror up in front of him and the photo beside it, I let him check out his fresh new cut.

"Oh, wow! I look just like my daddy! Thank you!" he said, and I smiled down at him.

"It was my pleasure. And when you see him, he's gonna love that you wanted to look just like him," I said, looking at his mama with a wink. "Now, you make sure you come back and see me again, OK?"

"Yes, ma'am. I'm gonna do all my chores so that I can use my allowance to come to you!"

"Nah, your money's no good here," I said, reaching into my apron and pulling out a couple of dollars. "As a matter of fact, why don't you take this over to the counter and get yourself one of those snacks. I mean, if that's OK with your mama," I said, throwing the ball that she'd tossed at my ass back at her and showing her more respect than she deserved wit' her messy ass.

"Can I, Mama? Pleeeaassseee!" he begged. Now, if she were rude to her child when I had been anything but, that would say so much about her character. However, she just nodded her head, and he took the money from my hand and ran toward the front of the shop.

As soon as I was sure that he was out of earshot, I picked up my broom and started sweeping the hair up from around my chair. It wasn't much, but I needed to get my words together so that I could let her ass know.

"Now, for you. You two came into my shop to start some shit. That was petty and juvenile as hell. And to use that cute little boy to do so says a lot about you and your sister or whoever the fuck this pasty white bitch is. You have a great son, and even though he was made by you being a whole ho out here in these streets, he'll find out the kinda woman his mama is soon enough. I ain't got no beef with you, and whatever beef you got with me, you need to take that shit out, thaw it, cook it, and eat it. 'Cause it ain't welcome on my table. Take your issues up with Keel. I ain't the one who knocked you up and dropped yo' ass."

"Bitch—" the white girl started, but Liza stepped up beside me, shaking her head as a warning.

"Aht! Aht! This ain't yo' fight, little whitey. Don't getcha ass beat behind some dick yeen even smelled," she said, and the white bitch shut the hell up.

Out of the corner of my eye, I could see Jasheem coming back with a bag of cotton candy. His mother reached into her purse to pull out the money to pay so that she could keep up her front for her son.

"Nah, don't worry about it. Keep that little change. Maybe you can go down the street and around the corner and buy you some fuckin' class," I said, and Liza giggled. I was big mad as all fuck, but I couldn't come unglued in front of this bitch.

"Now, you make sure to come and see me next week, OK, Jay?" I asked, and he nodded his head before coming to hug me. "And make sure your mama takes you to see your daddy so that he can see how y'all twinning, OK?"

"Yes, ma'am!" he said, and I wanted to ask if he'd ever met his daddy, because Keel had never mentioned meeting the little boy to me. But that wasn't my business. At least not anymore. This encounter had confirmed for me that I had to let Jakeel's ass go. That nigga would be the cause of me having gray hair and heart palpitations. I wasn't about to have a stroke behind his wandering-dick-having ass.

"Thank you, ladies, for coming. Hope to see y'all again soon," Liza said, waving at their asses and letting them know that it was best for them to take their leave before the hood bitch that was itching to be let loose hopped out and all over their asses.

Jasheem's mama took his hand, and she and the white bitch made their way out of the shop. As soon as I heard the door close, I made my way to my office. I was sure that Liza was gonna check on my client for me, but then she would be hot on my damn heels.

I hadn't gotten in the door good before I broke down. I collapsed on the couch in my office and buried my face in one of the throw pillows and cried my eyes out.

"You deserve some retail therapy, ho!" Liza said, coming into my office. "You handled their asses like the real boss bitch that you are! Ooooh, baby girl, I'm so sorry. Are you OK?" her tone changed as soon as she saw me shaking and crying on the couch.

She came and sat down beside me, rubbing my back as soothingly as she could. I was so over this shit, but for some reason, I still felt like Keel had a hold on me. I hadn't really realized the amount of damage that he'd caused to my heart with all that he'd taken me through until now.

"How many clients you have after this last one?" Liza asked, and I finally sat up. I couldn't speak, so I just shook my head, telling her that I didn't have anymore. "Well, then, I'm taking you shopping. You need a new wardrobe for this new stage in your life. I'm soooo proud of you, boo. I can't say that I could've played that shit like you did. And you told that bitch to keep her li'l money and go 'round the corner and buy herself some claaaass," she said, and we both laughed. "That shit was epic, bitch. I wished I had recorded that shit. Wait—I did!"

She pulled out her phone and showed me that she'd set her camera up and recorded the whole encounter. This bitch was a stickler for evidence. She was the recording and screenshot queen.

"You know what? You're a trip!" I said, shaking my head, and she looked at me like I'd offended her.

"Girl, listen, you needed this shit so that you could see how you read that bitch. You showed her why you're the main, and she was just a side thang. And you never know what might've happened. What if they'd provoked you, you'd beat both their asses, and they broke asses had tried to sue you and take this damn shop? Not on my watch, boo. My camera is *always* watchin'."

I hugged her, and we both leaned back on the couch while she pressed *play,* and we watched the replay of the encounter that had just proven my level of grown woman-ness. I had to admit, watching my personal growth made me smile. I had really grown a lot from the little girl who was beating up bitches who said they'd been fuckin' my nigga, even when it was proven that they'd been fuckin' my nigga.

"Wait . . . wait . . . wait . . . Here's my favorite part! Watch this pale bitch turn red as all fuck," she said, and we both laughed. This was much needed and made me feel so much better. Moments like this made me happy to have a true friend in Liza.

"You were right. This was *just* what I needed!" I beamed at Liza. We had been shopping for three hours, and I was so glad that I'd chosen to do this instead of going home and crying about that fuck nigga.

"Yeah, I knew it was. But could you go easy on a bitch's bank account? You got me swipin' this strip like we fuckin' or some shit," she said and rolled her eyes playfully.

I waved her off with my hands full of bags. I knew she had it. And if she didn't have it, then her sugar mama, who happened to be Keel's sister, Toya, sure as hell did. I think the thought of spending Toya's money was what made this shit that much sweeter. Call me petty, but I had to get my happiness where I could.

The realization that she was dating his sister hit me and made me feel dumb as hell at the same time.

"Liza, you know where Keel is working?" I asked her, and the way she turned her head to the side let me know that she was about to give me the same spiel that she did every time I tried to get information from her.

"Now, you know that even if I did, I wouldn't tell you. You my best bitch, and you know that. But I don't bring my house business and pillow talk outside my house. That's how we've been happy this long," she said, and I knew that was what she was about to say.

She was telling the truth, though. She kept that shit separate. I respected their relationship, honestly, and respected her even more. She wasn't gon' tell me shit that Toya told her, and she never repeated shit that I told her ass to Toya, either. Otherwise, I'd be in a hole in the ground, because she was the only other person who knew about Mel and me fuckin' around. Liza was as solid as they came, and that's why I would always love and respect her ass, even though I didn't think I would ever understand her not liking dick. But to each her own, I guess.

"Bitch, look!" Liza elbowed me in the side, bringing me out of my thoughts and making me wanna punch her ass in the face. When I followed where her eyes were looking, I instantly forgave her and turned my aggression on the muthafucka that she was lookin' at.

"So, that nigga ignoring my calls, so that he can skin and grin in some old bitch's face?" I asked, not really expecting an answer. I wouldn't have heard shit she'd said anyway because I had started to walk toward TGI Fridays. The nigga must've been embarrassed by the bitch, because they were in the corner, thinking that nobody would see them. But Liza had, and now, I had, and I was about to make that shit known.

"Bitch! Shontelle! Don't make a scene!" Liza yelled at my back while she struggled to keep up. I knew she was trippin' because there was no way that she didn't expect me to make a scene when she'd been the one that had pointed that shit out to me. You would think the bitch ain't know me at all.

Chapter Fourteen

Jakeel

I was sitting in TGI Fridays nervous as hell about this date with my probation officer. I'd asked for a booth in the far corner so that no one would see us because I wasn't trying to cause any issues for her. I didn't know what it was about her, but she was sexy as hell to me. I usually didn't date women older than me, but she ain't look like she was a day past 30, and that told me that she took care of herself.

I kept watching the door and looking at my watch. I didn't want to think that she was gonna stand a nigga up, but it had been two hours and three minutes, and she hadn't come in yet.

"You know what you want to drink, handsome?" the waitress came over for the third time, asking me. I could tell that she was the one who was thirsty as hell while she was asking me what *I* wanted to drink.

"Nah, I'm gonna wait for my *date* before I order," I said for the third time. She rolled her eyes and popped her mouth, giving a nigga plenty of attitude before walking away.

That was something else. If I had been meeting any other bitch, that shit would've caught my attention. But knowing that I was meeting Mrs.—my bad—Ms. Blake here tonight, there wasn't a bitch in here who could catch my attention. I'd caught wind that something had changed about her.

She'd gone from happily married with that big-ass ring on her finger, to there just being a tan line where the ring used to be. I'd peeped that shit but didn't say anything. I just tried to shoot my shot and was honestly shocked that she'd agreed to see me. I had thought about going home and changing clothes, but that shit woulda made a nigga look too eager, and that wasn't my move.

But when the hostess finally walked up, and I saw that she'd changed clothes and even put on some makeup and perfume, I felt like I wasn't doin' her fine ass justice in what I was wearing. Standing up from my seat, waiting for her to sit down, I smiled at her and took in that nice ass that was poking out from behind the wrap dress that she had on. We sat down, and I motioned for the waitress to come to our table to take our drink orders, but she looked away like she hadn't seen me. I hated bitches like that. She ain't get what she wanted, so now she wasn't gonna do her fuckin' job. I was gonna let her have a pass, but if she ain't make her way the fuck over here in the next couple of minutes, I was gonna call the manager on her ass.

"You know," I said, checking my watch, "if the roles were reversed, I would violate your ass. You're late," I joked, and she giggled. I wasn't sure how she was gonna be on this encounter, but I was glad that she'd left her hard-ass probation officer persona at the office.

"Well, I mean, it takes a little time to look this damn good," she flirted, leaning back so that I could see her better. I couldn't disagree with her there.

"Are you and your mother ready to order something to drink now?" the waitress's petty ass appeared outta nowhere and asked.

"I ain't his mama, but I am a MILF, and not only does he wanna fuck me, but your man would also—*if* you had one," Ms. Blake shot at her ass. I had to laugh because she was vicious as all fuck, and I loved that shit. She was getting sexier and sexier to me by the minute. "I can't stand little girls like you. I'm sure you been trying to get his attention while he waited for me. How does it feel to find out that he prefers a grown-ass woman to your teeny bopper trashy ass?"

The waitress stood there on stuck, not knowing what the hell to say to that. And if she knew what was best for her, she wouldn't say a damn thing. Ms. Blake looked like the type that would beat ass and ask questions later. And I wouldn't stop her, either. This bitch needed her ass kicked for trying to ruin my damn date.

"Now, what do you want to drink, baby," Mika asked me, reaching out and taking my hand in hers. My dick jumped in my pants, and it took everything in me not to say that I wanted to drink from the fountain that was between her fuckin' legs, but that was all that I wanted at this point. "I don't think that's on the menu here. But I'll be more than happy to oblige you later," she said with a wink like she was reading my mind.

"I want a double shot of Patrón, no ice," I told her.

"Oh, you're a drinker drinker, huh?" she teased me, and I nodded my head.

"That ain't shit but water to a nigga like me," I responded with a smirk.

"I heard that kinda shit puts hair on your chest."

"You can check that fact later on," I flirted with a wink. She blushed, and the waitress cleared her throat like our conversation was inconveniencing her. "Bitch, take a chill pill," I snapped, finally tired of her shit.

"I'll have what he's having," Mika said, and I swear that she had a direct line to my dick because every word that was coming out of her mouth made my shit jump.

Without a word, the waitress stomped off, and even though I wanted to shoot a cag under her ass, I fought the urge. I didn't wanna be thought of as an abusive nigga by trippin' that bitch on her way to get our drinks. Looking back at Ms. Blake, I could tell that she was irritated, but as soon as we locked eyes, her face relaxed.

"I don't know if I wanna drink anything that she brings us," she said with a nervous laugh, but there wasn't a lie in anything that she'd just said.

"I agree. That bitch 'bout gon' spit in our shit like Celie in *The Color Purple*," I said, and I could tell that my reference to the movie was a shock to her.

"What you know about *The Color Purple?*" she challenged.

"You told Harpo to beat me . . ." I quoted one of the famous lines from the movie, and she laughed a deep laugh. I could tell that she hadn't laughed in a while, and I was happy that I was the one that was giving her joy. "Don't underestimate me, beautiful. My mama used to have me watching that damn movie with her when I was younger."

"That's one of my favorites," she said, a broad smile on her face, and her eyes lighting up.

"Maybe we can watch it together, then," I offered, and it was then that I realized that she had never let go of my hand.

"I don't know about all that," she said, looking around like she was trying to make sure that no one she knew was in the restaurant. When she was satisfied with her scan, she looked back at me. "This was already a stretch."

"Yeah, speaking of . . . What made you say yes today? The last time I said something like this, you 'bout took a nigga's head off to hang in your office as a warning to any other nigga who dared to try your fine ass."

"Well, things change," she said with a shrug, looking toward the floor.

"What things, Ms. Blake?" I asked, not wanting to be nosy, but wanting to know at the same time.

"Mika . . ."

"Huh?" I asked, not sure who Mika was and how she was the thing that had changed. Maybe that was the name of the woman her man was cheating on her with. If that were the case, the nigga was dumb as fuck. You didn't step out on a bitch like her. These simple hoes I was used to dealing with, yeah. But not her. She was *everything* that a nigga needed. I could just tell from the couple of interactions that we'd had, and I didn't even know her ass.

"That's my name," she clarified for me. "Well, my name is Tamika. But call me Mika. If you gon' be all up in my business, then you might as well call me by my name."

I smiled and nodded, not responding immediately. A nigga felt like he was making moves in the right direction for her to be telling me her name and letting me call her by that shit. The waitress came back with our double shots, but the look that she had on her face made me not wanna drink that shit for real. As soon as she walked off, Mika's and my eyes met, and we both busted out laughing because neither one of us dared to put them damned glasses anywhere near our lips.

"Listen, I'm about to go to the ladies' room. What do you say we pay for these drinks and finish this conversation somewhere else?"

"Shiiid, you ain't gotta ask me twice," I said, a big-ass Kool-Aid smile on my face.

She got up and went to the bathroom, and I used the little machine that was on our table to pay for the drinks. I didn't leave that bitch a tip because she ain't deserve one. Not a monetary tip. Not the tip of my dick against the back of her throat, which was what she wanted in the first place. I was signing the receipt, waiting for Ms. Blake—Mika—to come out of the bathroom, when I was met with the last muthafucka that I wanted to see.

"Soooo, you decided that since you can't do right by me, you gon' get an old bitch, huh? 'Cause she so happy to have you that she gon' put up with anything, ain't it, Jakeel?"

"Hey, Liza," I greeted my sister-in-law, who was also, unfortunately, Shontelle's best friend. Liza waved subtly, and I could tell that she hated bein' put in the middle of this shit. She was a good girl, and I knew she was just being loyal to her friend. It was Shontelle who was in these folks' establishment actin' a fool.

"She the only one you see here?" Shontelle snapped with her hand on her hip.

"She the only one worth speaking to," I responded with a shrug, praying that Mika didn't come out while Shontelle was here cuttin' up. I knew for sure that would be the nail in my coffin and completely blow my chances.

"So, that's how you do me, Keel? That's *all* I meant to you?" she asked, sounding like she was hurt.

"Cut the shit, Shontelle," I said, standing up, wanting to get the fuck away from her. Leave it to her ass to make a damn scene. This was one of the reasons that I couldn't take her no-damn-where. "You put me the fuck out. Don't get mad 'cause I don't wanna keep putting up with your bullshit."

"Put up with *my* bullshit? *Really,* Jakeel? Your bitch brought your fuckin' bastard-ass son into my shop to throw in my face that she was the one who was blessed with your child and not me. But you're the one who put up with *my* bullshit?"

"What the fuck are you talkin' about, Shontelle? You really trippin' right now," I said, my face all balled up, not knowing what she was talking about for real.

"Liza, play that shit back," she said, and I had to laugh. Liza's ass stayed recording shit. I believed her ass missed her calling. She could've been a private investigator or some shit and made bank. She knew how to set that shit up without being detected and get the perfect angles so that you ain't miss a minute of what was goin' on.

"Shontelle, we can do this another time," she said, trying to talk some sense into her friend. I could tell she was just as embarrassed as I was right then.

"No, show him that shit *now!*" she snapped, and that pissed me off even more. I could tell that she was acting out, and it was coming from a hurting place, but she was really making an ass outta herself in front of all these folks.

Then I saw Mika coming from the bathroom and grimaced. That made Shontelle look in the direction that I was, and the smile that came across her face let me know that she was really about to cut up now. Liza grabbed her arm and tried to pull her away, but what had me fucked up was that now she knew what Mika looked like, and I had a feeling that the shit was gonna backfire. She was about to be on the rampage, and I didn't know how to stop her ass.

"This is what you want?" Shontelle shouted, looking Mika up and down with her face balled up. "This dry-ass geriatric-ass pussy!"

"You know, I'm 'bout tired of you young bitches," Mika said, and I could tell *she* was pissed. I didn't know if it was at me, or she was just tired of being picked on by these younger bitches for being with me, but I didn't think that Shontelle knew who she was picking a fight with and that she wasn't equipped for the battle she was about to start at all.

"You should be. We stay takin' y'all's men, huh?" Shontelle said with a laugh.

"No, the only men you take are the ones who never grew the fuck up and based their worth on a phat ass and a young face. And don't get it twisted. You gon' get older, and the men that you runnin' up behind, chasin' their pockets, are gonna leave yo' ass too."

"What-the-fuck-ever, bitch. *I* leave niggas—they don't leave *me*," Shontelle said, dismissively.

"Correction, apparently they *do* leave you because you're confronting one who is out with me. So, technically, it seems like *I* may have taken *your* man. Or maybe he grew the fuck up and decided it was time for an upgrade. Like somebody who knows that you handle your private business behind closed doors and don't air all your dirty laundry in public."

"Oh shit," Liza said before she could catch herself. Shontelle looked at her, and I could tell that she didn't expect Mika to come as hard as she just had for her. But she'd asked for that shit. "What? Keel tried to save you from this shit, but you wouldn't listen," Liza said with a shrug.

"I am soooo sorry, Mika," I apologized, not giving a fuck about Shontelle's feelings because, like Liza said, she'd done that shit to herself.

"It's cool. I know this comes with the territory." She shrugged coolly, letting me know that she was a beast in her own right, and this shit hadn't bothered her like I'd thought it would. The more I learned about her, the more I wanted her fine, classy, grown ass. "I'm just gonna go ahead and go back to the office," Mika said, and the fact that she told me where she was headed made me smile. She grabbed her clutch off the table, kissed me on my cheek, and walked the other way out of the restaurant as if Shontelle wasn't even worth her walking past.

I looked Shontelle up and down before shaking my head and walking out of the restaurant myself. If she knew what was best for her, she would take her ass the fuck on. On my way to my truck, I couldn't shake what she'd said about me having a child. There was only one person who could've possibly had my baby, and I knew her ass was petty enough to throw the baby in Shontelle's face . . . *Lauren.*

I made a mental note to stop by her spot in the morning. But tonight, I had a date to finish and a true boss bitch waiting on me.

"I didn't know if you were coming," she said, sitting in her car when I pulled up. The only reason that I knew it was her car was that it was the only one there outside the Probation Office at seven at night.

"I wouldn't miss the chance to get to know you," I said, smirking and keeping the last part of that thought to myself.

"Follow me," she said, and I was confused, but didn't get the chance to ask any questions, because she had already pulled off.

She navigated through the streets of Decatur until we reached a gated condo community. I was familiar with it because I used to serve customers out here. I hoped that she wasn't taking me to the house that she used to share with her husband. I didn't know if I would be able to handle an altercation with that nigga the way that she had. I was a beat-ass-first kinda nigga. I was over all that damn bickering. And only bitches bickered anyway.

When she put in the code, I pulled into the gate behind her. I followed her for what seemed like forever until we reached a cul-de-sac at the back end of the complex. I knew that she had to have just moved in, because these were new, like just built in the past seven years. They weren't there when I got popped, and I knew that she had to have been married longer than I had been locked the fuck up.

She parked in the garage, and I pulled up on the curb, turning off the ignition of my truck. She walked to the door, opening it and standing in it, waiting for me to get out. Her silhouette was sexy as hell, and I wanted to trace it with my hands so badly. But she wasn't that type of bitch, so I was gonna take my time with her. Learn her. I could honestly say that she was the first woman that I had wanted to get to know on a deeper level. She was appealing to a different side of me. Getting out of the car, I made my way up the walkway to her.

"Took you long enough," she teased, a shy smile on her face. I could tell she was nervous, and she had every reason to be. She was still married, and I was an ex-con and her parolee. She could lose everything fuckin' with me, and that was evident with the way them bitches had just acted at the restaurant. But for some reason, she was still giving a nigga a chance.

"I was admiring the view," I said, looking down at her.

"You tryin' too hard," she said, trying to dismiss the fact that I had just made her blush.

"No such thing with someone like you," I said honestly.

"Someone like me? What does that even mean?" she asked. She turned and led the way into the condo. I closed the door behind me and locked it, making sure that all the locks were engaged. When I turned around to follow her fine ass farther into the condo, I was too caught up watching her thick-ass hips sway to answer her question. "Make yourself comfortable," she said, motioning toward the couch.

I sat down and made myself comfortable. She went into the kitchen, and I just sat there, waiting on her to return. She had definitely just moved in because I couldn't see her living in a house that didn't have any personal touches or decorations. That put my mind at ease. When she came back, she handed me a glass and set the bottle of Patrón on the table in front of me before sitting down beside me, throwing back a glass of the clear liquid.

"So . . ." she said, pouring herself another drink. I could tell that she was nervous and trying to calm her nerves.

"So?" I asked, not sure what she wanted.

"What does it mean when you say 'someone like me'?"

"Oh," I laughed, realizing that she really wanted an answer to her question. I took the double shot of Patrón before answering her. "You're a woman who knows what she wants. I can tell that outside of that hard-assed work demeanor, you've got a heart of gold. I think that you're unappreciated and misunderstood. That most people don't want to know you beyond the surface and what you can do for them."

"Wow," she said, shaking her head.

"What? Did I say something wrong?"

"You picked all that up from two encounters?" she asked me in shock. "I was married to Rasheem for fifteen years, and he ain't catch on to half of that," she said frustrated. There was a sadness on her face that I wanted to relieve her of. I reached out and touched her face, and she lay into the palm of my hand.

"You are too beautiful, inside and out, for that not to be noticed by any man with eyes and common sense. I take it your husband isn't blind. So, I'ma just assume that the nigga rode the short bus when he was little," I said, and it made her laugh and hit me in the chest playfully.

"You make everything a joke, don't you?" she asked, and I shrugged.

"I was told that laughter was good for the soul. With everything that I've dealt with in my life, all I have sometimes is shits and giggles."

"Well, thank you for the giggles," she said, smirking. "And the shit. 'Cause Lawd knows that I done got my share of shit tonight with them little girls you got hangin' on ya dick."

I was shocked when she reached out and placed her hand in my lap when she said the word "dick." I didn't know how to react, but when she started to massage it and leaned over and kissed me, I almost pounced on her fine ass. But something in me told me not to. Not yet. So, instead, I pulled her into my arms and let her lay her head on my chest.

"Nah, we got plenty of time for all that," I said, and she looked at me like I was rejecting her. "I wanna try something different. Let me get to know you. The you that you don't let the world see."

She gave me a bright smile and looked up at me with something that I had never seen in the eyes of any other woman that I'd dealt with. It looked like love, but I wasn't sure, so I didn't wanna assume. I was hopeful, though, because I was convinced that I loved her ass from the first time I walked my ass up in her fuckin' office a couple of weeks ago.

The sunlight in my face woke me up. I looked down and realized that Mika was asleep in my arms. That made a nigga smile because I was sure that last night was a fuckin' dream. It had to be. This kinda shit ain't happen to a nigga like me. Shifting her to the side, I slid her off of me and onto her oversized couch so that I could relieve my bladder. It took me a couple of rooms to find the bathroom, but I did, just in time before I pissed all down my leg.

While I stood there peeing, I thought about last night. It had started with bullshit with the waitress, and then

Shontelle's ass, who I was sure had blown up my damn phone all night. But I had left the shit in the car so that we wouldn't be bothered by it. Mika and I had talked all night. We shared childhood stories, and I thought it was funny that she'd wanted to be a stripper when she was younger. Our stories weren't that different. She just chose to take the legal way to the money, and I chose the other route. When we'd finished the bottle of Patrón, she had challenged me to a game of *Grand Theft Auto* on the PS4, and that was the most fun that I'd had in a long-ass time. We'd laughed and cried together and eventually had fallen asleep. If it had been any other bitch, I would've been worried about violating because I wasn't at home last night, but since I was with my PO, I was hoping that I would get a pass.

Walking back into the room, I was shocked that she was still asleep. It seemed like this might have been the first time that she'd slept in a long-ass time, and I didn't want to wake her. But morning wood and her looking damn good in that dress had a nigga debating disrupting her beauty rest. Walking to the end of the couch, I kneeled and pushed her dress up around her waist. I didn't want to cross this line so soon, but I had to taste her. Looking down, I had to stifle a laugh. She ain't have no damn panties on.

Her pussy was bald and so fat and pretty. Ducking my head down, I wrapped my lips around her clit and started sucking on it. She shifted on the couch, and that made me suck a little bit harder. She wiggled around in place, and I took that as the go-ahead, putting my tongue as deep inside of her as it would go, while still sucking on her clit.

"Mmmm shiiiiit," she moaned, her hips moving in sync with my tongue stroking in and out of her pussy. "Mmmm . . ."

Reaching down, her hands landed on my head, and she sat up like a bolt of lightning had just hit her ass. I think she thought she was dreaming before now, but when she felt my head, she knew that this shit was authentic. I looked up at her, and the look that she had on her face was one of confliction. I didn't want to stop, but if she told me to, I would respect her wishes. When she didn't say anything, just kept staring at me, I went to pull away, but she wrapped her legs around my head and held me in place so tightly that my ass couldn't have moved if I wanted to.

"Please don't stop," she said, more like begged.

She pulled the string on her dress, and it fell off of her, revealing a body that would make a young bitch jealous as shit. She reached behind her own back and unhooked her bra. I wasted no time reaching up and squeezing her nipples in between my fingers. She arched her back in response, and in a matter of seconds, she was bustin' all over my face.

"Fuck, Jakeel! What . . . are . . . you . . . tryin'a . . . do . . . to . . . me . . ." she asked, while she shook in pleasure. I made sure that I licked up every drop of her juices before even trying to respond.

"Give you the pleasure that your company gave me last night," I admitted. I knew I sounded like a pussy-whipped-ass nigga, but with a pussy like hers, I would be that and be proud of the shit.

She smiled at me brightly and kissed me with so much passion that it made my dick press up against the zipper of my jeans. She reached down, trying to unzip my pants, but I grabbed her hand. I was trying to keep my word and not fuck her on the first night. She deserved better than that. She wasn't the kinda woman you used and threw away. She was the one that you kept. And if I had the chance, I would keep her ass and hold on to her as if my life depended on it.

"Why won't you fuck meeee?" she whined, and I had to laugh. She sounded like a spoiled-ass brat.

"Because you're the kinda woman who deserves a man to take his time. You ain't no one-night stand."

"If you do that shit right, it won't be a one-night stand," she said, and I looked at her to make sure she was serious. When I saw that she was playing with her pussy, waiting for my dick to take the place of her hands, I gave the *why-not* shrug and unzipped my pants, letting them fall to the floor.

I could tell that she wasn't used to a dick the size of mine because of the way she bit her bottom lip. She looked like she wanted to change her mind, but my shit was out now. Something was gonna go down, or a nigga was gon' be mad as fuck.

Sluuuurp.

Before I could say shit to her, she'd leaned forward, put my dick into her mouth, and sucked like a fuckin' vacuum. She ain't choke or gag on that shit, either. And the way that she reached down with the hand that wasn't massaging her pussy confirmed that the nigga she was divorcing was a fuckin' idiot for letting her the fuck go.

"Damn, girl! Ugh, shit!" I moaned and growled, trying not to nut too quickly. She was staring up at me with my dick in her mouth, humming on my shit.

She was tryin'a suck my soul out through my pee hole, and there wasn't shit I could do about it. I grabbed her head and started rough dickin' her face, and she ain't try to pull away. Instead, she ain't miss a beat. As a matter of fact, she went harder the harder I fucked her face. I felt my nut rising and didn't want to skeet down her throat, so I tried to pull away. She grabbed my ass, holding my shit down her throat, and I lost my mind. My toes curled, my head got light, and I came all down her throat. She didn't let go until my dick stopped throbbing in her mouth. And when I was done nuttin', she let go of my shit with a loud pop of her mouth.

"Now, fuck me," she ordered, and like my dick was under her control, it popped back up, ready for round two.

She lay back, her legs wide open like she was waiting for me to run up in her ass. I took off my shirt, and she took in the tatted, toned body that was under the too-big shirts that I wore. She bit her lip again, and I realized that was something she did when she liked what she saw. I was about to climb on top of her, and then I thought better of it. Instead, I picked her up, she giggled and then wrapped her arms around my neck.

"Which room is yours?" I asked, and she smiled, grateful that I was still determined to respect her in some way.

"The last one at the end of the hallway," she said, and I started to make my way down the hall. She traced the tattoos on my chest with her tongue, even nibbling on my nipples.

When I got to her room, I wasted no time placing her on the bed, then kissing her deeply when I got on top of her. I kissed down her neck and sucked on her pretty, perky-ass titties before reaching down and positioning my dick at her opening. She reached down and grabbed her legs, pulling them back until they were behind her head, and that shit made me pause. I had to lean back and take that shit in. Tamika Blake was the kinda woman that a nigga like me dreamt about when he was beating his dick as a kid. She was grown *and* a freak. There were no limits, and she wasn't selfish like some of these younger bitches were.

Leaning forward, I got back on top of her, ready to feel her insides. Before I did, I leaned down and gave her a fair warning.

"If I slide up in this shit, you mine, Mika. Period," I said, before sucking on her ear.

"I was already yours," she responded. "Aaaah!" she hollered out when I slid my dick as far inside of her as my body would let me.

"Fuuuuck! You're miiiiine . . ." I repeated, sliding in and out of her more and more quickly. "Say that shit, Mika."

"I'm youuuurs, Jakeel! I been waiting for this shit aaaall my liiiife!" she hollered my thoughts aloud. She was a one-in-a-lifetime kinda woman, and I felt like I had just hit the muthafuckin' lottery.

Chapter Fifteen

Mika

It'd been almost three weeks since I'd moved out of the house and contacted a divorce lawyer. After the last incident with Rasheem, I was determined to get away from him. I rented a two-bedroom condo for my daughter and me just until all the divorce proceedings were over.

This wasn't easy for me, and I knew it was hard on my daughter, moving from our home into a smaller place, but it was only temporary. I planned on getting a house in the near future.

Rasheem kept calling me nonstop. I guess he thought I was playing. I'm not going to lie, leaving him was the hardest thing I'd ever had to do. I loved my husband, but him disrespecting me like that was the nail in the coffin. There was no way we could come back from that.

"Mama, you okay?" Ky'Imani walked into my room and asked as she took a seat on the bed.

"Huh, baby?" I snapped out of my thoughts.

"Do you want to grab a bite, and maybe, we can catch a movie."

"Hmm, what would make you want to hang out with little old me?"

"First off, you're not old, and you haven't been out lately, outside of work. I think you've done enough moping around the house. You should get cute, dress up, and go out in the world. Probably turn the heads of a few dudes."

"Excuse me, but I'm not looking for no dudes. I'm good by myself."

"I know you are, Mama, but I know how much Daddy hurt you. I just don't want you to give up on love. There are good men out there. You just need to find the right one."

"Hold up. How old are you? I think *I'm* the parent, and I don't need to be taking advice from my teenage daughter. Now, go on before I take the belt out and whip that butt," I laughed.

"Sorry, Mama. I was only trying to cheer you up some."

"Well, you did—"

Her phone started ringing, so she hurried out of my room. I shook my head and busted out laughing. That child of mine was grown beyond her years. I really loved the bond we had developed over the years.

This was one of the days that I wished I could have stayed home. It was cold outside, and on top of that, it was raining. It was freezing in the office because these assholes still had the AC on blast. I grabbed my sweater that was hanging on the back of my chair and started putting it on when I heard the door open. I thought it was one of my associates . . . until I realized who was standing in front of me.

"What are you doing here?" I asked Rasheem with an attitude.

"I was in the building, dropping off some paperwork and decided to drop by to see my wife." This asshole walked into my office and took a seat.

"What do you want?" I got straight to the point.

"I'm here to talk with you about stopping the divorce proceeding. I mean, c'mon, we can both agree that we both messed up. Let's work it out and move on. That's what family does. I ain't no quitter, and I know damn well that you're not one either."

"Do you hear yourself? We *both* messed up? All I ever did was be a good fucking wife. But while I was doing that, you was out slanging dick around. You know I walk around here now, looking at all these females, wondering which ones you've fucked. You made a fool out of me all these years. People laughing in my face, and like a fool, I walked around here feeling proud . . . proud that I was married to the great detective," I chuckled. I was trying my best not to show any emotions. "But you didn't even cover your tracks worth a damn. Some detective *you* are."

"Mika, listen, most of what you're saying is straight-up bullshit. Yeah, I might've fucked around a time or two, but nowhere near what you're saying. And that shit means nothing to me. I love you. I married you. Do you know how many of these chicks would love to have me? But I don't want them. I want you."

"Well, lucky bitches. They can have you now because I don't want to be with you anymore. I'm divorcing you," I said, looking him in the eyes so that he knew that I was dead-assed serious. "Now, leave so that I can do my work."

"You fucking serious, huh? What you hope to gain out of this? You think you can just get the fuck up, walk away with my daughter? You won't get nothing from this. Nothing!" he yelled as he stood up.

"I walked away, didn't I? And you know what? Ain't a damn thing you can do about it."

Now *I* stood up. This nigga might be the fucking king over there where he at, but I was done being his fucking patsy. The longer I was in his presence, the more nauseated I started feeling.

"If you go through with this, you're going to regret this, Tamika. Think about how your life's going to change—"

"Get out of my office. I'm sure you got my lawyer's information."

He stood there with a wicked grin plastered across his face. Then he shook his head, turned around, and walked out.

"You're not going to like this," he said over his shoulder on his way out. He slammed the door so hard that it made the walls shake.

I opened the door and spotted him as he speed-walked down the hallway. I looked around and noticed a few coworkers in the area. I quickly eased my way back into my office and lightly closed the door. I then walked back to my seat and sat down. The nerve of this man. How dare he walk up in here, calling himself checking me. Lawd, I knew this was going to be a fight that ain't going to be easy, but I was so ready for it.

"Fuuuuck, baby! Who the hell would fuck around on pussy this good?" Jakeel asked in my ear while I rode his dick in the chair at my desk in my office. We had been sneaking around, fucking, and spending quality time since that night at TGI Fridays. I balled my panties up and stuffed them in his mouth to shut his ass up. The last thing I needed was to be caught fuckin' him at the job, on the clock, no less.

As much as I knew that this shit was wrong, I could see now how some of my coworkers had fallen for their parolees. He made that shit easy, too, because not only did he fuck me good, but also he went out of his way to make me feel special. I knew he wasn't making a whole lot of money at his job, but he still sent me flowers, Edible Arrangements, and shit. And because we weren't trying to be seen out in public together, if we weren't at my house when Ky was at her friend's house or some shit, then we were at a hotel, or he planned something sweet. This past weekend, he'd taken me to the country and laid out a picnic of a meal that he cooked for me—with the help of his mama—but still, it was the thought that mattered.

It didn't matter where we were or what we were doing, though, we just couldn't seem to keep our hands off of each other. Don't get me wrong. We had a good time. We talked about everything from food to music, and there was a lot more that we had in common than I would've ever imagined. I could tell that he spent a lot of time with his mother—who was only fifteen years older than me, by the way—and that they were really close. Even with all the shit he stayed into and her having to support two children as a single mom, they had a really close relationship. And I could tell by the way that he talked about her and his sister that he loved and respected them both greatly. It was apparent in the way he talked about them in comparison to the way that he spoke of the women that had been in his life. I could tell that the whole "tough-nigga persona" was a defense mechanism, and now that he'd taken that shit off, he was a softy. Well, maybe just for me, but I was the only one that I cared about. After meeting his most recent ex on our first date—yeah, I said *date*—I could see why he treated them like he did.

I tried to fight it, but I was falling for him with every encounter. And it seemed like the feeling was mutual. I didn't want him to be a rebound or a distraction from the shit with Rasheem, who still hadn't signed the papers, by the way. He was still trying to convince me to talk it out, inviting me to dinner and sitting outside of my damn office, trying to catch me coming or going from the building with flowers and cards and shit. But nothing that he did was gonna make me take him back. I was fed up and, even if Jakeel wasn't for me, I didn't deserve to be treated the way that Rasheem had treated me. He had fifteen years to get it right, but all he did was get comfortable and think that he could do what the hell he wanted to, and I would always be here. He must've forgotten who the hell he married. I may have been a little older, but I was still from NYC and would bust him in his shit. But because I had matured into a lady and had more to lose than gaining his ass acting right, I said fuck it. He wasn't worth it to me.

I kept telling myself to take it slow with Jakeel until things were over and done with Rasheem. I didn't want to bring any of that drama into our lives. Honestly, I was surprised that Sheem hadn't already found out about Keel. But he was so busy trying to "save his marriage" that I'd heard that he wasn't focusing on much of anything. His job included. But Jakeel was hard to let go of. And when I tried to pull away, even telling him why, he came at me harder, telling me that a real nigga ain't leave his woman to deal with her shit by herself. And just like that, I was back in it again. Like now, here he was, during his check-in, and I was riding his ass like I wasn't at work. And this nigga couldn't keep his damn mouth shut, so I had to stuff my drawers in his shit. I couldn't talk, though, because the shit got good to me, and I had to bite his damn neck just to keep from hollering when he raised his pelvis and hit my spot the way that no one but he had.

"I'm finna come, baby," I whispered in his ear before sticking my tongue in it. He grabbed my hips and started ramming upward into me so hard that I was sure someone could hear our bodies smacking against each other from outside the door. Throwing my head back, I could feel his southern head grow larger inside of me, and his dick got stiffer. The veins were bulging and rubbing against my walls like a ribbed condom. My breathing became labored. I bit my bottom lip so that I didn't let out the howl of pleasure that was threatening to erupt from my throat.

Boom! Boom! Boom!

Three hard knocks on the door to my office were followed by someone trying the knob to see if it were unlocked.

Jakeel and I looked at each other, and I hopped off his dick as if we'd just seen his mama's headlights through the window, and I wasn't supposed to be in his house. We both started fixing our clothes, and I hit the button on my phone for the receptionist's desk, putting it on speaker so that I could keep getting myself together. I needed to see who the hell was on the other side of my door.

"I tried to stop him, Mika. But he wouldn't stop. And your phone is on DND, so the calls were going straight to voicemail. I know you have a client in with you. He just—"

"Joanne . . . Joanne!" I yelled, trying to stop her ranting apologies.

"Yea?" she asked.

"He *who?*" I asked because she'd left that one important detail out. I was spraying Febreze all over the office, myself, and Jakeel. I was moving so fast I got some in the poor man's face.

"Damn, Ma. Don't blind a nigga. I wanna be able to see that beautiful face every day," he said, trying to calm me down with a compliment. But my ass was frantic. He took the Febreze bottle from my hand and went to town spraying it for me so that I could focus on the call . . . and putting my clothes back on.

I didn't know if I was about to have to face a supervisor or what, and I needed to know that more than her apologies. I knew she had tried to do her job and had tried to reach me. But I was busy getting dick and may have just fucked myself up in more ways than not getting my nut just now. I knew that Keel would more than make up for that later.

"Your husband," she said, and I popped my mouth.

"Thank you, Joanne. And I know that you tried your best to hold his ass off," I said, letting her know that I didn't blame her for the shit that was going on at all.

I definitely wasn't mad at her. But with Rasheem's ass, I was pissed now more than ever. How dare he come up in my place of work—and fuck up my nut in the process! There was less and less that I liked about this nigga by the day. It made me wonder what I'd ever seen in his ass in the first place. This was his nature. He wasn't doing shit that he hadn't always done. But at this point in my life, I wasn't making excuses for it anymore. And I sure as fuck wasn't gonna stand for it.

"Your *husband* is here?" Jakeel asked, and I could tell that he wasn't tryin'a be caught in the middle of no shit.

"Yeah, his ass is here, but he ain't got no damn business coming up in here," I expressed my obvious frustration.

Walking over to me, Jakeel kissed my lips and grabbed a handful of my ass. The way that he kissed me calmed me instantly, and I caught myself looking into his eyes. It was at that moment that I knew that I was in love with this nigga, and there was nothing that I could do about the shit, either.

"Act normal," I instructed him, walking to the door. He was already two steps ahead of me, sitting in the chair on the other side of my desk. He grabbed the paperwork and acted like he was busy reading over it. Taking a deep breath, I unlocked the door and snatched it open right as Rasheem was about to pound on it again. He was about to use so much force that when there was no door to hit, he stumbled into my office, almost falling on his face. I stepped back, in case gravity chose to be on my side and take his big ass down. I didn't want him to land on me or take me down with him. And, more than that, I didn't want his ass to touch me or get too close, because I didn't need him to smell Jakeel on me.

"What you got the door locked for?" he asked when he regained his composure. I was already more than halfway across my office and back to my desk by the time he got that question out of his mouth.

"What are you doin' at my job?" I asked him, not waiting for an answer before I lit into his ass. "I don't go to your place of work and question you about how you're doing things, do I? As a matter of fact, I don't go anywhere that you are and question shit that you do. I didn't at home, either. And maybe I should've because ya ass didn't know how to act!"

Jakeel looked up from his paperwork, giving me a look that told me to chill out. There was no reason for me even to be going back-and-forth with Rasheem, and he was right.

"I'm working with a parolee," I said, adjusting my attitude. I motioned toward Jakeel, who finally set the papers down and acknowledged Rasheem's presence. When he did, though, I saw the tension that crossed his face.

"What's up, man?" he said dryly, and I had to giggle because he had just checked me about my attitude.

"They let you out of the cage, huh?" Rasheem said, confusing the hell out of me. "I wish they had notified me. I woulda made sure that they heard the truth at that parole hearing."

"What truth? That you mad that we was fuckin' the same bitch, and don't neither one of us know whose kid she gave birth to? Oh, wait," Keel said, tapping his chin with his finger. "Or did you mean that you had me set up with a gun and drugs that you knew wasn't mine?"

"You would've gotten caught up eventually. I just accelerated the inevitable," Rasheem said, and if I had heard his ass right, he admitted to setting Jakeel up . . . *and* having a child. He didn't deny the shit, which an innocent person would've done.

"Child? You have a child, Jakeel?" I asked him, before knowing that I'd made my big slipup. I should've been asking my soon-to-be ex-husband that question.

"Why you questioning him? You fuckin' this nigga? Is that why your damn door was locked?" Rasheem asked so loudly that I was sure the whole damn office had heard his ass.

"Rasheem, this is my *job*. Why the hell are you in here causing problems?" I asked through clenched teeth. He was asking questions that were none of his fuckin' business.

"Nah, you're gonna answer me," he demanded, walking toward me. "Is this why you ain't tryin'a work shit out with me? 'Cause you out here fuckin' a goddamned ex-con? Your self-esteem is *that* low? This the *best* you can do, but you got the nerve to be telling me what you *don't* deserve?" he asked, looking at Keel with a scoff.

Jakeel was about to get up and say something to him, but I held my hand up, and he nodded that he would let me handle it before sitting back in the chair and crossing his legs. Lacing his fingers together, he put his hands in his lap, like he was about to take in a show. I couldn't take him seriously, because he was always making something a joke, but I had to say that I was happy that he was here at this moment.

"You know what pisses me off?" I asked, standing up out of my seat. "You come up in here, begging me one minute and threatening me the next. You just admitted that you set this man up *and* that you may have a child out there with another woman. That's the reason that I don't wanna work this shit out with you. You been slangin' dick all across the greater Decatur area, had a whole secret fiancée . . . and a *white* bitch at that. And now, you may or may not have a damn child out here . . ." I crossed my arms in front of my chest and shook my head in disgust. I knew we were loud as hell, and the door to my office was open, so I was sure people were standing in the hallway, listening to all this bullshit unfold.

"When did I say that I set this li'l nigga up?" Rasheem tried to deflect and flex on Jakeel at the same time. Keel didn't take the bait, and I had to say that I was impressed that he was able to chill with all that was happening right in front of him. Especially with it being the man who he thinks set him up and cost him seven years of his life. "And I ain't say that I had a child out here, either."

"You didn't say that you *didn't* set him up or that you *didn't* have a child out here, either, Rasheem," I pointed out to his dumb ass. *How in the fuck did this nigga get as far in his career as he has?* I asked myself, shaking my head again. "And we all know, something that *you* taught me, is that an innocent man denies any accusations, while a guilty man deflects."

He stood there with his eyes saucer-sized. See, the thing about Rasheem was that he was always talking, tryin'a put somebody up on game, but his ass never really listened. And because of who he was, he never checked himself, and his ego never let him think that no one would check his ass, either. And for the longest time, too long, I realized that I hadn't checked his ass. But today was the day that I was done and tired of the shit. He needed to get it through his thick-ass head that I wasn't coming back to him and to leave me the fuck alone.

"And the saddest thing about it all is that you had me out here lookin' like a whole fool, but you wanna question *me* about what *I'm* doin' with my pussy—pussy that you ain't even want? That wasn't enough for you to come home to. Hell, the wife, woman, partner, professional, cheerleader, confidante, mother of your *first* child wasn't enough for you to come home. So, while you try to play me like I'm out here bottom-feeding *if* I'm fuckin' my parolee, I'm just happy as all hell that I tested clear of AIDS and other STDs that my *husband* could've brought to me."

I bent down and picked up my purse, grabbing my keys out of them. I wasn't about to stay in this office and face all these damn people after the way that Rasheem had just embarrassed me in here. It wasn't until then that I saw that he had flowers in his hands. Shaking my head, I looked in his face to make sure that he heard me loud and clear.

"Rasheem Blake, I want you to hear me for the first time in fifteen years because I have never meant anything as much as I mean what the hell I'm about to say to you. Well, other than my wedding vows. But since you ain't take them bitches seriously, then neither did I. I don't want you—your name, your money, and damn sure not to be your wife. There is nothing that you can say or do that's gonna change that. So, one, stop making an ass out of yourself tryin'a salvage some shit that you threw away and sign the fuckin' divorce papers that I sent to your ass *weeks* ago. And take them damn flowers to the mother of your *other* child and give at least one woman in your life, who sacrificed her time and her body to bring forth your seed, something other than dick and grief."

Putting my bag on my shoulder, I tried to walk past him, but he blocked my path. Grabbing me by my arm, he leaned in and spoke through gritted teeth.

"You'll leave me over *your* dead body," he threatened, and I couldn't help but laugh. I knew this nigga wasn't standing his dumb ass here threatening me when he was the one who fucked up. That was the second time that he'd pulled this shit, and it would be his last. Or he wouldn't need a damned divorce lawyer, because he would be in a pine box some-fuckin'-where.

I saw Jakeel's jaw tighten, but only for a moment because my eyes shifted from my arm, where Rasheem had a firm-ass grip, to his face. I slid my purse down off of my arm and reached behind my back. I pulled out my baton and popped it, making it extend and click into place. I hit his ass in the elbow of the arm that he was gripping me with, and then when he let go, I caught him in the knee and the forehead. While he tried to ease the pain of those three licks that I'd just dished out to his ass, I walked the fuck out of my office, leaving both his ass and Jakeel's asses in there. I was over niggas at this point and didn't want to be bothered with either one of them.

I had to admit that hearing that either of them had a child, and possibly by the same woman, hurt me. I know that it was before I even knew that Jakeel existed, but the fact that they both had slept with the same . . . kind of woman bothered me in a real way. I needed some time myself to decide what the hell I wanted to do with my life. It was a whole mess right now, and I hadn't done a damn thing to start any of this shit. Jakeel wanted me. Rasheem wanted me. But I wasn't sure, at this point, if either of them deserved me. I was seriously considering moving back up north like Ky had suggested. I didn't think I would ever be able to show my damn face at work again. And if Rasheem and I weren't going to be together, there was nothing to keep me here for real. Getting into my car, I wasn't able to hold the tears back anymore. I'd planned to at least make it down the street and pull into a parking lot or alley and let it all go. But the stress was just too much, and the pressure broke me.

Tap tap tap.

I didn't know how long I had been crying. I'd lost all track of time and was pretty sure that I was halfway to the point of losing my mind. I didn't want to talk to anyone. I couldn't stand the thought of hearing what anyone may have had to say about how I had behaved. And I really think, what had me even more afraid was that one of the two men who had caused me all this grief and confusion might be standing beside my car. Or worse, both of them were.

Tap tap tap.

Whoever it was, wasn't letting up, so I looked in my center console and pulled out some Kleenex. Wiping my face and blowing my nose, I popped the lock and held my breath, waiting for that person to get inside.

"Biiiitch, what in the hell you got between them legs? We need to bottle and sell that shit," Joy said, easing into the passenger seat beside me.

I rolled my eyes but didn't respond right away. The shit would be funny later, but right now, I wanted just to have the shit removed so that I had nothing to offer these niggas since that seemed to be all they wanted. I knew that I was thinking in anger and grouping Jakeel with Rasheem, but it was moments like these that made women believe that all men were the same. I wasn't tryin'a be fair, because it wasn't like either of them was being fair to me. And neither was life. I was starting to feel like I was catching Karma of some sort for some shit that I had done in a previous life. As ridiculous as that might sound, it made more sense than any of the shit that had been happening to me.

"Joy, not right now," I said, letting her know that I wasn't with her shit at the moment. "My life is over," I whined, the tears starting to fall all over again.

"No love, your *marriage* is over. Your life is just beginning," she said, dabbing the tears from my eyes for me. "And if you want my honest opinion . . ." she said, pausing to see if I was up for any opinions. I knew she was gonna give me the shit regardless of whether I agreed to it. She was gonna say the shit, so there was no point in resisting.

"Sure," I said with an attitude that she ignored.

"I wouldn't walk away from my career and a man who has made me glow the way that Jakeel has had you glowing for the likes of Rasheem. He had you. He had his chance, and he fucked that up. Don't let him ruin your happiness because he sure as hell didn't let you being a great wife to him stop him from the shit he took you through and is *still* taking you through," she said, and I nodded my head. I was hearing her and knew that she was right. But I still had to take some time to get my head right so that I wouldn't make a decision based on emotions. I'd done enough of that to last me a lifetime.

"I just need some time to think, Joy," I told her honestly. "I mean, I don't even think that I can show my face in this place again after what just happened."

Joy busted out laughing, and I had to think back over what I'd just said to figure out what was so funny. I sat there and watched her, ready to hit her ass in the face, because she was supposed to be comforting me, and instead, her ass was laughing at my pain.

"What the fuck is so damned funny?" I finally asked, getting madder by the second.

"Girl, *everyone* in there was glad that you finally stood up to his ass. All of us didn't know what he was into, but we all knew that he didn't deserve you. Hell, *he* even knows that. That's why his ass was out there lying with roaches and rats. Because he knew he would never be able to measure up to the woman that you were to him. Those other bitches that he's dealt with, they didn't ask him for much and were happy just to get whatever he dished out to them. But not you. Not Miss Mika. You wanted him to match you, and that shit is almost impossible for a superhero, let alone a fuckin' man."

I didn't know if she was gassing me up, or if she meant that shit. But thinking about who Joy was, I knew that she wasn't just telling me something to make me feel better. I looked over at her and smiled. Those words were very much needed.

"And one last thing. You need to take leave, which I know you have a million days of, because you never take off work. You're gonna get your head the hell together and then run into the arms of that fine-ass young man who has done nothing but step up his game since he stepped foot in your office. You've changed too, and I know that he's the one behind it. He appreciates you, Mika. And even though he's not what you're used to, and the way that y'all met is kinda illegal, it's about time you broke a damn rule for once in your life. Why not do that shit for true happiness?"

Her words settled on my brain, and I planned to do just what she'd said. I didn't know that everyone could see the difference in me. I'd seen it in myself, but hearing that it was apparent meant a lot to me. And more than that, knowing that no one was gonna be looking at me crazy when I came back to work put my mind at ease. I kissed her on the cheek, and then she opened the door and got out. But before she closed the door, she looked at me with a big ol' smile.

"And just to make sure you get my full drift . . . When you stormed out of the office after giving Rasheem the cussing out and ass-whoopin' that he so rightly deserved, his bitch ass ran out to his car and sped off. But Jakeel, he pulled me to the side and asked me to try to talk to you and make sure you were good. He's been sitting in his car, over there," she said, pointing across the street. "He's waiting for me to check on you and come back and give him a report on how you're doing. I think the thought of losing you scares him more than death. Or more than being sent back to jail because of y'all's relationship violating the terms of his probation."

Jakeel flashed his headlights, letting me know that he saw Joy pointing at his truck. Blushing, I mouthed "thank you" to her before cranking my car up and putting it into gear. I watched her walk over to his truck, and the driver's-side window rolled down.

While she was updating him on my well-being, I decided to leave and get a head start on him. I wasn't gonna go home because I truly needed a break—and a bubble bath. But I would be seeing him soon. I laughed because my phone vibrated in my purse as soon as I'd pulled off. I saw that it was him, and I declined it, sending him a message instead.

Get a DNA test, and we'll talk soon.

Bet. I love you.

Reading those words made me almost run a red light. We'd never said them to each other before, and I knew that he wasn't just saying the shit to keep me around like Rasheem would try to do. I felt like Jakeel did love me and was saying it, in case I walked away from him and chose not to continue our relationship. Like he *needed* me to know.

Chapter Sixteen

Gina

"You sure you wanna do this, Lauren? The more I think about it, the more I realize that this kinda shit could get us killed," I asked my best friend, who was sitting on the couch staring off into space.

"Yep. This nigga thinks that he can cut me off, talking about he wants to make shit work with his wife? I got something for his ass," she said, and I looked at her, realizing that she cared more about Rasheem than I had, even though she never wanted to admit it. I needed her to know that she was playing with her life behind a little money and a broken heart. But if there was one thing that I knew about Lauren, it was that once she made up her mind about something, there was nothing that could change it.

"And you want me to take all this shit up there?" I asked, pointing to the thumb drive that had video, text messages, and even voice recordings of calls between her and Rasheem that would ruin his ass for what he did to Jakeel. This man was about to lose his career *and* his freedom, and I couldn't even feel bad for him. He brought this shit on himself.

"Yeah. And do me one more big favor, please? Take Jasheem with you. Jakeel just hit me up and said he wants to talk. I don't want his first time meeting Jasheem to be him cussing me the fuck out in case he wanted to check me about goin' up to that bitch Shontelle's shop."

I looked at her, hoping that she wasn't lying to me and planned to take her life when I walked out the door with her son. I had watched the once strong, beautiful woman become a broken shell of herself these last couple of weeks. She didn't eat or sleep. All she wanted to do was drink. She wasn't even spending any time with Jasheem.

"Bitch, chill. I ain't gonna kill myself. I gotta stick around to see that nigga's shit crash and burn," she said with a laugh that let me know that she really had lost herself in her desire for revenge. If taking Rasheem down was what it would take to get my main bitch on the path back to herself, then I was ready to get this shit cracking.

Picking up the thumb drive, I walked down the hallway to Jasheem's room. He was coloring something with so much passion that I almost hated to disturb him. Walking in, I stood behind him at his little artist's desk that I'd gotten him for Christmas a couple of years ago and looked over his shoulder. I saw that he was making a card.

"What you over here working on so hard?" I asked, making him almost jump out of his skin. "I'm sorry, baby. I didn't mean to scare you. I just didn't want to disrupt your genius," I said with a smile.

"I'm making a card for Mommy so she won't be sad no more. I want her to know that I love her and that I miss her being happy. See?" he said, holding up the card for me to view.

That motivated me even more to take Rasheem's ass out. He ain't do shit with Jasheem but throw money at his mama. He wasn't about to fuck the only loving parent that my nephew had because he was a selfish asshole. Maybe this was me tryin'a redeem myself for fuckin' around with him behind Lauren's back. But, even if it was, it was done from a place of love.

"That's nice, Jay," I complimented. He did have talent. He had drawn his 7-year-old rendition of him and his mother, sitting at a lake, looking at a rainbow. "But you wanna know what will make your mommy happy?" I asked, knowing that this would get him to go with me without too many questions.

"What?" he asked.

"She asked me to do her a favor and drop some things off. You wanna ride with me? And on our way back, we'll stop and get her some of her favorite Blue Bunny Ice Cream."

"OK!" he said, jumping up from his chair and running to sit on the side of his bed. He put on his shoes in record time and was at his door looking at me like *I* was the holdup. Jasheem would do anything for his mama, and I knew she would do anything for him. And that would make the dangerous shit that we were about to do worth it.

On our way out the door, we both stopped when we saw Lauren asleep on the couch. It was the first time that she'd slept in days, so we didn't want to wake her. Jasheem made a mad dash to the back and came back with the card that he'd made and a blanket. He placed the card on top of the table so that she would see it when she woke up and covered her before leading the way to the door. He was tiptoeing, so I played along and tiptoed with him. I eased the door open, and we left the house, using my key to lock the door.

When we were a few steps from the house, I challenged Jay to a race to my car, which I let him win. He needed a few wins in his life, no matter how small, with all that he'd seen in his short time on this earth, especially in the past couple of weeks. I made sure that he was seat belted and handed him the tablet that I kept for him in my car. Once I saw that he had on his headphones, I took my phone out and dialed a number that I rarely used.

I wasn't close to many of my family members, but this one would go to the moon and back for me. I was so happy that he'd picked up because I would feel better with him accompanying me instead of Jay and I going into the precinct alone.

"Hey, Uncle Bobby . . . It's me, Gina. Are you busy? OK. Well, can I come by your office, and you accompany me to turn in some evidence about a case that I feel like may land me on the cops' hit list?"

He agreed, and I navigated my way through the Decatur traffic toward downtown. I would make this one simple detour and then handle the business that would end all this—for us, at least. Then it would be ice cream and movies for my bestie, my nephew, and me.

Chapter Seventeen

Rasheem

"You might wanna put some ice on that. I hear them batons leave an ugly-ass knot," Jakeel had the nerve to say to me before getting up from his seat at my wife's desk. He thought this shit was a joke, but I was gonna get the last laugh. Standing up to face him, ignoring the pain that was throbbing through me, I reared my fist back, ready to punch him in his smart-ass mouth. All I needed was for him to hit me once, and his ass would be back in that cage, and then Mika would have no choice but to take me back.

"That's enough, Rasheem!" I heard from behind me, making me turn around. Standing in front of me was Mika's supervisor, Matthew Long, and the look on his face was one of pure disappointment. "That's all! Nothing to see here! Get y'all asses back to work. I don't pay you to stand around being messy," he spoke to his employees.

Mika's coworkers who had been watching the whole thing scattered like roaches, and he shook his head at them before turning his attention back to the people inside the room. He looked from me to Jakeel, and the faces that he gave the two of us were vastly different. Before he addressed me again, he spoke to Jakeel.

"Mr. . . ."

"Greene, sir. I'm Jakeel Greene," he said, extending his hand for Matt to shake. They exchanged a firm handshake before Matt continued.

"Mr. Greene, I apologize for this. If you would like to be changed to a different probation officer, I can arrange that for you. You have paid your debt to society, and from the glowing review that Ms. Blake gave me the other day, you are adhering to all of the rules that we have set in place for a successful transition."

"No, sir, it's cool. Things happen, and I have to say that a lot of the steps that I've made were because of Ms. Blake. I just hope that she's OK because I'm sure that this was embarrassing for her," he said, and I knew that he was taking a shot at me.

It was taking everything in me not to pull out my gun and blow both their brains out. Matt's for apologizing to a trash-ass nigga like Jakeel and Jakeel for subliminally confirming that he was fuckin' my wife.

"She'll be fine. She's tough, that one."

"Yes, sir, I got that same vibe from her. If it's OK with you, sir, I'm gonna head out. I have a couple of things to attend to before I have to go to work this evening." Jakeel laid it on thick as fuck.

"Yes, you're done here. And thank you again for understanding. Have a great evening," Matt said, escorting Jakeel to the door of Mika's office before closing the door and turning to me.

"I have to say that I'm surprised that you came in here acting like this, Sheem," he said, once we were alone. "You know you can't be doin' that shit, man."

Matt and I had been friends for years, and he knew about most of the dirt I did. He'd been preaching for what felt like forever about what would happen if Mika ever found out. I hated to say that he was right.

"I'm losing my mind without her, man," I admitted to him, rubbing my hand over my head in frustration.

"You shoulda thought about that while you were out here doin' your dirt, Sheem. Mika ain't the kinda woman you play with like you were. And now that you're about to lose her, you wanna act right. You know that's not how shit works, man," he offered advice that I didn't ask for. He was one to talk. He was on his fourth marriage, and it took three divorces sending his ass into bankruptcy for him to get the damn memo.

"And I know what you're thinkin'. I'm the last muthafucka to talk," he spoke my thoughts aloud.

"Long as you know," I confirmed with an attitude.

"But if you had any sense, you would listen to a nigga who has fucked up the same way you were fuckin' up because I can tell ya ass what *not* to do."

I walked over to Mika's seat behind her desk and sat down. Matt was still standing here talkin', but something caught my eye, and I blanked out. On the floor, under her desk, were a pair of Victoria's Secret panties. The only reason that a bitch would take her drawers off was to get her pussy ate or pounded. That was all the confirmation I needed. I was gonna kill Jakeel's ass and use her fuckin' an ex-con as leverage to make her take me back. We were still married, which meant that she was no better than I was for fuckin' this nigga before we were divorced. The thought of that nothing-ass muthafucka being inside of my wife filled me with rage.

"Did you hear me, Rasheem?" he asked, and I looked at him like I hadn't heard what he had just said because I hadn't.

"Nah, man, what you say?"

"I said, be a man about shit and sign the papers, bro. If you and Mika are meant to make up, then let that shit happen on its own. And you gon' have to let her do whatever she needs to in order to get past what you did to her. Don't let your ego cost you more than it already has."

"I hear you," I said, and he looked at me like he didn't believe me.

"A'ight man, be easy," he said, opening the door for me. I took my cue to leave because I had caused enough disruption in his place of business. But I was far from done with this shit with Jakeel and Mika. And I knew what I had to do. Heading to my car, I ran through the plan in my head. First stop, my lawyer's office.

"Mr. Blake, if I may speak freely . . ." my attorney Kevin Klein of Klein and Kristoff, said, looking at me across the desk. I nodded so that he could continue. "Thank you," he thanked me for the permission. "This has got to be one of the easiest divorces in my twenty years of being in this business. You get to keep everything. The house, the cars, the assets, the money in all your joint accounts, and even your pension that the state would require you to split with her if she hadn't waived her rights to it. Why rock the boat? I know men who have been battling in court for five years for *half* of this. They would give their left nut to be in your position right now."

"Fuck all that. She's fuckin' one of her parolees. I don't want my daughter around that shit! Make it happen!" I snapped, and he looked at me like I was losing my damn mind.

"Mr. Blake, you have had several affairs and even proposed to my niece during your marriage," he said, and I almost swallowed my tongue when he said his niece. Since there was only one white bitch that I'd dealt with and she was also the only person that I'd proposed to, I knew he was talking about Gina. "Don't worry," he said with a chuckle when he realized that the shit had just registered with me. "I still plan to represent you to the best of my ability. I just want you to know that what you've been doing is no secret, and even though Tamika isn't asking for anything, if the right judge gets wind of your indiscretions, they can still order her alimony and child support, as well as half of your pension."

He sat there, letting the shit sink in that he was spitting at me. I didn't want to hear any of that. All I wanted was for my wife to come home and drop this dumb shit. And I was tired of everyone telling me to let it go. She might be OK with letting fifteen years of marriage go, but I wasn't.

"As far as custody, do you have proof that she's having an affair?" he asked, and I shook my head no. He let out a heavy sigh like I was irritating his ass or something, and it was making me madder and madder. "Well, she had proof of yours, and in the state of Georgia, that means that she will win custody. Not to mention that you said Ky'Imani doesn't want anything to do with you, and she is of age to say which parent she wants to stay with. Being honest, this is a losing battle that you're trying to fight. Save your money, sign the papers, and cut your losses," he advised me.

My phone vibrated with a 911 text from Moore. "I'll think about it," I said, knowing that I wasn't about to sign them damn papers, no matter what anyone said.

"Please do," he said, and I stood up and shook hands with him. Leaving his office, I waited until I got in the truck before I dialed Moore's number.

"What the fuck you out here doin', man?" Moore's voice came over the speaker of my truck. I didn't know what he was talking about, but I didn't think I could take any more bad news.

"What the fuck are *you* talkin' about?" I asked, thinking that he'd heard about what happened at Mika's office.

"A bitch came in here saying that she had evidence that you set a man up, and she had your son with her," he stated.

I thought that was strange. If it were Lauren, he would've said that it was her. Since he didn't, I had no idea who the hell else would have my son and be trying to fuck me up. Except for—I know Gina wasn't that stupid. She just couldn't be.

"White bitch?" I asked.

"Aaaah, shit, man, yeah. What the fuck is goin' on?"

"I'ma call you back," I told him.

"*Don't* call me back. Handle that shit, man!" he snapped before hanging up in my face.

I tried to call Gina's ass back-to-back. Her phone kept sending me to voicemail, and that pissed me off to no end. She was playing with fire, and I was ready to kill her ass. I made a U-turn and headed toward the one place where I knew Gina would've been able to get any dirt on me. It looked like I was about to have a whole lot of blood on my hands tonight.

Boom! Boom! Boom!

I beat on Lauren's door with the butt of my gun. She had changed the damn locks on my ass. Otherwise, I would've just walked in on her ass and commenced to beat the hell outta her. I didn't see Gina's car, but I knew that all it would take was a call from Lauren to get her ass here.

"Who the fuck is beating on my door like the police—"

Whap!

As soon as she opened the door, I slapped the hell out of her with my revolver. I could've just shot her ass, but she needed to suffer for the shit she was tryin'a pull. She grabbed at air tryin'a to find something to help break her fall, and for some reason, that shit was hilarious to me. Then she hit the floor. I knew that if she had turned in what I thought she had, I was facing jail time and would lose everything that I'd worked for. If I'm going to jail, then it was gonna be for something other than setting up a nigga like Jakeel Greene.

Stepping over her, I went to her bedroom and got the duct tape and handcuffs that we would use when we role-played. This time, though, her ass was about to be held hostage in real life. I knew it was only a matter of time before the cops came for me, and I planned to make her ass tell them that she'd made it all up to ruin my name because I ain't want her ass no more and was tryin'a make shit work with my wife. If that didn't work, then she would become a bargaining chip. And as a last resort, if I were going down, then her ass wouldn't get the pleasure of witnessing that shit on this side of the afterlife.

Picking her ass up, I put her in a chair and handcuffed her hands behind her back while duct-taping her mouth. I had just finished taping her ass when I saw her phone vibrating on the table. Checking it, I saw that Gina had said that she was on her way back. This was about to be a two-for-one. And, as if God were on my side, I heard loud-ass music blasting outside the house. Going to see who it was, I couldn't believe my luck to see Jakeel whipping a tricked out Expedition into the parking lot. When I saw him get out and head toward the apartment, I hid behind the door, waiting for him to walk in. This shit was way too easy. It was almost like I was supposed to take these muthafuckas out the way they were all coming to me—without any hard work on my part.

Jakeel pushed the door open, and I let him take a couple of steps into the house before I drew back with all my might and slammed the butt of my gun into the back of his head. When that nigga fell face-first onto the floor, I swear my dick jumped in my pants a little. This shit took me back to my grimy nigga days. See, they'd let the rep and the badge fool their asses. They didn't know that they were crossing a real live, old-school-fuckin' savage. But they were gonna learn today!

Chapter Eighteen

Jakeel

Earlier

"When I saw you callin', I thought I'd had one too many glasses of Moscato," Lauren said, opening the door to let me into her house. "Then I thought that you were coming here to go off on me for upsetting your main bitch a couple of weeks back."

"Nah," I said, walking in and looking around. I had to say that her place was nice. It made me wonder how much of Mika's hard-earned money paid for it. "She ain't my bitch no more."

Hearing that seemed to make her perk up. I knew it would, but I didn't say that I didn't have a bitch . . . just that Shontelle wasn't her. You could tell a ho's intentions by speaking less and watching more.

"Then what do I owe the pleasure of your presence?" she asked, a smirk crossing her face. I hoped she ain't think I came to fuck her ass. But for some reason, I knew that was *exactly* what the hell she was thinking.

"I came to meet my son," I said, and her mouth dropped open.

"Really?" she asked like she was shocked.

"Yeah, but I have one condition," I said, and she rolled her eyes, crossing her arms over her chest.

"And what would that be?"

"Lemme test him and make sure that the li'l nigga mine," I said, expecting her to object. She smiled instead, and looking at her for the first time, I noticed that she seemed tired. She wasn't the same Lauren I remembered, but seven years could change a person—in a good or a bad way.

"No problem," she said, and it was my turn to be shocked.

"A'ight, I'ma be right back," I said, and she nodded her head. I didn't know why she didn't give me no pushback, but I wasn't about to ask too many questions, either. I turned and headed back out the door before she changed her damn mind.

I made a quick run to the store to get the tests that I needed and stood in line, waiting for the slow-ass cashier to finish ringing up the three people who were in line in front of me. Had to love the hood. Why did they have ten damn registers in a store but never had more than one of them open?

When I walked back to Lauren's apartment, I was shocked to see that the door was opened. I walked in and saw Lauren tied to a chair.

"What the fuck?" I asked, and she started bouncing around in the chair like she was trying to say something to me. I took several steps toward her before I was hit in the back of the head and knocked out.

Whap! Whap! Whap!

Three hard slaps to my face brought me to . . . and I found myself face-to-face with Rasheem. This nigga had a crazed look in his eyes, one that I knew all too well. I didn't think I was gonna make it outta here alive, and if I didn't, I was glad that I'd told Mika that I loved her before my life was taken from me—and by the nigga who coulda done right by her and fucked it up. Ain't it funny how a muthafucka will blame every-damn-body but the nigga in the mirror for the bullshit that he did? Whatever he had in mind and whatever he did to Lauren and me, I knew for a fact that Mika wasn't taking his ass back.

I was sitting on the floor with my hands cuffed in front of me, and my feet duct-taped together.

"So, you thought you could take my wife *and* my son?" Rasheem yelled at me, holding the gun to Lauren's head.

"I ain't tryin'a take shit. If you was takin' care of business with your wife instead of out here making babies, I wouldn't have been able to slide up in her—I mean, there," I taunted him. I knew I was at a disadvantage, and egging his ass on wasn't wise. But there were two rules that any street nigga knew could make or break a life-or-death situation. One, never show fear. Two, try to knock your opponent off his square and take the opportunity to get the advantage on his ass.

"You think you funny, huh, li'l nigga?" he snapped, turning the gun on me.

"Hey, best bitch! It's done! That nigga gon' be gone for a long-ass—"

POW!

The door opened, scaring his ass, and he fired without paying any attention. A white bitch fell into the house on her face, and a little boy, who had my whole face, rushed to her, screaming and crying.

"Auntie! Noooo!" the boy who I assumed was my son, Jasheem, yelled, hugging the woman in his tiny arms as she bled out from her chest. "Why you shoot my auntie?" he yelled at Rasheem, whose face was twitching.

I could tell that he didn't care that he'd traumatized my child for life. He was more concerned with the repercussions of shooting the bitch, whoever she was. If his ass wasn't goin' to jail before, he sure as hell was now. I knew that he was planning to kill us all now, and then try to get the fuck outta here before one of the neighbors called the police. Yeah, we were in the projects, but this wasn't one that had much gunplay, so it was only a matter of time before them red and blues came flashing.

Thinking fast, I eased up the wall while he stared at Jasheem and the white bitch on the floor. By the time he caught on to what I was doin', I was on my feet and lunging at him. I didn't care about getting shot. I just needed to get the gun off my son. That was all I could think about. He tried to move his gun hand toward me, but I swung my cuffed hands and knocked it away.

POW!

"Mamaaaa!" Jasheem's scream made me look over at Lauren, who now had a bullet hole in *her* chest.

Fuck, man! I thought. This nigga was reckless as hell and had just killed two bitches in this fuckin' house. I knew that if I didn't get the best of his ass, Jasheem and I were next.

"Look what you made me do!" he yelled at me, like any of this was *my* fault.

I didn't even entertain that bullshit. Clasping my hands together, I swung and hit his ass in the head with a double fist. He fell to his knees and dropped the gun, then fell backward with force into the chair where Lauren was, knocking her over with him. I managed to crawl over to him and started pummeling his ass in the face with my hands still clasped together. I was trying to kill that nigga with my bare hands but stopped when I thought about the fact that my son had seen two people already die today. I didn't want him to witness a third death and definitely not by my hands.

I was breathing hard, and my adrenaline was pumping. Trying to compose myself, the sound of my son's wails brought me back to my senses. Looking down, I pushed Rasheem's head to make sure that he was unconscious. When I was convinced that he was, I looked over at

Jasheem. He looked so helpless, and it was fucked up that he'd lost his innocence at such a young age. I could tell that he was a sweet boy like I was at his age—before the world got ahold of me.

"Jasheem," I called to him, but he was rocking back and forth, looking between his mother's limp body and the white woman who he had called his aunt. He was covered in blood, and his face was wet with tears. "Jasheem," I called out to him again.

He finally looked at me, but his little body was shivering so hard. I tried to stand up, but my feet were still bound. I needed to get to my child and comfort my son. Seeing him like this was killin' a nigga on the inside.

"Do you know who I am?" I asked him.

He nodded his head weakly, and that made me smile. I was happy that Lauren had at least told my son about me. And it was obvious that he was my son. A blind man could see that shit, and that let me know why Shontelle was so mad about it.

"You're my daddy," he said, and hearing that in his voice made my heart melt.

"Good. I need your help, OK? I need you to be a big boy for me, a'ight? I know this is hard, but I wanna try to see if I can help your mama and your auntie. Can you help me out?" I asked as calmly and soothingly as possible. It was strange how easily this fatherhood shit was coming to me. I never liked kids before, but I guess it's different when it's your own seed.

"Oh . . . O-O-OK," he said, standing up and walking toward me.

"You know where some scissors are?" I asked him, and he nodded his head, running off down the hallway. He came back with a pair of safety scissors, and it was so cute that I wanted to laugh, but I knew that this wasn't the time for all that.

"Here!" he said, proudly handing me the scissors.

"Those are great, but I need some that are stronger so that I can cut your mama and me free," I said, and he looked confused. "Do you know where any grown-up scissors are?"

"Mama said that I can't play with those, because she don't want me to get hurt," he said, still respecting his mother's wishes, even when it was clear that she couldn't do anything to punish him. Lauren had done a great fuckin' job with him, and it showed. That was definitely her doing, because having my DNA inside of him, his ass should've been happy to do some shit he ain't have no business doing. I knew I would've done the shit at that age.

"And she's right. But just this one time, I *need* you to get them for me," I said, then thought about it. "You know what? Can you tell me where they are?"

"I'll go get 'em. You can't walk. But only if you promise I won't get in trouble."

"I promise. If your mama gets mad about it, I'll tell her I told you to do it, OK?"

That seemed to be good enough for him because he took off again, but this time, he went to a different room from the one that he had gone into initially. I assumed the first room was his, and the one he'd just gone into was his mama's. He came out, carrying the scissors, walking with them slowly. It took a second for me to realize that he didn't wanna run with the scissors. I said a silent prayer that Lauren wasn't dead. I wanted to thank her for being a great fuckin' mama to my son.

While he was going to get the scissors, I searched Rasheem's body, looking for the keys to the handcuffs that he'd put on me. I couldn't find them, and that pissed me off. I needed to be fully capable of handling this nigga if he came to before the cops got here. I blew out a frustrated breath, shaking my head, looking down at this nigga. All this was because of him, and he was *still* ruining lives. One thing that my mama always told me was that a man's ego was the biggest weakness that he would ever possess. Rasheem Blake was proof of that shit.

When Jasheem finally reached me, he handed me the scissors like he didn't wanna chance getting caught with them. I smiled at him, and he stood there, big-eyed, watching my every move. I leaned down and cut my feet loose, finally able to stand. I tucked the scissors in the waistband of my joggers, picked my son up, and looked into his eyes. He gave me a tight hug, and I swear it was the best thing that had ever happened to me in my life.

"Nice to meet you, my nigga," I said to him, and he smiled at me. He being able to smile in the midst of what was going on showed me just how strong he was. Suddenly, I heard a moan and realized that it was Lauren. Walking over to the couch, I put li'l man down before rushing to the chair that Lauren was tied to. I cut the tape from her arms and legs first and then pulled the tape from her mouth.

She fell forward, and I caught her in my arms. She was barely breathing, but I was happy that she was breathing at all. I put her on the floor and went over to the white lady, but I could tell by the look in her eyes that she was dead. There was no saving her. I didn't want to make Jasheem panic, so I had to think of something to get him away from this situation. I didn't know if his mama was gonna meet the same fate that his "aunt" had, but I didn't want him here to witness the shit, just in case. And I didn't want him to be in harm's way when Rasheem woke up.

"Jasheem," I called to him, and when I looked up, I realized that he had been standing on the sofa, watching everything that I did.

"Boy, get your shoes off my couch," Lauren moaned, making us both look at her. I was happy that she was a fighter, and I was sure that it was because of our son. Either way, seeing her open her eyes, even if they were rolling back in her head and she was in obvious pain, them bitches were open. She had a chest wound that was bleeding pretty badly. But it wasn't in the same spot as the other woman's.

Jasheem slid down onto the couch and then off the couch and onto the floor. Running over to his mama, he kneeled beside me, grabbing her face in both of his hands and kissing her all over it. She gave him a weak smile, but I could tell that she needed medical help soon, or she would be meeting her maker.

"Get my phone, ca-ca-call 911, and go to your special place," Lauren said to Jasheem. I was glad that she had prepared a strategy to protect him in case some crazy shit happened to her, and he was home. She was grown as hell, and just like me, she knew the kinda life she was living and how the shit could go wrong quick as hell. But that didn't mean that our son had to be hurt because of it. I was getting more and more respect for her by the minute.

Without another word, he ran to the table and picked up his mama's phone and hurried off toward his room. I looked at her, and her eyes were starting to close again. I hated the fact that cops were always in a rush to lock up a nigga, but when we needed their asses to protect and serve, they were missing like a stripper's thong on a big-money night.

"Aaaah! Daddy!"

Hearing Jasheem scream out, I looked in the direction of the sound and felt my stomach drop. I had been so excited that Lauren had come to that I hadn't paid attention to the fact that Rasheem's ass had too. And this coward-ass nigga was holding my son by the back of his neck—with a fuckin' gun to his damn head.

"Yo, man! Yo' beef is wit' me, not my kid. Let him go, and you handle this shit with me like a man," I said, and he laughed like I'd made a joke.

"Nah, my nigga. You took something of mine, so I'm gon' take something of yours too."

"Rasheem, what the fuck are you doin'?" I heard behind me. I wanted to turn around to be sure that it was who I thought it was, but I didn't want to take my eyes off my son, or Rasheem because I knew this nigga was unstable, and I was trying to find an opening so that I could get my boy away from this muthafucka.

"I knew you would come sniffin' behind this nigga's dick," Rasheem said, confirming that it was Mika who had come into the house. I looked up to the heavens and prayed that we all made it outta this shit. But I had a feeling that, if Rasheem was going down, he planned to take as many of us as he could with him. He was already a body and a half down, and now, he had three more hostages. *Where the fuck are the cops?* I thought, hoping that Mika had called them since Jasheem hadn't had the chance to.

Chapter Nineteen

Mika

Previously

Right when I was about to pay for my room for the night, I had gotten a call from Ky'Imani saying that she was worried about me because her daddy kept calling her. This nigga was pulling out all the stops to try to make me take his ass back. She said she had a bad feeling and would feel better if I came home, so I did. The way my child hugged me sent a chill down my spine. I made sure to lock the door, set the alarm, and send Joy my location and a message to activate Plan B, in case some shit popped off. Today had been a crazy day, and I wanted to get ahead of anything else that might happen.

After a bubble bath, giving each other pedicures, and dinner, it seemed that Ky had calmed down some. We'd decided to make ice-cream sundaes and have a mother-daughter Netflix and Chill night to ease both our minds.

Beep-Beep-Beep! Beep-Beep-Beep!

"Dang, Mama, can't you turn that thing off?" Ky fussed, pausing the movie we were watching.

"Work calls, hon," I said, and realistically, the only reason that I was about to return the call was that it was Jakeel's mama. Anybody else would've just had to wait. Like Joy said, a bitch deserved a mini vacation.

"Hey, Ms. Greene, everything OK?" I asked, knowing that if she were calling me, it wasn't.

"No. Jakeel didn't come home from y'all's check-in. Is he with you?" she asked, and that chill came back.

"No, he's not. I left him at my office," I told her, and she got quiet. I didn't speak because I was racking my brain, trying to figure out where the hell Jakeel had gone. "Maybe he's at the girl's house that has his son."

That was the last thing that I'd asked of him, and I hoped that it hadn't been a mistake. If he had gone over there and slipped back inside of her pussy, that shit would destroy me.

"I don't know, baby. But I just got this weird feeling that somethin' ain't right," she said, and the worry in her voice made me check my location app that we used for all of our parolees.

"I've got his location here. I'll try to call him, and if I can't reach him, then I'll go check," I told her.

"Thank you, Mika. Please, let me know?" she almost pleaded.

"I promise," I vowed before ending the call. If I knew one thing, it was that a mother's intuition was rarely wrong. If she felt that something was wrong with her child, then that was probably the case.

"Mama, where you goin'?" Ky asked, and I could see the worry all over her face.

"One of my parolees missed curfew, baby. I gotta go get his ass," I said, trying to make it sound like a routine violation.

"Something don't feel right about this. Is this the parolee that Daddy keeps accusing you of sleeping with?" she asked, and I immediately became pissed. He knew better than to tell our child some shit like that!

"Yes, baby. But that's not for you to worry about."

"Are you sleeping with him?" she asked, and I nodded my head.

"But it's more than that, baby girl. I wanted you to meet him because, well, we're in love."

"Oh boy," she said, shaking her head. I didn't have time to discuss this with my child right now. And if her father weren't such a dumb ass, I wouldn't be discussing it with her at all, until the time was right. I didn't want her to find out like this.

"Listen, I promise I'll be right back. And then we can finish our mother-daughter night," I promised, hoping that I would be able to keep both the promises that I had just made to Ms. Greene and Ky'Imani.

"Mama, please be careful," she begged, and it made my stomach flip. She always told me to be careful when I went to violate a parolee, and it made sense because my job was dangerous. But there was something in her voice tonight that made me feel like it wasn't Jakeel that concerned her.

"I'm always careful," I said with a huge smile across my face. I was trying to calm her spirit, but I knew that she wouldn't be OK until I made it back home.

Giving my daughter a tight hug, I ran upstairs and put on my bulletproof vest, a black hoodie, black leggings, and some black steel-toed boots. I put on my waist holster and checked to make sure that both my Glocks were loaded before putting them in the holsters. I put my revolver in my left boot and made my way toward the door.

"I love you, Mama," Ky yelled at me, and the strain in her voice was breaking my heart. It made me want to stay here, but if I stayed home every time she was worried about me, I wouldn't have been as successful in my job as I had been. I turned around, running into the living room, and kissed the top of her head before heading out the door. I made a mental note to be extra careful because of the uneasiness that Ky was feeling about this particular encounter.

***

I made it to the location that Jakeel was showing in record time. I was driving like a bat outta hell, but it felt like something was on my side too. I hadn't gotten stopped by any cops or red lights. I just hoped my luck didn't end when I got there. I saw Jakeel's truck parked in the parking lot and pulled up to the curb. Throwing the car in park, I hoped that I would be able to figure out which apartment he was in. I put my badge around my neck so that I was identified as law enforcement, hoping that it would motivate someone to help me. Getting out, a woman frantically rushed up to me.

"What the fuck took y'all so long? I swear y'all don't give a damn about us down here," she fussed, and I could understand her frustration, especially if she had already called the police, and I had gotten here—from across town, no less—before they had.

"Ma'am, what's goin' on?" I asked, trying to get her to focus on what was most important.

"Somebody is shooting in my neighbor's house. There's a little boy in there," she said, and my heart dropped. I hoped that no one was hurt, not even Rasheem. I didn't want his ass, but I didn't wish him dead, either.

"Can you show me which apartment?" I asked, and she nodded, before walking toward the one that had the door opened.

"Oh my God!" she yelled when she saw the woman who was lying on the floor, bleeding from her chest.

"Ma'am, I need you to go to your house. What's your name?" I asked her, trying my best to keep my cool. I wanted to rush in there and see what the hell else had happened, but I had to play this smart.

"Norma. Norma Jean Hayes," she introduced herself, never taking her eyes off the woman's body.

"OK, Norma. Go back into your house and call 911 again. Tell them a white woman has been shot, and it looks like she's been fatally wounded. I'm gonna try to get the boy out of the house and send him next door to you, OK?" I asked, and she nodded her head, finally meeting eyes with me. As fucked up as it was, I knew that a call saying that a "white" woman had been shot would get the cops here, so I worked that shit. "Which one is yours?" I asked, and she pointed to apartment D. Pulling her phone out of the pocket of her housecoat, she dialed 911 and speed-walked toward her home.

I eased up to the apartment that had the injured woman in it and pressed my back against the wall by the door. Listening, I tried to gauge how volatile a situation I was walking into was.

"Yo, man! Yo' beef is wit' me, not my kid. Let him go and handle this shit with me like a man," I heard Jakeel plead, and I wondered who the hell he was talking to.

"Nah, my nigga. You took something of mine, so I'm gon' take something of yours too."

Rasheem, I thought, hearing a voice I knew better than my own because I'd shared my life with its owner for the past fifteen years. But what the fuck was *he* doin' here? Drawing my gun, I cocked it, making sure there was one in the chamber. Stepping into the doorway, I raised it to the head of the man whose last name I shared. I couldn't believe my eyes. The white woman was there, and I was pretty sure she was dead. Another woman was on the floor, who, I was sure, was the mother of the little boy, and she was in and out of consciousness. And then, there was Rasheem, holding a gun to a little boy's head who couldn't have been 10 years old.

Looking at the little boy, I knew he was Keel's. I didn't need the DNA test results. He couldn't have denied that damn kid if he'd wanted to, which let me know that

Rasheem was fuckin' around with his mama because he *wanted* to. There was no way that he could've possibly thought this little boy was his.

"Rasheem, what the fuck are you doin'?" I spoke, making my presence known. I kept the gun trained in the center of his head and would take the kill shot if I needed to.

"I knew you would come sniffin' behind this nigga's dick," Rasheem sneered, and I could tell that he'd lost his mind. "You should be at home with our daughter, but here you are, running up behind this fuck nigga!"

"Rasheem, what the hell are you doin'?" I asked again because he hadn't answered my question.

"What the fuck does it look like? I'm tryin'a save our marriage. If I get rid of this nigga and the bitches that I slipped up with, then you'll *have* to take me back!"

I squinted and cocked my head to the side like that would make the dumb shit he'd just said make sense. This nigga couldn't be serious right now. It was then that I realized that he had lost his whole mind, and I'd probably have to kill him for any of us to make it out of this shit alive.

"Rasheem, do you hear yourself? Are you *really* about to throw your whole career away because I want a divorce?"

"Career? What career?" he snapped, and I was confused all over again. "These bitches ruined that shit already!"

He waved the gun between the dead white woman and the black woman who had now slipped back out of consciousness. I didn't know what he was talking about, but I was sure that it was something that he'd caused, so I couldn't summon the fucks to care. Instead, I used my training. I knew that keeping him talking would keep us alive, one response at a time, and I was just trying to buy time until the cops arrived.

"Ruined it how, Sheem?" I asked, using his nickname to try to maintain a bond with him.

"They took evidence in that showed that I set this fuck nigga up," he said, and it took everything in me not to shake my head. I couldn't believe that, while he had me at home, he was so worried about who another bitch was fuckin' with that, he set a man up to be locked up.

I saw Jakeel's jaw clench and knew that what he'd just heard had pissed him off to no end. Stepping forward, slowly, I eased past Rasheem before Jakeel reacted in a way that would surely get us killed.

"You're a decorated officer, Rasheem. One of the best homicide detectives in Decatur. I'm sure your career ain't ruined behind the lies of two bitches that we both know are just mad that they can't have you," I appealed to his ego, hoping that it would give me the advantage that I needed. I even lowered my gun slightly to remove some of the threat and show some submission. Instead, he busted out laughing.

"You think I'm stupid, don't you?" he said, looking at me with malice in his eyes. "I had the same training you did, Mika. Look at you, placing your body between that nigga you been fuckin' to block my shot and me . . . appealing to my ego. But you don't give a damn about me. If you did, you would be by my side, ready to get rid of these muthfuckas who are trying to ruin *our* lives, instead of tryin'a save one of them."

"Nobody has to die, Rasheem," I said, trying to reason with him. "And they didn't ruin our lives. *You* did—"

Before I could say another word, Jakeel grabbed me and snatched the other gun from my holster, placing it to my head. I knew that he was reacting desperately and completely understood and respected that if it came down to his son or me, he would choose his son, even if this was his first time meeting his child. I would've done the same thing if someone had a gun to Ky'Imani's head.

"Let my son go," Keel seethed, pressing the gun to my temple.

"This the kinda nigga you want, Mika? One that will put a gun to your head?" Rasheem asked, laughing again.

"I don't want either one of y'all," I said, and *that* made his ass stop laughing.

"Oh yea?" he asked, a smirk coming over his face. "You hear that, my nigga? She just like these other two bitches. They use us and throw us away when they don't have no more use for us."

It was appalling that he was trying to bond with Jakeel. And I could tell that the shit wasn't working. Keel didn't respond or flinch. That shit wasn't what he cared about at the moment. It was what Rasheem cared about. All Jakeel wanted was to get his son away from the madman that I was embarrassed to have ever called my husband. Placing his knee in the back of mine, Jakeel knocked me down to the floor, now holding the gun to the back of my head. I put my hands behind my back and sat back on my heels. Trying to move as little as possible, I reached into my boot, pulling my revolver out.

"Let my son go, or I'ma kill this bitch," Jakeel hollered. It was apparent that he was tired of the back-and-forth.

"Shoot her ass, and I'ma kill this li'l bastard, and then take yo' ass out too."

Rasheem cocked his gun, letting Keel know that he meant business. Out of the corner of my eye, I saw someone in the window. I tried not to turn my head too much, but it looked like someone was holding something in their hand and was watching the whole thing. That was just like a nigga. Recording shit instead of calling the cops. Muthafuckas would place themselves in harm's way just to get a couple of views on social media these days.

"Do it, Keel. I don't want your son to die because of me," I begged, pissing Rasheem off.

"Well, let me do the honors, then," Rasheem said, taking the gun away from the little boy's head. "You're my *wife*, and you out here fuckin' lowlifes and shit. That's what you wanna do? That's why you wanna divorce me? Because of *this* nigga?" he snapped, giving me the opening that I needed.

Pow!

Pop!

Pow-Pow!

"Daddyyyy!"

Chapter Twenty

Shontelle

Using the Find My iPhone app, I tracked Jakeel's location. If he thought he could get rid of me that quick, he had me fucked up. I'd devoted too much of my life to his ass for him to just walk away from me like that. If anybody was gonna be with him, it would be me! Not some old bitch with dried-up-ass prune pussy.

I had found his car parked at a CVS, and it made me wonder what he could need outta there. Probably some condoms. Or some lube because I knew that the old bitch that he was fuckin' with's shit ain't get as juicy as mine did.

Sitting outside of the apartments, parked two places down from his car, I kept my eyes peeled on the apartment that he'd just entered. I saw that he was at that bitch Lauren's house and had a bag.

"Y'all niggas ain't shit," I said, as soon as the countdown to begin my Live ended. "Y'all can have a bitch that holds you down, and you'll leave her for a bitch that wouldn't even look at your ass twice. Why is that?" I asked, letting my frustration show. I watched as my views started to pick up, and that encouraged me to keep talkin'.

"I mean, look at me! I'm a bad bitch with a good pussy, who's loyal and makes my own money. And yet, I'm outside a bitch's house where *my man,* who I held down while he was locked the fuck up for seven years, by the way, may or may not have a child with. And that ain't the worst of it," I said, popping my mouth. "He ain't even with that ho no more. Now he with an old-school, 1982-pussy-havin'-ass bitch. What kinda shit is that? But let us fuck around on y'all, and y'all lost y'all's damn minds. If y'all can't handle that shit being done to you, then don't do the shit to us, either."

I was at 300 viewers in that short time, and I loved the attention. It was the ego boost that I needed after the way that Jakeel was doing me.

"Then y'all wanna talk shit when we have to become FBI agents and shit to catch y'all wit' y'all's pants down!"

The sound of what I thought were two gunshots made me stop talking. I wanted to go and see what was going on, but secretly, I was hoping that Jakeel had been shot or shot some-damn-body. No more would I hold down his ass. He'd have to do whatever time they gave his ass without me this time. Since he didn't appreciate my loyalty, I'd let him see what his life would be like without that shit. Reading the comments, I could tell that there were a lot of women who were going through what I was going through, or who had been through it. That shit was sad. What was a good bitch supposed to do these days?

Hearing a car screech to a stop not too far from where I was parked, I was shocked to see that it was the bitch that Jakeel was with at TGI Fridays that day.

"What the fuck is she doin' here?" I asked, more to myself than to my viewers. I realized that I might have just pulled up on something juicy, especially when she got out with a badge around her neck.

"Well, well, well, y'all. Looks like there's been a plot twist. There's the bitch he's been fuckin' wit' right there, and it looks like her ass is the law. Let's destroy a couple of lives tonight, shall we?" I said, my smile getting big as hell.

Turning the camera around, I pointed it at the bitch that Jakeel had left me for. She was talking to some old lady who had been outside since I'd pulled up. They headed toward the apartment that I'd seen Keel go into, and I got out of the car, planning to follow. I used Keel's big-ass truck to hide behind until the bitch had gone inside. Then I ran up to the apartment, standing in front of one of the side windows, recording the whole thing.

My phone was ringing off the hook. Between Liza and Mel, they kept calling me back-to-back. I slid my navigation bar down and turned on the DND for my calls so that they wouldn't keep pausing my Live. They weren't concerned about my ass before now, so they could kiss my big, round, juicy booty cheeks.

When I looked back up through the window, I saw that the woman had her gun pointed at a man's head who had the little boy Jasheem by the neck with a gun pressed against his temple. The two bitches who had come into my shop with him to start drama were both shot and lay on the floor. Jakeel was standing there, looking mad as hell, and that made me happy. No, I didn't want Jasheem to have to deal with this kinda shit. He was a great kid and didn't deserve that shit. But with the ways that his parents moved, it was only a matter of time before something caught up to them.

The old bitch walked up toward the man who was holding Jasheem, but she was also positioning herself in between the man and Keel. She was a better bitch than me because I wouldn't put my life in danger to save no nigga. Damn sure not no nigga like Jakeel, and he proved what I thought when he grabbed her ass, took one of her guns, and put that bitch to her head. That nigga wasn't loyal to nobody but his damn self, and that was what a lot of my watchers were saying.

The rest of their snitching asses were telling me that I needed to get off Live and call the cops and acting as if they had never seen no shit like this go down before. I was up to over a thousand viewers now, and I wasn't about to miss out on this shit because of some bleeding heart muthafuckas. They could call the damn cops themselves if they wanted to.

"Oh shit!" I looked up from the comments just soon enough to see that Keel's new bitch seemed to have seen me, but that wasn't what had made me cuss.

Pow!

Pop!

Pow-Pow!

"Daddyyyy!"

Three guns went off, and Jasheem screamed at the top of his lungs. I jumped so hard that I damn near dropped my phone. I wanted to run in the house and get that baby, but my feet felt like they were stuck in cement. I couldn't move.

"Freeze! Put your hands up!" I heard behind me, feeling a gun pressed against my back.

I threw my hands up immediately, and the cop who had snuck up on me snatched the phone from my hand.

"Officer, I think I just caught a triple homicide on my Live," I told him. "End it and save it so that we don't lose that evidence," I said, playing the good citizen.

There was silence, and it made me nervous. I didn't know what he was doing, but as I stared at Jakeel on the floor bleeding, tears came to my eyes. I knew I acted like I ain't give a fuck about him, but I loved him. And now, I wished that I had called the cops instead of being an attention whore. Maybe they would've gotten to him sooner and saved his life.

"Turn around," the cop said, and it was then that I saw cop cars all over the street. They hadn't used the red and blue lights or the sirens because they didn't want to let the people who were holding guns and shit around a kid know that they had arrived. "Come with me."

Obediently, I followed him, and he walked me to a cruiser, opening the back door for me to sit inside.

"What are you doin' out here?" he asked me, his eyebrow raised.

"I was following my boyfriend because he's been cheating on me," I said honestly, and he shook his head.

"Why not just leave him alone? Why would you run behind a man or put yourself in harm's way to catch him doing something that you knew he was doin'?" he continued to question me. I didn't respond right away because I watched as the woman next door met a cop right outside and picked up a crying Jasheem, holding him in her arms.

Then I watched the ambulance jump the curb and pull almost up to the door. They raced inside and started wheeling bodies covered in sheets out of the house. I didn't know if one of them was Keel, and that was fuckin' with me.

The nigga who had been holding Jasheem hostage was led out in handcuffs, and he was saying something that I couldn't hear to the cops that they weren't tryin'a hear. They led him in my direction, and I felt my heart rate increase.

"I'm telling you, it was life or death," I heard him trying to lie.

"This lady here got the whole thing on camera," the officer who had just been lecturing me, said, holding up my phone. The way that the man in cuffs looked at me made my blood freeze over.

"I only got the last shooting," I admitted, looking everywhere but at the cuffed man, as they led him past me and put him in another cruiser. But unlike me, he wasn't sitting in the back with the door open. They slammed the door on his ass, and the cruiser took his ass away.

"I got the rest of it," the neighbor who was holding Jasheem said while the medics checked him out. Being real, I was surprised that her old ass knew how to use a damn camera phone, but it looked like the cops would have all the evidence that they needed to close their case between the two of us.

I kept my eyes glued on the door, and right when I was about to lose my shit and accept that the only man that I'd ever loved was dead and gone, and it was partially my fault, another gurney came out with him on top of it. He was bleeding from his head, but there was no sheet over him, so at least he was alive. He was followed by that old bitch who wasn't letting him out of her sight. She hopped in the ambulance with him but then got out and walked over to where the neighbor was holding Jasheem. After a brief conversation that I was too far away to hear, the neighbor lady handed Jasheem off to the woman, and she carried him to the ambulance that his father was in. They slammed the doors once she was inside and turned on the sirens, speeding out of the complex.

"Are you through with me?" I asked. I wanted to find out what hospital Keel was going to so that I could be there when he woke up. I felt like it was my last chance before I lost him to that bitch forever.

"No, ma'am. I'm taking you downtown so that you can give us a full statement. I don't know if you realize what you stumbled on, but this is a lot deeper than your man sleeping with another woman."

I hung my head, knowing that I had just lost Jakeel forever. Instead of being there for him, I was focused on self, and that shit could've cost him and his son their lives. Accepting that reality, I turned my legs so that he could close the door and escort me downtown. All I could do now was hope that Jakeel made it because his son needed him. He'd just lost his mother, and Keel was all that Jasheem had left.

Epilogue

Mika

"Homicide Detective Rasheem Blake is facing several charges, including two first-degree murder charges after two videos surfaced of him shooting two women in cold blood. The women, 28-year-old Gina Klein and 30-year-old Lauren Mason, are believed to have been attacked by Detective Blake after they turned in some information that proved Blake had set up Mason's child's father, Jakeel Greene. Greene was sentenced to seven years in prison because of the actions of Blake. The police are keeping some details of this case closed, including a surprise witness, who they say will make sure that Blake never sees the light of day again. The chief of police said that Blake's actions are deplorable and are not a reflection of the way that the Decatur police operate. He said that he feels that a pending divorce, as well as the surfacing of this evidence, were too much for Blake, and he snapped. We will keep you posted as we get more information on this high-profile case."

I turned the TV off and looked over at Jakeel. He was sedated. They'd had to remove the bullet that had been lodged in his skull. It had been touch and go since he'd gotten out of surgery, and I refused to leave his side because I felt like the minute I walked away, I would lose him. The door opened, stealing my attention from his handsome face for just a moment when Joy came in. Behind her were Ky'Imani, who was holding Jasheem in her arms. I'd pulled some strings and got CPS to let him stay with me until his father came to, letting them know that he was the only surviving relative that the little boy had. And it had worked—for now.

"Daddy! You're awake!" Jasheem yelled, almost jumping out of Ky's arms.

"Well, hey, there, handsome," I said, leaning forward to kiss his lips. Joy left the room to get a doctor, and Ky handed Jasheem to me. He was almost fighting to get to his father, and I didn't want to deny him any longer.

I sat him on the side of the bed, and he lay on Jakeel's chest. I couldn't help but smile, and Ky came up beside me and rested her head on my shoulder, watching the two of them interact. She hadn't been surprised by what had come to light about her father, and that bothered me a little bit. It seemed like everyone knew how fucked-up Rasheem was but me. I hoped that I wasn't missing any signs with Jakeel now because I didn't know if I could survive another night like this one.

"You must be Ky'Imani," Jakeel spoke to my daughter, while lovingly rubbing his son's back.

"Yes, sir. Nice to meet the man who gave my mama the ability to see herself the way we all do," she said with a smile, making me blush.

"She's an amazing woman, and anyone who don't know that don't deserve to breathe the same air she does," he said before the doctors and nurses came in to check his vitals. We left the room, well, all of us but Jasheem, who refused to let his father out of his sight. And rightfully so.

When we reached the hallway, I saw the Shontelle girl who had acted a fool at TGI Fridays and who I'd learned was the person I thought I'd seen standing there recording the whole thing tonight, getting off the elevator. I wasn't in the mood for no bullshit and would shoot her ass and just take the charge if she tried me after the night I'd had. She saw me and came straight toward me, but I couldn't read her demeanor. When she got to me, she grabbed me and pulled me into a hug. I didn't hug her back at first, because I thought the bitch was gonna try to stab me in my back or some shit. But when I saw that she wasn't gonna let me go until I returned the act of affection, I wrapped my arms around her.

"Listen, I know I'm 'bout the last bitch you wanna see after the night you've had, but I had to come and make sure that Keel was good," she said, once she'd finally let me go. "He was all that I've known all my life, so I thought that my actions were my way of fighting to keep him. But if there's one thing that watching that shit play taught me, it was that you can't make someone stay who doesn't want you."

I nodded my head and smiled at her.

"The doctors are checking on him now, but you can go in as soon as they're done," I offered, making Ky and Joy both look at me like I was crazy. I could tell that they thought I was crazy, or maybe that I hadn't learned my lesson about letting bitches too close to my nigga. I had learned my lesson, but that wasn't it. I'd learned that if a nigga wanted to do you dirty, they would find a way. So I wasn't about to break a sweat tryin'a keep them from doin' what the hell they wanted to do.

"Thank you," she said, looking through the window of the door. "How's Jasheem?"

"As well as he can be after seeing his whole family shot right in front of him and having a gun to his head," I said honestly.

"Yeah. That was fucked up. But I want you to know that I plan to testify for the prosecution and make sure that psycho nigga never gets out."

I didn't waste my breath telling her that the psycho nigga was my soon-to-be ex-husband. Nor did I waste my breath telling her ass that I thought it was fucked up that she stood by while all that shit went down. I'd gotten the details of the whole scenario, and she showed her true colors with placing Facebook likes over the well-being of a man that she claimed to love. Even with all the dirt that Rasheem had done to me, I would've tried to do something to help. Not just stand by and watch. Just like earlier, when I could've killed his ass. But I wounded him to the point that he wouldn't bleed out, but he wouldn't be able to come after any of us again until the cops arrived.

When the doctors came out, she didn't stand by and wait for them to tell us the details of his condition. She rushed into the room and to his side. I saw Jasheem leap into her arms and give her a tight hug. The amount of love that little boy still had with all that he'd just experienced gave me hope. Turning away so that negative thoughts wouldn't consume me, I faced the doctors.

"So, what's the verdict?" I asked, and the neurologist had a strange look on his face.

"He's gonna make a full recovery," he said like he was surprised.

"That's great news," I said, beaming.

"It's a miracle. He shouldn't have made it out of surgery."

Nodding my head, taking in what he was saying, I had to fight back the tears. Just then, Shontelle came out of the room and touched my shoulder. She was holding Jasheem and looked at me with a smile on her face.

"He's asking for you. *Just* you," she said and motioned with her head for me to go on in there.

"You know you gotta be some kinda angel," Jakeel said, as soon as I entered the room.

"Why you say that?" I asked with a giggle.

"You saved my life."

"I mean, I was just doin' my job," I said with a shrug.

"No, you gave me a reason to live, to beat the odds, to want more. I done had a hard-ass life, ma. But from the first day I met you, I felt like I was bein' given a second chance at life, and I knew it would only work with you in it."

I felt the tears start to fall because he was speaking the same truth that I felt about him. There wouldn't have been any life for me without Jakeel. Before I met him, I didn't know that I hadn't been living—just going through the motions. But with him, I felt every beat of my heart. I had a reason to smile. I felt like I mattered.

"I was tryin'a finesse you outta them drawers, and you finessed a nigga outta his heart," he said with a chuckle. "But that's cool. 'Cause I know it's in good hands."

I leaned down to kiss him with all the love that I felt for him.

"Aye! That's enough of that. Let the li'l nigga heal, so he has the strength to handle all . . . that . . . ass . . . Dayum, baby bro. I see why you was willing to die for this one here," a woman said, bursting into the room.

"Toya!" Ms. Greene said to her daughter, hitting her arm playfully.

"I'm just sayin'," the woman who I assumed was Keel's sister, said. "Happy to see you still alive," she finished, dapping her brother.

"It's all because of her," Jakeel said, pointing at me. Ms. Greene pulled me into a tight hug.

"Thank you," she whispered in my ear before walking over to the side of her son's bed. I decided to leave so that they could have a little privacy. I knew they'd been worried to damn death.

"Hey, Tamika!" Jakeel yelled at my back right when I reached the door.

"Yea?" I asked, turning around.

"I love you."

"I love you too," I said, smiling and blushing, blowing him a kiss. I knew that I'd made the right decision *for me* for the first time in my life.

Also available
by Racquel Williams . . .

Carl Weber's Kingpins:

Jamaica

Out in stores now!

Prologue

Donavan, aka Gaza

"Compound is now open for breakfast," Lieutenant Rodriguez yelled over the loudspeaker.

Fuck. How did I sleep this late? I've waited ten fucking years for this day to come, and my dumb ass fell asleep. I jumped off the top bunk onto the floor. I grabbed my shower bag and rushed toward the shower. To my disappointment, the shower stalls were already packed. Mostly with niggas going to work at Unicor or to the gym for their daily workout routine.

"Damn, homie. This yo' day, ain't it?" my homie Big Cee said to me as we exchanged daps.

"Yeah, you know it, mon. Yo, soon as I touch down, my nigga, I gotcha. You hear me, yo?"

"Man, I already know you got me, bro. Aye, yo, get out there, fuck some bitches, get money, and stay out the motherfucking way. Nigga, I don't want to see you back in here. You heard?" He grabbed me up in a bear-type hug.

"Yo, my nigga, you already know, I'm focused as fuck," I said. "Fuck the Feds. I ain't never coming back to this shit. My nigga, keep yo' head up. You know they passing these laws and shit. Yo' day comin', homie."

"My nigga, I got fifteen bodies on me. Ain't no motherfucking law can get me up out of here unless they drop the motherfucking charges, you dig? All I need you to do is bless a nigga with some change when you send me some pussy pictures. Other than that, go live life, my nigga."

I nodded. "A'ight, man, I got you. I love you, my nigga."

"Yo, lemme go. You know how I hate missing breakfast," he said, trying to hide the tears that were coming down his face. I watched as he ran out of Unit 8H, into the dimly lit federal compound.

I used e'erything in me to fight back tears. Cee was my big homie, my partner up in this bitch. The only nigga that I had confessed a lot of shit to. But he was right; he been down for fifteen years, and the judge had sentenced him to life. E'erybody knew life in prison meant just that: life. The best I could do for homie to show him how much I appreciated him was to keep his books stocked and send him naked bitches. . . .

"Shower open," a dude yelled, interrupting my thoughts.

"Here I come." I squeezed through, not giving a fuck who was next. I was ready to get the fuck up outta here.

"Nigga, how the fuck you goin' to just cut? You see all these motherfuckers waiting to get in," someone said behind me.

I stopped dead in my tracks, then turned around to face the little pussy nigga that had had the balls to say some shit like this to me. I stepped a little closer to his face. "What the fuck you say to me?" I had my fist balled up. Before he could respond, I hit him dead in his mouth. Before I could get another hit in, I felt someone grab my arm.

"Yo, chill out! You goin' to let a bitch-ass nigga take yo' freedom away?" It was Cee holding on to me.

"Nah, bro. Fuck that nigga. I 'on't give a fuck."

"Man, shut the fuck up. Get in the shower, so you can dress and get the fuck up outta here. You in a mother-fucking position that myself and other niggas would kill to have." I saw the seriousness in Cee's face, and I knew he meant business.

"A'ight, man." I snatched my arm away and walked into the empty stall.

I was still fuming. But I felt where the big homie was coming from. I had a chance to walk out of here a free man today, and here I was, trying to fight. I cut the shower on, releasing the water on my head. I need to get my mind right before I stepped out today. . . .

Twenty minutes later, I was dressed and ready to go.

"Donavan Coley, to R & D. Donavan Coley, report to R & D."

This was my time, I thought as I strutted to the main building. Niggas were passing by me, giving me daps and reminding me to keep in touch. I assured them I would and kept it pushing.

Freedom at last, I thought.

When average prisoners left prison, they'd either go to a halfway house or go straight home if they maxed out. However, for me, it was different, I was on my way to an immigration holding facility, where I would stay until they shipped me back to my home country of Jamaica.

I was ten years old when Mama and I made our way to the "land of opportunities." Those were my mom's words for the United States. Since I was born and raised in the Kingston slum of McGregor Gully, my destiny was already carved out for me. Mama was a higgler who bought and sold clothes, shoes, and whatever else she could get her hands on to support her five children. There wasn't no Daddy, and the few no-good niggas that came around didn't stick around, especially when it was time to come up off that paper.

After watching Mama struggle by herself for a few years, I decided that I had to go out there and get money by any means necessary. I and two of my partners started hustling weed. The business started off slow, but as time went on, it grew. At first, I was able to help Mama with our food bill. Eventually, I was able to afford more. I remembered the smile on my younger siblings' faces when I bought our first television and brought it home. Then I purchased a nice bed, and before you knew it, our little two-bedroom board house was decked out. I smiled as I thought about the joy on my mama's face. . . .

At some point, a relative of ours in the United States offered to help Mama out. So Mama, my oldest sister, and I came to New York one summer, with no intention of going back to Jamaica. The rest of my siblings remained in Jamaica and lived with my grandmother. Mama quickly married some dude and got her green card in no time. About a year later, my sister and I got ours also.

I wasn't no book-smart nigga, not that I didn't know a little something, but my focus wasn't on that. I wanted to make money fast—not a few dollars, but plenty of them. I started off small, with an eight ball, and worked my way up. At first, things moved slowly for me, because I was the new kid on the block. One night at a club in the Bronx, I met two cats from Jamaica, Leroy and Gio. We became a trio and were inseparable. Whether we were grinding or fucking bitches, if you saw one of us, you saw all of us. It didn't take me long to convince them that we could make this money and start running shit. Later, we made friends with a Trini dude, Demari, who would forever change our lives.

It took me about six years to get shit moving the way I wanted it to move. I found a connect out in Cali to supply me with pure, uncut coke. Within a year we were copping twenty-five kilos on each run. Putting in that work, me and my crew of five niggas had the East Coast on lock. We were supplying niggas in Jersey, Delaware, Virginia, and as far away as Florida. Money was flowing in, and so was the hate from other niggas. That didn't stop shit, 'cause after a few altercations and niggas getting dropped, the word was out there that we were not to be fucked with. Shit started getting hot, but that didn't deter me and my crew. Matter of fact, we started going harder at the grind.

I was so caught up in the grind, I was oblivious to the fact that one of my runners, Demari, had got torn off in Delaware by the Feds and had decided to rat on me. What made matters worse was that I had fucked with this nigga hard. Had brought the nigga to my crib, had gone on trips with this nigga, and had even bought this nigga a brand-new Lexus truck. Demari hadn't been moving no way different, so I had had no reason not to trust him or believe he was anything short of loyal.

A year later, I was on my way to one of the trap houses when a black SUV cut me off. I pulled my gun, getting ready to bust at this clown, before I exited my Range Rover. Five other black SUVs pulled up. Niggas jumped out and ran up on me.

"US marshals, get down! Get down!" one of them shouted.

Fuck! I just shook my head. I thought about trying to shoot my way out, but I was surrounded. I looked up and saw a helicopter flying low. It was like in the movies. These motherfuckers were everywhere. They put the cuffs on me, and just like that, my life was changed.

As it turned out, all the trap houses were raided, my niggas were locked up, and accounts were seized. As I sat in my cell in MDC Brooklyn, I kept wondering how the fuck the Feds knew so much about my operation. The answers soon came to me in my motion for discovery. There was an undercover confidential informant. A bitch-ass nigga that I fed had crossed me! My lawyer fought, but in the end, the Feds had too much shit on me. From hours and hours of wiretapping, they had amassed a mountain of information about my drug activities and discussions of shootings. My lawyer advised me to go ahead and plead out.

In the end, the judge sentenced me to 180 months in prison, which was equal to fifteen years. I heard Mama screaming out after the sentence was passed down, but I, on the other hand, was feeling blessed. I wasn't happy, but, shit, with all the evidence that they had on me, they could've easily given me life in prison.

I whispered "I love you" to Mama as the marshal led me away. Within weeks I was shipped to Beckley, West Virginia, to do my time. That had been my home for the past thirteen years. Until today . . .

"Let's go, Reid," a marshal yelled, interrupting my deep thoughts.

I opened my eyes and realized the plane had landed. We were in Rhode Island. This was where the immigration prison was located. Mama had told me that the lawyer said I shouldn't be here for nothing over two weeks. But shit, you know how fucked up the system was; these motherfuckers did what the fuck they wanted to do. But fuck it. I done did my time. This shit right here was nothing compared to the shit I had done went through in the pen.

As I exited the plane, I stopped and took a long breath. This shit felt good.

"Move it, Coley," this pussy-ass marshal yelled, as if I was his bitch.

I looked at that nigga, smiled as I kept it pushing. In another lifetime, this nigga would never come out his mouth at me like this. I walked off to the van that they had waiting. We all climbed in and sat there waiting in the hot-ass van, laughing and talking.

"Yo, it's fucking hot in here," a nigga in the back hollered.

But his plea fell on deaf ears. The marshals continued on about their business, ignoring us.

"Yo, pussy. It's hot up in dis van," I yelled.

"What the fuck you just said?" said a white, redneck, bitch-ass nigga as he stepped in the van.

"Nigga, you heard what the fuck I said." I looked that nigga dead in the face. We stared each other down for a good two minutes. This nigga finally backed away. I knew he'd seen in my eyes that there wasn't no bitch in my blood.

Minutes later the other bitch-ass nigga got in the van and pulled off. About thirty minutes later, we arrived at the immigration prison, climbed out of the van, and marched inside. I was eager to get in there, to get a shower, and get something to eat. This small prison was nothing compared to the one I had come from. It was quiet, and I welcomed that. After being in the pen all those years and being around niggas, being in a quieter place was far better. Once you got in bed in the pen, you could never really get a good night's sleep, because niggas were constantly getting killed. You had to be on guard all the time, or you might just be the next victim.

Being the nigga I was, I was always on guard, 'cause I had promised Mama that I would come home to her alive, and not in a body bag, and that was a promise that I could not break. . . .

Chapter One

Gaza

It was surprising how shit had changed in the thirteen years that I'd been gone. I had left Jamaica with Mama and my sister at the age of twenty-two, and here I was, returning at thirty-five, a grown-ass man. I felt kind of funny as I stepped off the United Airlines flight that had taken me from Rhode Island to Kingston, Jamaica. Yes, I was born at Jubilee Hospital and raised in McGregor Gully. When you mentioned the Gully, niggas automatically knew what you were all about. If you were from the Gully, you already knew we were all 'bout our paper. Either we were slinging them rocks, sticking up other dope boys, or pimping bitches out. We were goin' to get it one way or the other. . . .

It was humid as fuck, but it felt good. I stood outside, inhaling and exhaling the air on this hot August day. I looked around me; nothing seemed familiar. The last time I was here, in my country, I was a little-ass young man. I ain't goin' to lie: I started feeling crazy as fuck. I felt everyone was staring at me. I knew they were aware that this was the plane that carried the deportees.

After going through customs, I finally walked out the door. People were everywhere, and cars were pulling up to the curb. I felt like I wanted to run back inside the terminal, hide from all this chaos around me. . . .

"Donavan." I heard someone yellin' my government. I immediately recognized the voice without seeing the face.

I looked at the crowd of people that were standing around, and there was my mama, my queen, waving at me. I smiled and pushed through the crowd, trying to get to her.

"Oh my God. My baby is free!" she screamed as she hugged me. Then she started planting kisses on my forehead.

Seconds later a car pulled up, and dude started honking his horn at us.

"Go the fuck around. You see me hugging ma child," Mama said and flicked the man a bird.

"Come on, Mama. 'Cause if him, that pussy, say anything to you, it's gonna be bloodshed out here today." I was so serious, and I let it be known.

She finally let me go out of her tight embrace, pointed to her car, and climbed behind the wheel. I threw the envelopes that I had in my possession on the backseat and then got in the front passenger seat. Mama pulled off, still cussing the man out with her raw Jamaican accent, which seemed to get stronger the older she got.

"Damn, Ma. Ain't nothing change. You still a gangsta," I joked.

"Baby, don't yuh start, now. You know yuh mama can handle herself."

Her ass was nothing but about four feet five, but you couldn't tell by her voice, which was strong whenever she spoke. Mama was the type to whup on niggas and bitches. I remembered how she used to beat this nigga Tony that she used to fuck with back when we lived in Jamaica. I mean, Mama used to use a broomstick on that nigga. It was funny as hell, because this nigga was big and bulky. He used to run out of the house, yelling cusswords until he got outside the gate. Thinking back on those good old days, I couldn't help bursting into laughter.

"What the hell so funny, boy?"

"Ma, you remember how you used to run after Tony, hitting him with a broomstick and shit?"

"That damn fool Tony. You know he got killed a few years back? Gunmen ran up in his house in Portmore and killed him and his son. Word had it, him and his son was wrapped up in that scamming thing."

"Really? That's fucked up."

"Boy, watch yo' damn mout'," she said with her raw Jamaican accent.

"My bad, Mama, but you do know I'm thirty-five years old now, right?"

She swung that neck around so fast and looked at me. "And what's that supposed to mean?"

"Just easy yo' self. You done know how do things set already."

"Uh-huh. So how it feel to be among the free?"

"You know, I don't really feel it as yet. Ask mi dis same question in about a month."

"Well, I'm just happy you are here. I pray night and day fi God to let you come home to me safe and sound. And here you are, my baby," she said.

"You done know mi a God bless and Father God not leaving my side."

"Well, everybody is at the house, waiting fa you. They are so happy you home."

"Oh yeah." I smiled.

It had been thirteen years since I'd seen my family. As I said, my mom, my oldest sister, and I were the only ones that had made it to the United States. The rest of my family had stayed in Jamaica, with my grandmother. I was really excited just to be in the presence of people that I knew genuinely loved me. . . .

I watched as Mama pulled up at a gate outside the three-story crib that my money had helped build after we left

Jamaica. This was one of the first things I had done when I started making money in New York. I was as proud of it as I was of the big house in New York that I had bought Mama. When the Feds had got me, they couldn't touch neither house, 'cause Mama worked, had money in the bank, and had the houses in her name, and they couldn't prove she knew anything about my illegal activities. My mama wasn't no fool, and she handled her shit like a real G.

"Oh shit! This is it, Mama?" I said as she punched the code in the keypad. She waited for the gate to open and then drove up the marble driveway.

"Yes, son, this is it," she answered as the gate swung shut behind us.

After she stopped the car and turned off the ignition, I stepped out of the car and just stood there, looking. This house was more beautiful in person than it was in the pictures I had seen.

"Gaza is here," I heard one of brothers yell.

All I saw out of the corner of my eye was people rushing out of the house. Not just any people, though. Familiar faces ran up to me and almost knocked me to the ground.

"What's good, family?" said the same brother who had announced my arrival. He hugged me tight. See, this was the brother that I was closest to, and he was the one that everybody said was my twin. We hugged for a good minute before my grandma interrupted.

"Mi grandbaby. Come give yo' grandmother a big hug." She pushed my brother out of the way.

"Grandma Rosie, what a gwaan?" I tried to use my rawest patois on her.

"Welcome home, mi baby. Come. I know you must hungry." She took my hand and led me into the house. That didn't stop everyone else from following behind us. The treatment that I was getting was nothing short of that afforded royalty.

My grandma ushered me into the dining room. On the long table were large bowls of curry goat, white rice, oxtails, and jerk chicken, as well as a big jar of sorrel punch. Wait, it wasn't even Christmastime, and sorrel was being served. I smiled as I looked at the family members surrounding me. This was the place I need to be, among real family. . . .

It was a little after 11:00 p.m., and all the festivities had died down. I kissed Grandma on the cheek after she gave me a very serious tongue-lashing about my troubles with the law. I guessed this was long overdue.

I walked out on the balcony, with a Guinness in hand, and rolled me a blunt. I welcomed this serene feeling I was experiencing right now. I took a long drag of the weed and instantly started to choke. I mean, a nigga ain't smoked in a few years. When I first got to the pen, me and one of my cellies used to hustle the weed inside. But just as on the outside, niggas started snitching. After my cellie got caught and more time was added to the twenty years he was doing, I decided to chill out. My black ass was trying to come up out of there, not add a single day to what that bitch-ass judge had done gave me.

The house was up in the hills of Cherry Gardens and overlooked the entire downtown. The view was spectacular to a nigga that had had to look at brick buildings for over a decade. I sipped on the Guinness, took a few more pulls, being careful not to choke.

"Yo, Father, what's the pree?" said a male voice behind me.

"Oh shit! My nigga," I exclaimed as I turned around.

It was my right-hand man, Gio. He was my partner from back in the day, had run with me in New York.

"Yo, Father, how freedom feel?"

"Feel motherfucking good. This is what I been waitin' on."
I looked around, inhaling the fresh Jamaican air.

"Welcome home, nigga." He gave me dap; then he handed me a key fob and a cell phone.

"What's this, yo?" I shot him a suspicious look.

"Go out front and see fa yourself."

He walked back inside the house, made his way to the foyer, went out the front door, and headed down the steps to the driveway. I followed him. Outside of the crib sat a black BMW with rims. I walked over to it and stared at the beauty.

"This is your ride. Welcome home, Father," Gio said.

I looked at him to see if this was a big joke, but he stood there, with a serious look plastered all over his face. I looked down at the key fob in my hand, didn't see a key. "Yo, where's the key?"

"Oh shit. I forgot you been gone for a minute. This a keyless, push-button car. Yo, we don't drive vehicles if they not push button. Press the button on the fob and open it up."

This was dope as shit. I looked down at the key fob, pressed the UNLOCK button. I then opened the car door, climbed in, and pressed the START button. Nothing. "Yo, what the hell? Why it ain't starting?"

He leaned in the car. "Put yo' foot 'pon the brake pedal."

He then pushed the button. The car started. Yo, this was new to me. I hadn't driven in years, but I was eager to test out my new whip.

"Hop in, nigga," I told him.

He jumped in on the passenger side, and I pulled off. The ride started off a little rough, 'cause this baby had power and a nigga was rusty, but I quickly got it under control. I went around the block a few times, catching the stares of bitches and niggas that were hanging out late. Then we went back to the house, and we drank a bottle of Patrón that he had brought over and smoked blunts back-to-back on the balcony. It felt good to have in my presence one of my niggas who had been rolling with me from day one. It was a little after 5:00 a.m. when he rolled out and I left the balcony and went back into the house. I took a quick shower before going into my bedroom. It felt so good to be in a real bed, and not on that cot they had in jail. Before I knew it, a nigga was out. . . .

I heard banging on the bedroom door, which woke me up out of my sleep. I jumped up, looked around. That was when I realized I wasn't in prison. I had been in a deep sleep when the knocking startled me. . . .

"Donavan, you still sleeping?" Mama's voice echoed through the crack in the door.

Oh shit. I had forgotten she was leaving, was going back to the States today. I was supposed to take her to the airport. I grabbed my phone and looked at the time. It was well after 12:00 p.m. "I'm up, Mama. Give me a few minutes."

I rushed to the bathroom, took a quick shower, and grabbed one of the white T-shirts and jean shorts Mama had brought down for me. In no time, I was dressed and ready to go. I walked in the kitchen, where my grandma was sitting with an older-looking woman.

"Doris, this is the man of the house, Donavan. He will be your new boss."

Doris stood, walked over to me, and shook my hand. "Nice to meet you, young man. I hear all good things 'bout you."

"Nice to meet you too, Miss Doris."

My mother walked in just then. "Your breakfast is on the dining-room table," she said.

"Thanks, Mama, but I'm ready to take you to the airport."

"Donavon, is who car parked out in the front?" my mother asked.

"It's mine, Mama."

"Is yours?" She stopped dead in her tracks, turned around, and looked at me.

That lady's look had never changed over the years. Whenever she was displeased with any one of us, she had a special look that she would shoot our way. This time was no different, but the only thing was, I was no longer a little boy and I wasn't afraid to face her.

"You late, right? You 'on't wanna miss that flight," I reminded her.

I left the kitchen, grabbed her bags in the foyer, carried them out, and then placed them in the trunk of the car. I got behind the wheel and waited for her. She finally appeared and got in the passenger seat, and then we drove off. I could tell she was feeling some type of way, 'cause her mood had changed drastically.

"Donavan . . . I know you're grown and I can't tell you how to live ya life, but Jamaica is not a nice place. You left here when you was a young man. Now it's more killing. Don't come down here and get wrap up with these bwoy down here."

"Mama, listen, you need to stop worrying. I'm good, trust me."

"You betta be, 'cause I don't want to lose you. Don't you trust none of these people down yah. You been gone too damn long to come down yah and lose your life."

"Mama, come on. You worry too much, mon. Relax. I want you fi go home and focus on enjoying life. Trust me, I got this."

"All right. Me warning you. My mother always say, 'A hard head make a soft ass.'"

I burst out laughing. "Mama, you have always said the same thing too."

She didn't respond; instead, she turned her head and stared out the window. I cut on the music to kind of mellow out the mood.

When we reached the airport, I pulled over to the curb and unloaded Mama's luggage. When she got out of the car, I turned to her and said, "I love you, Mama." I hugged her tight as she professed her love for me and repeated that these people were no good.

Then I watched as she strutted into the airport terminal. When she looked back, I waved one last time. After she had disappeared inside the terminal, I hopped back in the car and pulled off.

Chapter Two

Gaza

Six months later . . .

Pop! Pop! Pop!
Gunshots rang out at Club Mirage, one of the most popular nightclubs in Kingston. I grabbed my gun as I ducked by the side of the table where me and a few niggas had been drinking liquor and vibing.

"Yo, what the fuck is that?" I said.

"Yo, some niggas up front a shoot in a di place," my partner Gio answered.

"This the shit I'm talkin' 'bout. This why I don't like to be round niggas like that," I muttered. "Now the fucking police goin' to definitely come through."

"Yo, let's get out of here," Gio urged. "I know the back way."

"A'ight, bet."

We all got up and made our way to the back entrance. I guessed we were not the only ones aware of it, 'cause bitches and niggas were making their way out the door also. Soon as we got outside, multiple police cars were pulling up.

I dashed to my car, jumped in, and sped off, wanting to get far away from the chaos that was taking place back there. My phone started ringing. It was my nigga.

"Yo."

"Man, I hear it's the nigga Yellow Man from Grants Pen that got killed tonight."

"Yellow Man? I don't remember him, but damn, that's fucked up, B. These niggas making the spot hot as fuck. I'm glad we got the fuck up outta there, yo."

"Yeah, yo, anyways, I'ma head to this catty house on Waltham. Link you in the a.m."

"A'ight, yo."

Shit. It was late, and after all that had happened tonight, I guessed I was going to call it a night. I got some shit to do in the morning, and I needed a fresh mind in order to execute these plans.

Being back in Jamaica was cool and everything. I had been trying to stay out the spotlight because it had been years since I lived here. But shit was getting hectic now; money was getting tight. I had started out fucking with the ganja, but truthfully, there wasn't no big money in it. It was just chump change compared to what I was used to making. So it was time to put some big plan into motion, and I already got some niggas in mind.

After eating some breakfast, I decided to meet up with my big homie Gio around the way. I'd hadn't been to McGregor Gully since I got back to Jamaica. But my niggas still frequented the area and had a stronghold on everything that went on around there. So that was where I was headed today.

I jumped in my car and headed out. Money was on my mind, and there was nothing or no one that was going to stand in the way of that. I was a boss that was used to four or five cars at a time, multiple houses in different cities. This poor shit, living dollar to dollar or depending on Mom Dukes to send money from the United States, was not for me. I was a grown-ass man, and I was going to get rich by any means possible.

As I cruised through the slum of the Gully, it saddened me to see how people were still living even after all these years. What made it worse was the fact that these politicians would come out here close to election time and would offer fake-ass promises, give out a few jobs, distribute a few bags of flour and sugar, and hand out a few dollars, just enough to grab the attention of the poor people. In return, the people would go out and vote for these dishonest politicians, thinking that a better life was going to come for them if they voted. The truth was, after the election was over, the politicians disappeared, along with all the promises that were made to the people. See, this was the reason why the community was so fucked up. There was no money coming in, and all the youths could do was turn to a life of crime, killing, raping, and robbing their own people in order to survive.

On my way, I drove past a few niggas. They were young, so more than likely, they didn't know me. I cruised to the address of my partner. I spotted him and others sitting outside a cook spot that he had. It was really a front for all the other shit he had going on.

I pulled up, then tucked my gun in my waist before I exited the car. See, the Gully was not a nice place and was definitely no place to be without a strap. I walked up to the niggas sitting outside. I noticed they were playing dominoes and talking shit to one another.

"Yo, what's up, niggas?" I said as I approached.

"Yo, Father, bless up," Gio said.

"What's up, mi linky?" my nigga Leroy said. Shit, I was happy to see Leroy. He was one of my riders in New York. He had got less time than the rest of us 'cause they really didn't hear him discussing anything on any of the tapes. He had got ten years, while the rest of us had got fifteen or more.

"Trevor, my nigga, what's good, dawg?" I said. We exchanged daps.

"Yo, boss man, we've been waiting on you so we can figure out our next move," Gio said.

"Shit. Let's get to it, then, niggas. We got shit to do."

"Yo, let's go to the back. Yo, Camille, hold the front down," Gio said.

After he said that, I saw a sexy, dark chocolate chick walk to the front. "All right, boss. I have it under control," she said as she sashayed past me, hips swinging to the sides and ass bouncing up and down. She looked familiar, but I couldn't recall where I knew her from. Our eyes locked for a quick second before she disappeared.

Damn. Who the fuck is that? I thought.

"Yo, Father, you good? You look zoned out still." Gio tapped me on the shoulder.

"Yeah, I'm good, nigga. Yo, is that shawty yours?"

"Who? Camille? Hell nah, nigga. You don't remember her?" He laughed.

"Nah. Her face looks familiar, but it's been so long, I can't call it."

"Come on. We need to handle this business first before you start worrying 'bout pussy."

Shit, that nigga was tripping. I had been gone for years, and other than the bitch he had brought to the house a few nights ago, I ain't fucked nothing else. Yeah, I was worried about getting this paper, but I planned on smashing bitches in the process.

I entered the room in the back, where I immediately spotted cameras. I noticed that they surrounded the entire building and also were focused on the street. I loved how this nigga had the shit set up. You could see everything that went on up front just by watching the TVs.

"Yo, what's the pree, Father?" Gio said.

"Yo, my niggas, y'all already know we on some money pree. Not no little bit of money, but enough money where we can live comfortably out this bitch. Y'all know how the system out here work more than I do. So we need fi put we head together and come up with the perfect plan how to get this money. The weed business too slow right now, but if it pick up, den we can dabble in that also. My main focus is the coca. Me 'ave a few connects in Miami that's willing to fuck wit' me on it, but the ting is how to get it to them without customs intercepting it—"

"Father, I love this idea, but mi 'ave one betta than that," this younger nigga, Dee Lo, said, interrupting me.

"And yuh is?" I quizzed.

"Yo, a my nephew dis, Father. 'Im cool still, and 'im know 'im ting."

"Cool. What idea you 'ave that is betta than the one I'm talkin' about?" I asked in a cold tone.

I didn't like that the little nigga didn't have the sense to shut the fuck up and wait until I was finished with what I was saying. See, these niggas must be sleeping on me, 'cause my accent ain't as raw as theirs, or maybe 'cause they felt like I wasn't one of them since I'd been gone so long.

"No disrespect still, mi genna, but coke money is good, but di scamming money is way betta," Dee Lo replied.

The entire room got quiet as the little young head spoke. I looked at him. Whatever he was saying sounded foreign to me. Since I'd been back, I'd heard niggas talking 'bout this scamming shit here and there, but I had no idea what the fuck it was, and I didn't even care. Shit, I was a drug dealer and a killer. I didn't scam people. However, since this nigga felt the need to bring it up, I decided to see what the fuck he was talking about.

"Scamming money? Nigga, I'm tryin'a build a 'millions of dollars' empire, not some five grand and bullshit-ass change."

"Father, trust me, the youth know him ting," Gio said. "Di scamming ting is the big thing now. Why you think you see all these big houses and big foreign cars popping up? A nuh drug money. Mi 'ave a brethren that make over six million in one week. One week, Father, by just using his phone. A Mobay and St. James niggas dem a eat off of it. A just now town niggas catching on. I mean, we can push di coke and start fuckin' wid di scamming ting too. A rich, we a try get rich."

His words were spinning around in my head. *Over six million in one week.* That shit seemed a little suspicious, but I knew my nigga knew his math, and we'd been rolling so long that I trusted his judgment.

I nodded slowly. "A'ight, my niggas. Y'all have me interested in dis shit. I'm fresh to this shit, so how does it work?"

"Yo, the Africans started this shit many years ago," Dee Lo informed me. "Is like you buy a spreadsheet from a connect in America or Canada. On it are names of people and their phone numbers. It's mostly rich white people. You have somebody on di team that will make the calls, informing the person that they win thousands of dollars, maybe millions, and that they'll have to send money first to process the amount they about to get. You can tell them the processing fee is anywhere from a hundred to five thousand US dollars."

I frowned. "Yo, this sound like bloodclaat fuckery to me."

"Yo, I'm a telling you, it's the business now."

"So you tellin' mi, people in America are so fucking stupid that they willin' to send money to a fucking stranger in hope that they're going to get thousands and possibly millions?"

Dee Lo shook his head enthusiastically. "Hell yeah, my genna. That is exactly what we saying. Because of dem stupid asses, we can be rich young niggas."

By the time the meeting was over, I was feeling optimistic. I had a few thousand US dollars that I had stashed away. It was time to hit the niggas up in Miami. I was ready to get shit started. They also had me sold on the scamming shit. So before I walked out of Gio's back room, I called my sister in New York and told her that I needed four brand-new laptops shipped down to me. I also copped a few new phones, which I would use for the scamming thing. The only thing I needed now was a chick to pick up the money at Western Union. This was the hard part, because I didn't know too many bitches down here and definitely none that I could trust. . . .

After I got off the phone, I walked out to the bar area, and there was that sexy bitch Camille sitting down, pretending like she was so occupied on her phone.

"Yo, shawty, lemme get a shot of Patrón," I said to her as I took a seat at the bar.

"My name is Camille," she said with a slight attitude.

"My bad, Camille. Can I get a shot of Patrón?"

"You sure can." She got up, poured a shot of Patrón, and placed it in front of me. "That will be a thousand."

I handed her a five-thousand-dollar bill. "Keep the change," I said and winked at her.

She went back to doing what she was doing before I walked in. I took out my phone and texted my nigga in Miami, letting him know that we needed to link ASAP.

"Can I get you another drink?" Camille asked me a while later. Her sexy voice echoed in my head.

"Nah, gorgeous. But how 'bout yo' number?"

"Excuse me?" She looked at me like she was shocked.

"Yo, B, stop playing games. I wan' yo' number." I spoke with my raw Jamaican accent, which was still mixed with an American accent.

"No, I don't want to give you my number. Sorry, baby," she said and then walked off.

I wasn't tripping. I knew her ass was just being careful. I took the last sip of my drink and got up from the bar. Walked out to join my niggas.

"Yo, my niggas, I'm out. I hit my nigga up, so soon as he link, things will start rolling. Also gonna check out some laptops," I announced.

We exchanged daps. Then I jumped into my car and left out. As much as I liked being around the niggas, I didn't feel too safe in the Gully. Niggas were just too grimy there, and I had learned the last time around that I couldn't trust nobody. . . .

Chapter Three

Camille

I'm so tired of living in this slum, I thought as I walked home from work. Even though it was evening time, Kingston, Jamaica, was still burning up from the hot sun.

I had been busting my ass lately, working long hours at the bar and going to various parties on the weekend and doing dance competitions. I competed against other area dancers. Lately, I'd been killing the game and winning most of the competitions, which had earned me the privilege of saving over fifty grand. However, that was a far cry from what I needed to get a nice place somewhere uptown. While the Gully would always be my home, things were starting to get out of hand. With area dons beefing with other areas, people barely wanted to be out and about after dark in the Gully. Many nights when I left the bar and walked down to my lane on Robert Avenue, I prayed to God.

Shit didn't seem like it would get any better anytime soon, 'cause it seemed like even the police were scared of coming down here. I often heard the police commissioner talking 'bout how he goin' to clean up the area, but that was just a bag of shit. Crimes had been going on down here even before I was born. Plus, the way the police were lately, they were more criminal than the dudes.

I held tight to my little purse as I walked down the street now. I had a little knife in it that couldn't do much damage, but I planned to stick it as far as I could if one of these boys ever tried to attack me. I was dead-ass tired; feet was hurting and everything. I was not goin' to complain, though, 'cause Gio had given me the job, even though a lot of other bitches had been lined up to get it. I knew Gio from when we were growing up. He moved to America but came back a few years ago, when they dipped him.

I was almost at my gate when I heard a vehicle coming up behind me. I heard the car horn honk, but I kept walking. In Jamaica, most times it was best to just hold your head straight and just mind your own business. The car pulled right in front of me and stopped.

"Yo, what the bumboclaat you doing?" I yelled, not giving a fuck who the driver was or what the repercussions were going to be for me cussing at him.

The driver's door opened, and I quickly dug into my purse and grabbed my ratchet knife. I was ready to fight for my life or die fighting.

The tall, dark, dreadlocked dude that was in the bar earlier stepped out of the car and asked, "Yo, you good?"

"Yo, what is wrong wit' yo? Why you cut me off like that?"

He was smiling like this shit was a joke, but my ass was angry as fuck. My heart was racing because I hadn't been sure if I was about to be raped, robbed, or shot.

"Yo, chill out, shawty. Get in. I'll take you home."

"You pull in front of me, and now you thinking I'm foolish enough to get into a car with a stranger? This gyal is no fool. I'll walk home. Matter of fact, my house is two houses down, so I don't need a ride."

"Yo, Camille. That's yo' name, right? Why you playing hard to get? Yo, I see you and I like you, so what's the problem?"

I stood there looking at him. I knew who he was. I remembered us growing up together. He was, like, three or four years older than me, but I remembered him. I didn't when I first saw him, but while he was back in the office area, I asked Jimmy, the bar boy, and he gladly let me know that this was the nigga that was making big moves in America and who had got torn off by the Feds. After his time in America, they had deported him to Jamaica. So yes, he looked good and all, but he had just got deported, so I knew his ass ain't got shit, and I barely got anything, so what the fuck would I want with him?

"Listen, Donavan, or Gaza, as they call you. I'm not looking for no man, and you is wasting my time. Mi tired and need to go home, so no disrespect. You look good and everything, but I'm not interested." I started walking off on him. This nigga was obviously wasting my time, and I was hungry and about to be angry.

"All right, shawty. Remember, though, I'm not giving up. I'ma make you my woman." Without saying another word, he jumped in his car and pulled off.

Who the fuck this nigga think he is, telling me he is not going to stop until he gets me? I thought. *Shit. He really got me fucked up if he thinks I'm one of these licky-licky Jamaican bitches that is frightened for a Yankee bwoy. Shit, he better ask his niggas. Camille is the real deal. . . .*

When I reached my house, I noticed my best friend and partner in crime, Sophia, was sitting on my verandah, waiting. *Oh shit.* I had forgotten I told her to meet me at my place.

"Yo, my girl, you too wicked. Why you tell me say, you walking down the lane. You 'ave me sitting out here with all these mosquitos tearing my ass up."

"My girl, I'm so sorry. I was almost at the gate when a bwoy pull him car in front a mi. Trust mi, you don't know how mi vex."

"A which bwoy that, and what he wanted?"

"Gyal, is a bwoy from foreign name Gaza. Him grow up round here, but he went to America since he's young. He just get dip, and now he's back in the place with Gio and him crew. "

"Really? How I don't know 'im?"

"He left ling time before you move round here."

"So what he want with you?"

"The bwoy is looking me," I muttered through my teeth.

"So nothing is wrong wit' that. It's not like you 'ave a man. Shit, it's been a while since you get any dick."

I whipped my neck around and looked at this bitch. How the fuck she just going to say that shit?

"Gyal, you really serious right now?" I said.

"Like a heart attack. Bitch, it's time you start fucking again. Omar gone fi 'bout a year now. He's not coming back, boo boo."

I hated that she would bring up my ex, Omar. He was the one that had taken my virginity, and we'd gone steady for 'bout six years. I had thought everything was going good between us. That was until I saw posted on his WhatsApp a picture of him and a girl and someone congratulating him on his marriage. I'd never forget that Saturday. It was like my world had stopped at that moment. I remembered running from my house to Sophia's house. When she'd come to the gate, I couldn't even speak. I had just stood there and had started crying and had shown her the picture. Being that she was my bestie, she'd led me inside her house and had me lie down. I'd stayed in that position until the next day. Just the memory of that shit hurt my soul. Up to this day I hadn't laid my eyes on Omar to ask him how he could do me like that. . . .

"Hello, bitch. Back to earth," Sophia said.

"Yo, sorry. Was caught up thinking 'bout Omar and the shit he pulled."

"Bitch, let Omar go suck his stinking pussy mother. I hate that bwoy with a passion."

Sophia was not joking when she said that. After the shit went down, she'd gone to war with him on WhatsApp, IG, and Facebook. I think Omar had ended up blocking her, and since he had never made it back to the area, he didn't have much to worry about.

"I hear you, my girl, but after all di shit I went through wit' Omar, I'm not sure I'm ready to date another man so soon."

"Bitch, you know who you are? You is Camille, the rassclaat best dancer in town and country. When gyal see you, they salute you. You better boss up and take what's rightfully yours. Stop worry 'bout a dirty, no-good-ass bwoy. Omar fi dead long time."

I looked at her and smiled. I swore I didn't know what I would do without her. Some people in the community said she was messy and stayed in drama, but I saw it differently. Sophia was originally from Tivoli Gardens, and she was just real. She didn't bite her tongue and would tell you exactly what was on her mind. Trust, this bitch was not scared.

"Anyway, I'm dying of hunger. Do you want to walk out on the scheme and let us see if di chicken man is out there?" Sophia said.

"Yeah, let me change my clothes real quick."

"All right, Muma. Hurry up. Dem mosquito are deadly bad."

I opened the door to my little one-bedroom apartment and rushed inside. I grabbed a pair of little shorts and a small tank top and quickly got dressed. Within minutes, me and my bestie was walking up the road, gossiping about everything that went on in the Gully.

After we got the chicken, we walked back to my house, where we sat down on the verandah and ate. The entire time we were eating, my mind was thinking about what Sophia had said. I mean, I'd been trying not to date anyone, because I was still hoping and praying that Omar would come back to me. But my friend was right. That nigga had dissed me and now belonged to another bitch. What the fuck was I waiting for? It might be too late, though, 'cause I did blow Gaza off twice. A nigga like him could get any bitch he wanted, so what the fuck this nigga wanted with little old me . . . ?

When we were done eating, Sophia stood up. "Yo, bitch, it's getting late, so I'm going to my yard. You know how Oneil get brindle when he come in before me, and true, I'm not in the mood to fight him tonight. Plus, tomorrow night your show, and I need mi money from him to do my hair and my nails tomorrow."

"A'ight, goody. Text me when you reach inside the house. I'm going to have a bath right now."

"All right, boo."

I watched as she walked down the street. When she was no longer in sight, I unlocked the grill and walked into my apartment. I was tired as hell, and I needed to shower and rest up because tomorrow night was a big night for me. I had a dance contest, and I would receive fifty grand if I won. I knew that one of the girls I was competing against was a big-time dancer who used to roll with the Spice dance crew, so the pressure was on. I knew I had to practice my moves and also come up with some new moves that nobody had ever seen before. I looked in the mirror. Was I ready for this?

Hell yeah, bitch, you ready, a voice echoed in my head.

My freshly done weave was in a bun, and my body was looking good dressed in a bodycon. I planned to perform tonight in a white jumpsuit from Victoria's Secret. This was my night, and I was shining like the diamond I knew I was. Some of these bitches in the dance contest did this shit to pass the time, but this was my way of getting out of the ghetto. The more battles I won, the more my name would circulate. I was hoping that one day one of these entertainers would come looking for me to be in their videos or go on tour with them. Yeah, I was only a girl from the ghetto, but that didn't stop me from dreaming big.

I watched as bitches pointed fingers and whispered among themselves in the club's lobby. I didn't even acknowledge them. Instead, I swung the little ass and hips that God had blessed me with and made my way to the dressing room. Then I dialed Sophia.

"Bitch, where you at?" I asked when she answered the phone.

"Yo, I'm two minutes from the club. Are you there?"

"Yes. I'm in the changing room. Hurry up and come on."

I hung the phone up and changed my clothes. I was almost finished dressing when this one bitch that I had beaten numerous times walked in. I could smell trouble from a mile away. This bitch, Anika, had been salty the last time I beat her, and she had kept yelling at the judges that they were cheating for me. The bitch had gone as far as threatening me. I hurried and put my legs into the pants part of the jumpsuit and pulled it up. I pretended like I was stunning the bitch, but all along I was reaching for my razor in my wallet. I placed it under my tongue. This was a trick that I had learned early on. See, when you grew up in the ghetto, you had to learn how to defend yourself.

"Yo, Marie, see the dutty gyal here that steal my spot last time?" Anika yelled to a bitch that had walked into the dressing room behind her.

"Eh, is that her? Look on the old parasite. They stole yo spot, goody. After this gyal don't even look like she can dance," her big, bad friend commented.

"Yo, bitch, I win that fair and square," I told Marie. "I beat your friend three time, and tonight I'm going to beat her for the fourth time. I'm a good dancer. I don't have to steal anything."

Marie glared at me. "Is it me this underprivileged gyal talking to?"

This bitch Anika stepped to my face. I didn't think twice. I pulled the razor out of my mouth and just went in.

"Oh my God! This gyal cut you, goody!" was all I heard.

I opened my eyes and saw that I had blood all over my dance clothes. I looked over, and I saw the bitch holding her face. She was screaming.

I grabbed my bag and stuffed my things in there.

"She a try to leave. Hold the gyal and beat her," someone said, pointing at me.

"Nobody better not put a bloodclaat hand on her. Yo, come on." Sophia grabbed my hand and pulled me through the crowd that had gathered in the dressing room.

We raced to the lobby and then out the front door of the club. The people in front of the building were not aware of what was going on, because they had been standing around, talking and drinking. The second we were outside, Sophia started flagging down a taxi. The taxis that went by zoomed past us, so more than likely they were filled with customers. I happened to look back and saw security running into the building. I knew that by now everybody was aware of what had gone down in there.

"Come on! We have to get away from here," I told Sophia.

We decide to run across the street in front of the club, but that meant we would have to dodge all these speeding cars. We waited for a gap in the flow of traffic and then ran as fast as we could. We had made it to the other side of the street when I noticed the BMW. It was the car that Gaza drove. I walked over to the car and looked inside. He was sitting in there. I guessed he had just pulled up. I didn't know he frequented this scene.

He climbed out of the car when he saw me. "Whaddup, shawty? I see we meet again." He smiled at me.

"Listen, I need a ride out of here," I told him.

"What's good?" He looked at me suspiciously.

"I got into it with a gyal in the club, and I end up cutting her. Now they're after me."

"Oh, word. Get it in, yo." He looked around.

I was about to get in the car when Sophia grabbed my arm. "Who is this? You know him?" She was looking at me suspiciously now.

"This is the same youth that I was telling you about. The other man. Come on," I said.

We all got in the car, and he pulled off. He drove past the club, and the crowd was gathered around the entrance, but we couldn't see anything else. This was some bullshit.

"Yo, what happen in there with you and the bitches?" he asked once the club was in his rearview mirror.

"Yo, I come up here to compete in the dance contest. This gyal that I beat three times have it in for me. She jump up in my face, along with her friend. I tried to ignore them, but the bitch start disrespecting. So I pull the razor out my mout' and slice di gyal in her face. A long time, I give that gyal. Whole lot of passes."

"Yo, goody, I'm sorry I was late. 'Cause, trust mi, if I was there, that gyal couldn't come up inna yuh face like dat. Trust me," Sophia said. I could tell by her tone that she was pissed off.

"I didn't know you is a bad gyal, mon." He burst out laughing.

"Why you laughing like it's a joke thing? What if they call the police? I'll be locked up," I said in an annoyed tone.

"Yo, relax . . . A Jamaica this, so them bitches ain't callin' no police. If anything, you just have to be prepared to fuck them up again."

"I'm not afraid of these bitches. I'm angry because tonight I'm s'pposed to get fifty grand if I won. This is how I make my money. I'm an independent gyal, and this gyal come fuck with me and fuck up my thing. Yo, I'm vex bad."

"Yo, chill out, babes. Fifty grand? That's nothing, babes. Just easy," he said.

He was saying that shit 'cause he probably got money, but I didn't have money like that. I made a few dollars at the bar, but dancing was my thing to get me up out of the ghetto.

"Y'all ladies going home?"

"Yeah, if you don't mind. Drop me home please. I 'ave this gyal blood all ova my clothes," I said.

The rest of the ride was quiet; I was too fucking upset to keep on talking. With the anger that I was feeling right now, I could definitely kill that bitch. Why the fuck would she decide to mess with me? I was not a troublemaker. I made my little money and took care of myself. Tears wanted to flow, but my pride wouldn't let me cry in front of a nigga that I barely knew. So I used everything in me to hold it in.

Twenty minutes later he pulled up at the house. But wait, how the fuck did he know exactly where I lived at? *Hmm. Let me find out this nigga been doing his homework*, I thought.

"Here you go, ladies."

"Tanks," Sophia said and jumped out.

"Thank you. I appreciate it," I told him. I was about to exit the car when he grabbed my arm.

"Yo, B. Take my number and link mi."

"Come on, Gaza. Mi appreciate what you just do for me, but I just tell you I don't want no man."

"Camille, fuck that nigga that hurt you. I'm a man, not him. Yo, take this number and link mi," he said in a serious tone.